O

"The ⟨...⟩ Bull, "every b⟨...⟩

Burgess, known to the Sioux as Sitting Lizard, realized that Red Cloud was right. The white man had conquered every single thing, including his own heart.

"But I have heard something else," Sitting Bull continued. "I heard that you have seen a man who has a magical shield. The Sioux who traveled with you said they have witnessed a ghost wall."

Burgess had tried to think of a better way to describe the invisible wall that had surrounded the mystery scientist's camp, but there really was not one. "Yes," he said.

"And has small magical men that will not die when hit with arrows. And he has flame that does not flicker and is not warm."

"I did not see them myself, but yes, I heard of them."

"The best Sioux warriors will return to find this man," said Sitting Bull. "I will lead them. When we find him, I will tell him I want his ghost wall and his men that cannot die and his thunder noise. These are weapons that can frighten even the famous Professor Marsh. These are apparently things that are beyond what the other white men out here possess."

"But it will be very hard to get these things from him. What if we fail?"

Sitting Bull's eyes glared afresh. "What if we fail? What if we do not try? How can I ignore this chance? The white man spreads from one end of the world to the other. I was not born to accept crumbs from a white man's table. The Great Spirit may be bringing this man here with his magical weapons just so that I may take them and defeat the white man. How will we know if we do not try?"

Burgess could not argue with him. He looked at his knees in shame.

"We leave tomorrow," Sitting Bull said. "You lead us to where the man can be found, and we will find him. This could change the world."

BAEN BOOKS by BRETT DAVIS

The Faery Convention
Hair of the Dog
Bone Wars

BRETT DAVIS
BONE WARS

BAEN

BONE WARS

Copyright © 1998 by Brett Davis

A Baen Books Original

Baen Publishing Enterprises
P.O. Box 1403
Riverdale, NY 10471

ISBN: 0-671-87880-8

Cover art by Bob Eggleton

First printing, June 1998

Distributed by Simon & Schuster
1230 Avenue of the Americas
New York, NY 10020

Printed in the United States of America

To Andrew and Ashlyn,
who know a thing or two about dinosaurs.

ONE

Othniel Charles Marsh squinted at the heavens and saw a falling star flash like a water bug over a pebble bed of constellations. He couldn't see it exactly; he had left his spectacles in his tent and had wandered out to relieve himself without bothering to fit them to his nose.

The meteorite was a cottony ball to his eyes, but his mind turned it this way and that and focused it into a pleasingly sharp image. He had seen falling stars before, had seen most things before, in fact, and so his mind was rarely at a loss to sharpen up the sometimes fuzzy pictures his eyes could gather. He found his wire frames generally uncomfortable in the field, especially in this sort of cold. Might as well fasten a tiny torture device to his face.

At any rate, sharp images were not necessary to find one's way to a scrub bush suitable for his purpose. The sputtering fire, fueled by lignite coal dug from the surrounding rocks, illuminated only the raggedy straw-colored grass at the edge of camp, and he contented himself with the first bunch he came across.

He finished providing fertilizer for the bush and hugged himself under the armpits, shivering involuntarily. Summer barely over, and it was already cold at night. Summer gave up early in Montana, packing up and heading off further west or south to finish out its days

1

in comfort before some of the hardy stock around here even knew it was gone. The fire was outmatched by the darkness, but it did the best it could, snapping and crackling occasionally with the effort.

Marsh had the slightest headache, a tiny sliver of pain that lived somewhere in the middle of his balding head. It had shallowed his usual deep sleep, waking him ceaselessly, reminding him that he was not back in Connecticut where he wanted to be but was out in the emptiness of Montana, where he did not want to be at this particular time. New Haven had fires and boxes of bones for intellectual pursuit; Montana had rocks, towering peaks of sandstone and shale that only grudgingly gave up their prizes, and not without considerable pain to the extractor. In his pain-flavored dreams he had heard the cries of the great beasts from the stones that rose above the camp like ancient fortresses. Even though entombed for millennia, the bones of the hulking reptiles had groaned in sympathy for his discomfort.

And then his bladder woke him up and he went outside, where the noises of the great beasts turned out to be nothing more than the whispers of the wind. He placed his pudgy fingers at the small of his back and stretched his head up toward the stars, trying to ease a kink out of his back, a throbbing cousin of the sharper pain in his head. No amount of blankets could make the ground in Montana comfortable, and he did not have as many as he would have liked. All he needed were aching feet and he would be well represented with pain.

He imagined he saw a thin wisp of gray smoke off in the distance, up the river. He would not be able to see such a thing even if it existed, but his imagination overrode his eyes and put it there just the same. The smoke marked the camp of Cope, the lair of the enemy. God had given boundless energy to Cope, which had taken him out into the field on numerous trips, more than Marsh could recount. Cope could dig all day, every day, and would dig all night if he could. He was formidable in the way a rat was formidable—small, but tenacious. Cope even resembled a rat to some extent. God had given Cope persistence, that could not be denied, but Marsh was comforted that the superior mind had been reserved for himself. Cope could dig up bones forever, but he couldn't always tell what they were. He was like a child with a complicated jigsaw puzzle, quick to see patterns that were not yet clear, quick to cram pieces together and say he had solved it.

Marsh heard a rustling to his left, behind a stand of the stubby, stubborn pines that managed to scratch a living out of the thin soil. Gen. Custer was barely cold in the ground, and any rustling in these parts was cause for concern, lest other white men be destined to join his ghostly troops. The two armed soldiers that Marsh had cajoled the Army into loaning him were forty feet or more away, probably dead to the world. He had passed the sleeping form of one of them on his way to his nocturnal errand, and now wished he had awakened the man. He squinted into the dark, unable to see anything beyond the black wall of pines. He mentally ran through his speech, trying to get his sleep-addled brain to remember the key points to say to show that he was a friend of the Indian. He hoped it was a Sioux, rather than a Crow; it was easier to demonstrate his friendship for the Sioux.

"I didn't mean to scare you," a thin voice said, and a small, dark figure stepped into view.

It was Stillson, a young man Marsh had hired in Fort Benton to care for the horse team. He would really have preferred someone larger, but then again he was running behind schedule and needed the large men out in the field even more, digging the bones. Stillson—

and in the early hour he could not remember whether that was a first name or a last name—had shown himself without recommendations of any sort, but seemed good with the horses and was hired aboard. There were not many people willing to come into Indian country these days, so Marsh had decided to risk the hire.

"What are you doing creeping around at this hour?" Marsh asked, in a voice that started harshly but then grew quieter as he remembered the sleeping men in camp.

Now that he knew an Indian attack was not imminent, he didn't want to wake them. They needed to be fresh in the morning.

"I believe it was the same urge as you, sir, but then I saw someone moving around, and you can't be too careful these days, what with General Custer and all. So I decided to investigate. It was you, of course."

Stillson came forward and the fire strained to cast some light his way. Marsh squinted down at what looked like the flickering image of a human face. Then he remembered that this boy, not a man, really, just a boy, had a tendency to keep his face dirty. Even in town, when he came up to ask for the job, his cheeks had borne flecks and streaks of mud. These had only increased in size and shape as the party headed into the countryside. Water was scarce enough in this extreme land, but not *that* scarce, and now they were camped within spitting distance of the Judith River. The other six men he had hired were not exactly ready for a dinner party at Yale, but they at least managed to be only slightly grimy, not out-and-out dirty. Maybe Marsh could catch young Stillson standing beside the river one day, and accidentally bump him into it.

"Well, good night, sir," Stillson said in his boyish voice after Marsh had stared at him for several moments without saying anything.

"Wait one moment," Marsh said.

Stillson had faded back out of the reach of the fire, and Marsh couldn't tell exactly where he was. This seeming invisibility had given him an idea.

"Stillson, do you see anything over there on the horizon? Up the river?"

"What sort of thing?"

"Any evidence of a fire. Smoke, or a glow, or anything like that."

"Hmmmm. No, sir. I don't. It's too dark."

"Stillson, have you ever heard of a man named Edward Drinker Cope?"

"No, sir."

Marsh stifled his momentary irritation. For all his failings, Cope was one of the premier naturalists in the world, although his work was constantly bettered by the likes of Marsh himself. Still, for such a prominent, albeit flawed, scientist to go so unnoticed by much of the population was an affront to Marsh. The public seemed content to be agog at the likes of George Armstrong Custer, who had displayed a talent only in getting himself killed.

"Mr. Cope is trying to dig up the same sort of bones that we are. The bones of sea reptiles, Pterodactyls, Titanotheres. Ancient horses big as elephants. Maybe even the bones of dinosaurs. Have you heard of dinosaurs, Mr. Stillson?"

"I believe I have, sir. Giant lizards."

"Sort of, yes. Anyway, I am trying to dig them up and so is Mr. Cope. I believe I should get to them first because I am a better scientist than Mr. Cope and could do a better job with them. Do you understand me?"

"Yes, sir. I hear you are a good scientist."

So the Stillson nose was brown from more things than dirt.

"Thank you. You seem to be good at slipping around

at night, and you're small. You can fit through the ravines up in the sandstone. I want you to do something for me. Wander around tomorrow up on those bluffs. Find Mr. Cope's camp and let me know where he is and what he is doing."

No response.

"I'm not asking you to risk your life. Just find out where it is and see what you can see. And you don't have to go tramping all over the world. It is nearly directly east of here, from what I have heard, and it's probably not far from the river. That should narrow things down for you."

"Does this mean I still have to take care of the horses?"

"Of course. I don't know how much we'll need them tomorrow anyway. Just feed them in the morning and then you can slip off after that."

"I'm worried about being able to do both at once."

Finally it occurred to Marsh's tired, pained mind what Stillson was driving at. Perhaps the lad had his hand out, but Marsh couldn't see it in the dark.

"There will be extra pay in it for you. If you find him and give a good report, I will double what we agreed to."

Every aspect of paleontological research was getting more expensive these days. He had to pay for specimens against Cope, who had gotten his paws on his dead father's money and was therefore able to pay a pretty penny. Now Marsh was even reduced to paying to find out what Cope was up to. It would be galling enough to pay to find out what a gentleman scientist was doing, but it was downright offensive to waste valuable resources on monitoring such as Cope. Still, it had to be done; it was the rat you didn't watch that would bite you in the rear.

"Do you agree?"

"What about the Indians, sir? Double pay doesn't help if I'm not here to spend it."

"I don't believe there are many around here now. Take one of the soldiers with you if you are that nervous. I will also give you a letter for them, telling who I am and what I am doing. Rest assured it will be enough to see you through safely, especially if they are Sioux."

"You're good with the Sioux, then."

"You could say that. Do you agree?"

"What if they can't read?"

"Stillson, the fact that I am willing to pay you double indicates there may be some modicum of risk involved. Otherwise I wouldn't pay you at all. If you are unwilling to perform this task, then say so."

"I'm not, sir. I mean, yes, I'll do it."

"Good. In the future, just be forthright with me and don't beat around the bush. Get some sleep now, and we'll talk it over a bit more in the morning. I'll tell you more about Mr. Cope so you don't accidentally bother someone else."

He laughed, letting Stillson know that was a little joke. White people hadn't come around these parts much since Lewis and Clark, especially not when winter was on its way and Sitting Bull and his deadly Sioux were still at large. Stillson barked out a half-hearted laugh. The boy was trying.

"Good night, then," Marsh said.

"Wait, sir. Are you sure the camp isn't to the south a bit? Over there?"

Marsh could not see where Stillson pointed, or even if he was pointing. He saw nothing on the horizon, and nothing even in the foreground save for the feeble orange glow of the fire.

"I don't think so. What do you see?"

"It's hard to tell. Nothing really. It just looks like a faint green glow, shining through the cracks in the middle of one of those ridges. Like a tiny little smudge halfway up the hill."

That would be a good phrase to describe Cope, Marsh thought; a little smudge on the hill. But this could not be him, unless his earlier sources were all wrong, and he hoped that was not the case.

"*Green*, did you say?"

"Yes, sir, it looks that way. I can barely see it."

"Hmm. I cannot imagine anything he might be burning that would be green. Perhaps it's a trick of the light, such as it is. The air up here can do odd things, you know."

"I know."

"Anyway, let's get some sleep now. And, Stillson—"

"Sir?"

"Please don't tell anyone about our deal. They'll all want to be out looking for Mr. Cope, and I won't get any digging done."

TWO

Edward Drinker Cope jabbed the tip of a cotton-gloved finger into the wall of sandstone, sending fragments skittering down. Nothing. What he thought was the tip of a fossil turned out to be just more rock. Further over was something more promising, a wall of sandstone and shale studded with tiny points of light. Could be nothing, could be the claws or vertebrae of a beast that died millions of years ago.

The way things had been going out here, it was likely the former. He decided to chance it. The ledge underneath his feet was only a foot and a half wide, the nearest cliff face behind him ten feet away. Below was nothing but air for five hundred feet, followed by razor-sharp rock and spiky pine for another hundred. The pines were mere green dots from this height. Fall down there and it would be easier just to wait for the ravens to locate all your parts. All around him, streams of rock grains shussed their way into the abyss, as if to show him how easy such a fall could be. Of course, this being the Montana badlands, there was another obstacle. Before him was a spike of rock, jutting out right at face level.

Going over it was impossible, but he thought he could fit underneath. Only one way to find out. Gritting his teeth, he took a breath, swayed his torso and head

9

underneath the spike and rammed his pick into the
wall on the other side. It was like driving a blow into
water. The pick head disappeared up to the shaft,
releasing a fresh flood of rock fragments. He felt the
immutable pull of gravity, trying to show him those
distant pines and razor-sharp rocks up close. It was
not a warm day, but his body broke out in sweat. He
saw the headline: FALL CUTS SHORT BRAVE
GEOLOGIST'S CAREER. A mute parade of all the
creatures whose bones he hadn't yet found clumped
before him, wagging their cumbersome tails, flashing
their eyes; at the end of the line stood a chortling Othniel
Marsh, gleefully writing down their names on a legal
pad.

"Lord!" Cope said, and grabbed at the spike, the only
other option besides falling.

His fingers scrabbled on its top, knocking dust and
rock chips onto his face and moustache. He sneezed,
which actually helped by driving his fingers harder into
the rocks atop the spike. He sneezed again, and realized
that he hadn't fallen after all. The spike was sandstone,
not shale, or he would even now be reunited with his
creator, something he wasn't quite ready to experience.
Slowly, slowly, he eased back to the left of the spike.
Now that he wasn't going to fall, he didn't intend to
retreat. He pulled the pick out of its dusty sheath with
a trembling hand and leaned against the rock wall, secure
on the ledge, at least as long as the ledge remained
secure. His knees were trembling, but there was
nowhere to bend down and relax. He would just have
to keep working. If he looked to the left, he could see
a tiny portion of the Missouri River, near where it joined
the Judith. The Missouri ran thin and shallow here,
its mild demeanor making up for the violent upthrusts
of rock all around it. The Missouri rolled on, indifferent
to whether Edward Drinker Cope could see it or not.

"I thank you, Lord," he whispered, and closed his eyes for a moment.

When he opened them again he saw more rock, and nothing but rock. The light spots he saw in the black shale turned out to be shadowy depressions and nothing else. He had risked his life for shale pits. Perhaps the Lord had taunted him with near death, and no reward, to remind him of the puniness of his efforts. Ferdinand Hayden had found dinosaur bones in these very rocks two decades back, stacking them up at the Smithsonian like so much cordwood. Perhaps he had gotten them all.

He glanced up at what he could see of the sky. They called this the big sky country, but the black ravines offered him only slices of it. It was getting darker and colder, and it would not do to be caught in the ravines once the sun went down. They dug into the earth like dark veins, sometimes continuing like broad avenues for miles, sometimes narrowing to a few inches and coming to an abrupt end. Sometimes they stopped over empty space. He had gotten close enough to that already today.

He walked back up the ledge—slowly—until he got back to the top, where the horses waited with the rig. Charles Sternberg was waiting for him there, sitting atop the wooden plank. Sternberg was young but eager to look for fossils, so it was a shame their luck was not running high. Empty rags filled the back of the cart. On a good expedition, there would be huge bones stacked underneath them. On this trip, they slouched like flat ghosts.

"Thought maybe you wanted to forgo supper tonight," Sternberg said, his mouth tilting up faintly at the corners to show he was not altogether serious.

His shirt and vest were covered with tan streaks. He was lame in one leg and deaf in one ear, but he worked harder than most men who had all their senses and limbs working properly. He had been working a flatter section of hills and had collected more dust—but no more bones, Cope noted a little ruefully.

"I see you had fun today," Cope said.

"As much as possible," Sternberg replied. "I found a tooth. One single tooth. Herbivore, probably Hadrosaur. Fits in a pocket, easy to carry. And yourself?"

"Why, I found nothing at all but had adventures nonetheless. I nearly fell right off the cliff today, but the good Lord could not see his way clear to leave you in a helpless state without me around, so he plucked me back from the precipice. He rewarded me not with bones, but with my own life."

With a tug of the line, Cope nudged the quartet of horses forward. The empty cart rattled behind, as if in reproof.

"No disrespect, but perhaps you should pay me up front," Sternberg said. "In case the Lord changes his mind."

"I'll think about it. But I thought perhaps I would work the lower ground tomorrow and you can take the ledges. Or maybe we'll both work the ledges and we'll see whom the good Lord prefers for company."

They rumbled away from the cliffs, down a broad, gentle ravine that looped around and headed back for the river. Once the cart got to nearly level ground, they could see smoke rising from the campfire.

"I wonder what Boston has cooked for us this evening," Cope said.

Boston Mickle had a round face, which Cope assumed meant he was a good cook, and indeed he had turned out to be that. He could do justice to whatever the guide happened to bring down.

"Perhaps Jenks has shot us a Titanothere for supper," Sternberg mused.

Cope heard his stomach rumble. No food had entered its domain since breakfast, and no water either. His eyes had gazed all day on empty sandstone and shale, a nourishment that did little to fill either brain or belly.

"I believe they are extinct," Cope said. "But I also believe I could eat one right about now."

Once they stopped the cart, Sternberg hopped out to unfasten the horses.

"No luck today, Boston," Cope shouted to the cook. "The land gives up its bones most grudgingly."

"Come over here and eat these sage hens and you'll soon have some fresh bones to play with," Mickle shouted from the fire near the main wagon.

He hovered over the camp stove like a hairless bear, his face red with sweat. Jenks Dart, the guide, was nowhere to be seen, probably off hunting something else for breakfast. At the edge of the stove were two pies, sending steam into the air. Mickle's meals were usually more fit for a Philadelphia drawing room than the badlands of Montana. Cope and Sternberg ate better than anyone in the territory.

"Not just yet," Cope said.

He and Sternberg walked the quarter mile to the river to wash themselves, then returned and rolled out the pickle barrels that doubled as seats. Jenks Dart had returned and nodded at them, but he was more interested in showing Mickle the latest beasts he had killed, so Mickle could figure out how to cook them. Dart was a tall man who said little but was quick with a rifle, capable of bringing down any critter that flew, walked or crawled. If future scientists uncovered fossils of this era, a good many of them would have been put there by Jenks Dart.

Cope had fetched his tattered Bible from his tent, and held it in his left hand as he thumbed its pages. Sternberg waited patiently for him to read. The young

man never seemed to mind hearing the word of the
Lord at the end of a long day, which made Cope glad.
So many men his age did not care to hear it. Cope
came to rest on a page at random and started to read.

"Hast thou entered into the springs of the sea? Or
hast thou walked in the search of the depth? Have the
gates of death been opened unto thee? Or hast thou
seen the doors of the shadow of death? Hast thou
perceived the breadth of the earth? Declare if thou
knowest it all."

A rumble from his stomach drowned out the next
verse, and Cope shifted uncomfortably on the pickle
barrel.

"I declare that I knowest your food is getting cold,"
Mickle said with a chuckle, but Cope glared at him.

It was hard enough to take time out to be reverent
without the cook making fun of you.

"It would not do you a great deal of harm to pull up
a barrel and hear a bit of the word of God now and
then," he said harshly, and Mickle's face reddened
beyond what the fire could do.

"I'm sorry. But please come eat, it really is getting
cold."

Cope nodded to Sternberg and closed the Bible. The
verses he had stumbled across were not that comforting
to a paleontologist anyway. They were more than
halfway through the hens and were starting to eye the
pies when Dart wandered back into the camp. He had
one hand on his everpresent rifle and the other gripped
around the neck of what appeared to be a small, dirty
person in the indeterminate years somewhere between
boy and man. Dart had big hands and his fingers nearly
met around the front of his captive's skinny throat.
The youth had a scruffy black hat shoved down over
his unkempt black hair, and his face had not been
acquainted with water in some time. Dart marched

him to the makeshift dinner table, a rough plank stretched across two pickle barrels. He stood blinking at Cope and Sternberg. Cope put his fork down, a chunk of sage hen still on it.

"I don't know, Jenks, that looks a bit big to eat," Cope said.

"You need to wash it off a little, too," Sternberg contributed.

The young man's face was dirty but his eyes were bright, glowing with either fear or rage, or both.

"I caught him skulking around in the ravine over there," Dart said, motioning with the rifle. "He seems to take a great interest in the camp."

"He's in dire need of entertainment, then," Cope said.

He brought his face in close to that of the intruder. The young man flinched.

"What's your name, son?" Cope asked.

"Al Stillson. Sir."

"Are you by any chance an Indian, Mr. Stillson? Our cook is a little nervous about Indian activity."

"I am not."

"I thought you looked a little pale for that. So if you are not an Indian up to some mischief, why are you looking in on our camp?"

The young man shrugged.

"I was just wanting to see who were here, is all. Not many people come through these parts."

"You live around here, is that it?"

"Yes, sir."

"Right out here, in the middle of nowhere."

"Yes, sir."

Cope picked the fork back up and reclaimed the bite of sage hen, chewing slowly. He noticed Stillson was eyeing the plate.

"Don't feed you too well in Mr. Marsh's camp, do they?"

"Excuse me?"

"The soldiers at Fort Benton said nobody lives out here. The only other people out here besides the Indians are Mr. Othniel Charles Marsh and his crew. It is not unheard of for Mr. Marsh to spy on me. I've been expecting it, as a matter of fact. And here you are. You are being paid by Marsh, are you not?"

"No, sir."

"Jenks, I wonder if you can touch the tips of your fingers together."

Dart tried. The young man's bright eyes grew just a little brighter, and a little bigger.

"Don't be so slow, Jenks. Just go ahead and touch 'em together. In fact, see if you can make a fist."

The boy suddenly grabbed at Dart's fingers with both hands, and simultaneously let out a blast of breath that ruffled Cope's moustache.

"All right! All right! I'll tell. You're right. Mr. Marsh told me to come find you and see what you were doing."

He rubbed his throat. Cope nodded at Dart, and he removed his big hand entirely.

"I do not enjoy hearing lies," Cope said. "Do you understand that?"

The young man answered with a cough and a nod. Cope gave him a hard look for a long moment.

"Boston, get this young man a plate," he shouted finally.

The cook, pleased to be able to present his work to a new mouth, huffed and puffed busily around in his tent. He did not take meals with the prospectors, because he ate nearly all day, sampling bits of everything while he cooked. Dart ate by himself, too, out of habit. Mickle finally produced a clean plate, piling it with still-warm food and placing it carefully on the plank beside the others. Sternberg scooted over on the pickle barrel to make room, although the boy didn't take up much.

"Have some supper with us," Cope said. "There's usually more than enough to go around. Jenks, thank you."

"I'm going walking around," Dart said.

He cracked his walnut-sized knuckles, creating sharp reports that sounded like distant gunfire.

"I'll make sure he doesn't have some friends, hiding in the ravines."

The mysterious young Stillson ate ravenously, giving the hens no chance at all. Cope was glad; Mickle always appreciated hearty appetites, and a happy cook led to happy stomachs.

"Othniel really *doesn't* feed you."

"No, it's not that," the young man said between bites. "It just took a while to find you, and hiking these ravines makes you tired."

"Amen to that," Sternberg said.

Suddenly Stillson stopped and put his fork down and looked at Cope, his eyes narrowed.

"Why are you feeding me? I'm spying on you."

He didn't wait for an answer before he resumed eating.

"Mr. Stillson, have you ever been to Kansas?" Cope asked.

Stillson paused for a second, and then resumed finishing off his hen.

"No."

"Well, I was out there a few years back digging up some fabulous creatures that swam in the prehistoric seas. It was a small group, and I ended up working with some men who were employed by your professor Marsh. I had identified some bones that I wanted, and showed them some that they could have, but when all was said and done and dug up they walked off with some finds that I had made."

Cope knew he should keep his voice down, but he

couldn't contain his emotion and it grew louder the longer he spoke. He could feel his moustache hairs fairly quivering with indignation. He was probably frightening the young man, which was not his intention, but he couldn't help it. He noticed that any fear the boy may have felt was not enough to keep him from starting in on his slice of pie.

"I just want you to know the sort of man you're working for. When did he hire you?"

"Three days ago, sir. In Fort Benton. To care for the horses."

Sternberg snorted, and patted the young man on the back.

"The horses! My word, son, you're a bit small for that."

"I'm good with them, though."

Cope smoothed his moustache with his fingers, as if soothing the savage inner beast he had so recently disturbed.

"That's no doubt true, but don't you think it would be more exciting to uncover the mysteries of the ages? To dig up, with your own hands, the bones of some of the most fantastic creatures that ever walked the earth?"

His voice was rising again, but Cope couldn't help it. His enthusiasm didn't seem to be catching.

"I'm not sure I'd be all that good at digging, sir. I can't tell the difference between the bones and the rocks."

Cope stuck his finger in the air. He always liked to lecture, and sensed an opportunity.

"Charley, do you have that specimen you uncovered today?"

Sternberg put down his fork and rooted around in the pocket of his vest. He produced a small cloth bundle.

"Here you go. The product of a whole day's work."

Cope took it and hopped off his barrel. He walked

around, eyeing the ground, before selecting something and picking it up. He walked back to the plank table, unwrapping Sternberg's find as he came. Cope placed two small objects next to Stillson's plate, and even in the rapidly fading light the difference was easy to see. One of the objects was sharp and sand-colored, obviously a rock. The other was darker, and although bits of rock clung to it, it was obviously much smoother.

"Which one is the fossil?"

It really wasn't a fair opportunity. Only an idiot would point to the rock. He had the young man trapped. Stillson really had no choice. He aimed his finger towards the brown chunk, but Sternberg grabbed his skinny arm.

"No, no," Sternberg said. "Don't touch. A gust of wind can break these things."

"Oh, let him touch," Cope said. "We can find more."

"The way it's going, I wouldn't be so sure."

Stillson ran a finger over the fossil.

"It's a tooth," Cope said, and the youth nodded, as if seeing it at last.

Cope pointed up at the craggy rocks that glowed copper against the darkening sky.

"Three or four million years ago, these rocks weren't here, young Al. All around where we are, right where we are standing, there was a great inland sea. Monsters that would make your head spin swam there in the deep, and the air was full of leathery creatures that looked like reptiles but flew like birds. And on the edge of this sea, reptiles the size of three grown men put together ate plants, and in turn were eaten by enormous meat-eating dinosaurs more ferocious than anything seen on earth today. When the sea dried up, and these creatures died out, some of their bones slowly turned into minerals. Those are what we find today. That right there comes from one of them," he said, pointing at the brownish lump. "It's a tooth from a Hadrosaur, a creature that looked like a giant leathery duck."

For some reason, the boy did not seem excited. He kept his head down, looking at the fossil. When he was a young man, it would have taken a team of horses to have kept Cope out of the field after hearing a description like that. How the young had changed. The new generation was shaping up to be a real disappointment.

"I don't know," Stillson said.

"I'll be blunt with you," Charles Sternberg chimed in, trying the direct approach. "Mr. Cope had hired two other men to help us out, but they didn't want to come out here because of the Indian situation. So right now it's just him and me, and we only have four arms between us."

"Join us," Cope said. "We'll pay you half again as much as old O.C. Marsh is paying you."

The young man was obstinate. He ran a finger over the fossil again, then said in a small voice, "I can't. I'm sorry."

Cope considered whistling for Jenks and having him threaten the lad again, but that probably wouldn't work and he really didn't have the heart for it. He had no choice but to let the boy go, right back to the enemy camp.

"All right," Cope said. "Your loyalty would be more admirable had you chosen a more admirable person to be loyal to, but that's your business. It's dark now. You'd be as likely to bump into an Indian patrol as find your camp now. Spend the night here, and head out first thing."

The boy would have to be an idiot or suicidal to leave now, and he nodded his head to indicate he agreed. Cope was glad he had not lost all powers of persuasion.

"If you won't help us dig, could you do us one thing? We'll pay you," Cope said.

The boy looked at him suspiciously, like he knew what was coming.

"Slip off once in a while and tell us what Mr. Marsh is finding. You know where we'll be, at least for the next couple of days. Don't risk your life, just let us know what sort of stuff he's digging up."

Stillson blinked a couple of times, considering.

"Remember what a really good dinner you had," Cope said. "There's more where that came from."

THREE

"Well, did we have a good night's sleep?"

Al Stillson had hoped to sneak back into camp and be found with the horses, like he had been there all night. The birds had barely noticed it was dawn but O.C. Marsh was already up, sitting with the flaps of his tent pulled way back to let the sun shine in, whisking dust off an ancient leg bone with a shaving brush. The bone would have looked like it belonged in a chicken leg except it was dark brown and mottled. If it had been gnawed on, it happened a long time ago.

Marsh had hired guards but didn't seem to use them as sentries. Stillson hadn't seen either one as he came into camp. Apparently they had been hired purely for their guns. It was just barely daylight and already the camp was alive with activity. Marsh had selected a flatter section of land for his camp, some three miles upriver from Cope's meager accommodations. Stillson had wandered in quietly, but apparently Mr. Marsh's ears were better than his eyes.

"Good morning, sir," Stillson said, and Marsh frowned.

"Young man, didn't you come from the direction of the river? Did you know there's *water* in the river? Did you think to perhaps dip your face in that water to experience its cleansing effect?"

"No, sir."

The fastidious Marsh gave him a look that contained more than just a hint of disgust, but he soon let it pass when he remembered what young Stillson had been up to.

"Were you able to find Mr. Cope's camp?"

"Yes, sir."

He paused, wanting to see how badly Marsh wanted the information. Edward Cope used a plank set over pickle barrels for his camp table, but Marsh had brought along an actual table, an oak drawing-room refugee that looked alien in the midst of the dusty tent. The table itself was a very efficient dust-gathering device, but Stillson had noticed that Marsh wiped it fastidiously every morning and evening. Marsh set brush and fossil to the side of the table, so he could lean on his elbows and give full attention to Stillson's report.

"Pull up a chair, please," he urged. "Tell me what you found."

He had brought along chairs, too, stained dark to match the table. Tiny leering faces were carved into the ends of the arms.

"They're camped about three miles from here, down the river. Where the bluffs are higher."

"How many are there?"

"Just two. Just Mr. Cope and Mr.—" he started to say Sternberg, but then remembered that he shouldn't know their names. He didn't want to imperil his steadily growing revenue stream by revealing to Marsh that he had been caught.

"—and another man. And a cook and a scout."

Marsh gazed off into the distance as he pondered this information.

"Just two men, you say? That's odd. He can usually scrounge more than that, and he got here before me. And a scout, you said? Did anyone see you?"

Stillson shook his head.

"So a cook and a scout, but not a very good scout. Did they seem to have found anything? Did you see any great bones lying around their camp?"

"No sir. In fact, I overheard them talking. They said they aren't finding anything."

Marsh mulled his over for a while, but slowly a smile crept onto his pudgy face. His brushy moustache and beard nearly hid it entirely, but couldn't hide the smile wrinkles around his eyes.

"Well, this is not bad at all, then. I was worried I would get here late and not come away with much. Cope had the lead, but as usual managed to squander it."

Stillson rose to go.

"I'd best see to the horses, sir."

"Yes, do that, please. Some of the men are going to take the rig about two miles north, so please get them ready for that. But you look tired. Where did you sleep?"

"In one of the ravines. Under some bushes. It wasn't bad."

"Goodness. It can't have been comfortable. I can barely sleep in my tent. I didn't mean for you to work that hard at it. See to the horses and get yourself something to eat. And then take a nap. That's an order. You won't need to go back to keep an eye on Cope until tomorrow."

"Yes, sir. Thank you."

Marsh was so merry at Cope's predicament that it seemed a good time to ask for some pay up front, perhaps a little extra for the fictitious night spent in a ravine, but no sooner had Stillson risen from the chair than Marsh was back brushing the fossil. He eyed it with such a joyous intensity that Stillson thought it best not to disturb him.

He got the horses harnesses to the cart and ready for their daily job, which was not really very onerous. They walked to the digging site, waited around until dusk and then carried it back. They had been in camp less than a week, but the cart never seemed to be very full. The horses got good rations and lots of time off in return, so Stillson figured they had one of the best jobs in the camp. He finished the task and wandered back to his tent. It was the smallest in the camp but plenty big for him. Marsh had planned on using it to store tools, but gave it to Stillson once he was hired, since he didn't have a tent of his own.

Inside he wiped off his face, although he kept a small box of dirt nearby in case he needed it again. He lifted up the folded blankets he used for sleeping to expose a small plank of wood, about a foot long and eight inches wide, covered lightly with dirt. Underneath it was a battered notebook. He pulled out the notebook and replaced the plank and the blankets, and then stretched out on top of them. He hadn't jumped ship to join Cope's camp because he didn't want to lose the notebook. He pulled a small pencil from his pocket. He kept it sharp with his knife, but didn't do a very clean job. The pencil looked like a small animal had gnawed at it.

Al Stillson had never met a real scientist before, but Edward Drinker Cope and Othniel Charles Marsh were not what he would have expected. He had thought scientists rarely left their dusty laboratories, where they pored over ancient texts and examined the bodies of dead animals. There was Charles Darwin, of course, who had gone off in his boat and kicked up quite a fuss, but when he conjured the image of a scientist Stillson still pictured someone like Isaac Newton, relaxing in his finery under a tree, waiting for the apple to fall.

Othniel Marsh looked more the part, sitting at his fine oak table brushing up his fossils. Stillson suspected he would have worn evening dress to the field if he could have, but the dusty conditions would not allow it. Cope looked a little less scientific to Stillson's eye. Marsh had described Cope as looking sort of like a rat. He parted his hair in the middle and brushed it back. His moustache flowed into his beard, and both flowed away from his face. The general rearward sweep of his hair made him look as though he constantly faced into the wind. Stillson thought this made him look more like a badger than a rat, and an angry badger at that.

Then again, Cope was the only one who had talked to him in any sort of scientific terms at all. Marsh, for all his airs, had said virtually nothing about the bones he sought but instead seemed more interested in Cope. Cope had at least spun his vision of the inland sea and its giant reptilian residents; Marsh had described Cope as if *he* was a dinosaur, a frightening beast to be avoided.

From what little Stillson had seen, the science of paleontology was not drastically different from ditch digging. At the business end it seemed to involve a great deal of sweating and no small amount of swearing, at least judging by how the deed was described by Marsh's men. He suspected it was not that much different with Cope, although there was probably considerably less swearing.

Sternberg had told him, before going to sleep, that there was much more to it than that. He had described the museums back east, where the bones were reassembled into some semblance of how they must have been in real life. The scientists were forced to imagine the flesh and muscles, and sometimes were forced to imagine missing parts of the skeletons. In some cases they were forced to conjure nearly the whole animal from just a few brittle bones. They were helped along by artist's sketches, but even the puniest of bones were magnificent enough all by themselves.

"Mr. Cope can do this better than most," Sternberg said. "I've heard that he can identify and picture a

completely new dinosaur just from a vertebra or a bit
of a skull, or even a tooth. He can look at a tooth and
see how it fit into a jaw, and from the shape of the jaw
he can imagine what the rest would be like. Sometimes
he's wrong, but usually he's right. Marsh can do that,
too. But you won't get Cope to admit it."

Sternberg had explained all this in low, resonant tones,
while Stillson sprawled in a spare tent to the left of
him, a tent that belonged to a camp worker who had
abandoned them. Edward Cope slept on the other side
of Sternberg, if what he did could be called sleep. The
excellent meal he had eaten seemed to disagree with
him at night. He snorted like a horse and bucked in
his sleep. Stillson felt sorry for his wife back home.
She must have bruises up and down her legs if he kicked
that way when he was there.

"It's like all the beasts we dig up during the day attack
him at night," Sternberg said, and from outside the
tent it did sound like Cope was being mauled in his
sleep. "I'm deaf in this ear, so I sleep on this side of
him, but it doesn't seem to help much. He's loud enough
for two ears."

Cope's kicking and snorting kept them awake for a
long time before exhaustion took its toll, so while they
waited to drop off Sternberg told him the story behind
the rush to Montana. The beds around the Judith River
had been explored some decades before, and had yielded
some good bones, but had then been left alone for a
long while. Then one afternoon in the spring a priest
who had been doing some missionary work among the
Crow and Piegan Indian tribes happened to go for a
walk through the ravines. A huge storm had come through
the area a week before, washing rocks and silt towards
the river and also uprooting what appeared to be a column
of smooth rock, unlike any rock the priest had seen
before. It was three feet long and knobby on both ends.

He kept track of the occasional news of scientific findings, and correctly reckoned it a dinosaur bone.

A certain professor Othniel Marsh at Yale was known to pay good money for such bones, so the priest sent it to him, with the thought that the proceeds could extend his time in the field. Somehow another scientist, a Mr. Edward Cope of Philadelphia, got wind of it and cabled to the priest that he would pay more. The bone was already on its way, but the priest sent along a cable instructing Mr. Marsh to forward it to Mr. Cope. He wrote that he was sorry for the trouble, but the Lord's work sometimes had to go to the highest bidder.

"Of course, Cope suspects he opened the box," Sternberg said. "There were some scuff marks where it was sealed, but we don't know if the priest did that, or Marsh. Looked at one way, Marsh got the best end of the deal if he did open it. He saw the bone and discovered where it came from, but he didn't have to pay for it. Just between you and me, if the situation were reversed, Ed Cope would have opened that box."

Just as he said that there was a ferocious exhalation and a thump from inside Cope's tent. Stillson half expected Edward to leap out of the tent, shouting that his good name had been defamed, but he was still just wrestling with his nocturnal attacker.

"The bone was a femur from the rear leg of an animal, but it didn't seem to fit with anything anyone had found before. It wasn't from one of the Hadrosaurs and didn't seem to match any of the meat eaters like Laelaps. It was something from a big plant eater, a heavy one that walked on all fours and couldn't rear up on its hind legs. We still don't know what it is. So here we are."

A mysterious femur, found easily in rocks from whence other good bones had come; Edward Drinker Cope did not need to hear much more. He had arranged to go, and Sternberg had begged to go with him.

"He had been back in Philadelphia, doing some desk work," Sternberg said. "He lives there most of the year, but I don't think that sort of work agrees with him. He likes to be out in the field. I met him in Omaha and we rode the train together to Utah and then took a coach into Montana. When we got to Helena the Army men said we would be crazy to come out here after what happened to Custer. Cope would not hear of it. He said the Sioux would be too afraid of the Army to try anything more, and so far he's been right. We've had a few Sioux come by, enough to scare off the two other men Cope hired. But we've had no trouble, and Cope loves it here. He's probably worth a million dollars in scientific knowledge but he's hanging all over these hills like he's some kind of monkey. I'm more than a decade younger than he is but I have trouble keeping up with him."

"Why is he so afraid of Mr. Marsh?"

Sternberg laughed.

"He's not *afraid* of Marsh. He just doesn't want him to find any bones first. They don't get along. They used to, though. Can you imagine that?"

Stillson shook his head, which made a rustling sound on the blanket. He was lying on his back with his face barely sticking out of the tent, just far enough out that he could see the stars. They seemed vast and awesome, and supremely unconcerned with whether Cope and Marsh could find ancient bones. Charles Sternberg spoke from within his tent. Stillson couldn't see him at all, could only hear his voice, a calming counterpart to the violent barks and snorts that emanated from Cope's tent.

"Yes, they were friends, less than ten years ago. They went looking for fossils together in New Jersey once. I think they found a Mosasaurus and some other things. Do you know what a Mosasaurus is? It's an ancient seagoing lizard that's sort of like a cross between a snake and shark."

Stillson tried to picture that, which was difficult. He had seen snakes but had never even seen a picture of a shark. The beast his imagination conjured resembled a stretched-out goldfish with big teeth and pop eyes.

"They also named some of their early findings after each other. I think Marsh actually named a type of Mosasaurus for Mr. Cope, and Mr. Cope named a Colosteus for Marsh. That wasn't that long ago, but those days are gone. I shudder to think what vile creatures they would try to name after each other now."

Stillson figured Marsh would have some sort of rodent in mind for Cope, although he might also find a cross between a snake and a shark acceptable.

"What happened between them?"

Sternberg waited a little while to answer, and Stillson thought he had perhaps fallen asleep. Cope had settled down, making the night a good deal quieter.

"I don't know, to be honest, but it's not doing either one of them any good. I leave it to them to have their fights back east. I just dig up the bones."

"How did you get started looking for dinosaur bones?"

"It's kind of an odd job, isn't it? My family moved from New York to Kansas when I was about your age. We were farming and ranching, but I didn't care much for that. I got so tired of fooling with the goats and the cows and the horses. I like my four-legged animals long dead and in the ground. I barely like to handle the horses we have here. But there I was. I started seeing things in the rocks, odd things I couldn't place, but I didn't have time to fool with them much. Then one night I had a dream. I was walking by a big, slow river, and I came upon a huge tree, unlike anything I've ever seen. So big it could block half the sky. It had leaves a foot across, and the moon lit it up really nice. I couldn't recognize much in the dream, but I did see this particular hill, that's shaped kind of like a cone. The next day when I woke up I walked out to that hill. There was no river, there was no big tree, but I found that hill and walked around it, just looking. I found a place where the hill was split open in the side, probably from frost. There had been a lot of ice and snow already that year, and it was playing hell on the rocks. Inside that break was a fossil leaf there, a foot across. A foot across."

"Wow," Stillson said.

"It was just a dream. Don't read too much into it. But I figured if I was dreaming about this stuff, I sure must be interested in it. So I quit ranching and started digging. That was just at the beginning of this year. I was desperate for support so I wrote to Mr. Cope and asked him to fund me. I told him why I wanted to do it, pretty much just like I told you, although I didn't tell him about my dream. He didn't know me from Adam but he sent me three hundred dollars and I've been at it ever since. When I found out he was coming here, I begged him to let me come along. He did. Thank God."

His voice drifted into silence, just as that leaf had drifted into mineral immortality. Stillson had fallen asleep then, too, and writing about sleeping was making him drowsy again. He closed the notebook and replaced it under the plank, carefully brushing some dirt over it. He stretched out on the blanket and went to sleep with his hat still on his head. No monsters came to him in his dreams, and he didn't see any trees.

FOUR

Sounds of shouting woke him from his sleep. He sat up and rubbed his eyes and started to leave the tent, almost getting beyond its flap before he remembered his box of dirt. He spat on his fingers, dipped them in the dark brown contents and then smeared them across his cheeks. He was getting used to the feel of dirt of his face. It had a comfortable weight that made him feel protected.

One of the soldiers was walking towards his tent when he came out.

"Come on, little man! Big news at the dig. Marsh wanted me to send for you. Get on my horse."

Stillson clung precariously to the horn of the soldier's saddle as his big gray horse trotted across the pocked ground for what seemed like forever. His feet couldn't reach the stirrups and flailed unanchored at the horse's sides. Montana had never seemed so vast. Stillson was glad as they neared the ad hoc quarry where Marsh's crew had been digging; he didn't think he could have held on much longer.

He had never been to a dig site, and was sort of glad, after seeing it. The men seemed entirely focused on the work. There was no luxury of any kind to distract them, no shelter except the shade of the cart. It made the camp seem like a hotel by comparison. O.C. Marsh stood at the pit's side, pacing the periphery, watching as four of his men tugged and strained at something in the loose shale.

"Pull!" Marsh shouted. "Pull!"

He looked like he was nearly ready to get in there himself. Stillson saw a furious storm of dust, as the men pulled at something, and then they stepped back and let the dust clear.

"That is fabulous! Fabulous! Good work, men!"

The skull of a loathsome monster beamed out from the pit of black shale, which was at the base of a gentle rise. The earth all above it was scarred with the bites of pickaxes, and the ground in front of it was trampled where the men had hauled it out. Its bones were battered, some were obviously missing, but it was still frightful. A long, slender half-skull, one of its eye sockets obliterated, was capped near the mouth by two curving teeth, one of which was broken off in the middle. The teeth were nearly long enough to be tusks, as if the beast was some sort of predatory elephant. Stillson stared at it, mouth agape. Charles Sternberg hadn't told him they were digging up monsters that looked like *this*. He tried to imagine what such a creature would look like encased in flesh, but his imagination wasn't up to the challenge.

"Look at this, Mr. Stillson!" Marsh shouted gleefully at him as he hopped down off the horse.

Marsh extended an arm to the hideous skull like a carnival barker showing off his prize freak. Stillson walked closer, staring in fascination. The skull pointed straight ahead, like the beast was about to leap from its underground lair and eat the entire camp. The diggers stood around it, their sweaty faces displaying broad smiles. They looked like hunters he had seen in pictures from African safaris, only their quarry was long dead.

"Isn't it amazing? Come closer, my dear Stillson," Marsh said.

Stillson complied, never taking his eyes off the wonderful beast. Marsh put an avuncular arm across his shoulders, pushing him into the paunch of his belly.

"This is what it's all about, young man. That creature there is probably a ferocious predator, and we are the first living men to see it. Not one living being has set eyes on it from the day it died until now, and here you are to witness it."

Stillson nodded and smiled. Well, maybe paleontology was a little better than ditch digging.

"Shall we look for more of it?" one of the men asked, and everyone else laughed. "There are probably some nasty claws back in there, as well."

Edward Cope would have been in there after it without hesitation, but Marsh looked up at the sky and shrugged.

"No, that's discovery enough for today. It's getting a bit late. Let's knock off and get an early start tomorrow. Good work, men."

The men laughed again. They seemed to be in unusually merry spirits. Perhaps they had hidden some liquor in their collection bags. The soldier was waiting to give Stillson a ride back to camp, but he opted to jump in the cart. The cart was not at all comfortable, but at least he wouldn't have to worry about falling out of it. It would ordinarily house some bones wrapped in burlap bags, but there didn't seem to be any bones around except for the monstrous head, and that was being left behind. There was lots of room in the cart. Marsh sat on the platform in the front of the cart, next to the driver, a usually taciturn man named Digger Phelps. *Everybody* must have been into the liquor; Phelps and Marsh smiled like they were off for a ride in the park.

Marsh turned around so he could face Stillson.

"What did you think of our find today?"

Stillson shrugged and smiled.

"It was wonderful. I've never seen anything like it."

Marsh laughed.

"Neither has anyone else."

Phelps laughed at that.

"I believe I told you to take the day off after seeing to the horses, didn't I, Mr. Stillson?"

"Yes, sir."

"Have you made any plans, by any chance?"

He didn't like where this was going.

"No, sir."

"Would you do me a favor, then? Have a look in on Mr. Cope's camp. Since we made this fantastic find, I want to know if they have found anything similar. Just give a look around and tell me what they're doing. And for God's sakes don't let them catch you. We've got a big lead on them now. I don't want any word of this to get out until I'm ready."

"Yes, sir."

"And, Stillson—"

"Yes, sir?"

"Please don't stay out all night again."

FIVE

Black clouds of acrid smoke from the torch almost gagged him, but he dared not cough. Actually, it probably wouldn't hurt much more than the torch itself. He might as well build a little railroad out here, ride up in the caboose and toot the whistle. Maybe O.C. Marsh himself would come out and help him climb down from the car.

Edward Cope hoped the exploratory pink glow of dawn would come soon; it was hard to see out here, even with the half moon shining. The moon lit the tops of the low hills but did nothing to illuminate the loose rocks or patches of scrub grass under his feet, patches just waiting to trip a man and send him face first into root or rock. That's where the torch came in, although it presented problems of its own. It was too cold for snakes, so he didn't have to worry about them, but it wasn't at all too cold for Indians and he did have to worry about them, especially when he was carrying around a flaming orange target. Fling your arrows a foot to either side of the light, men, and one of you will get him!

This appeared to be where Stillson said the great skull could be found. The skulking youth had appeared near dinner time, again, which Cope was beginning to think was on purpose, and said Marsh's crew had dug up the head of something out of Greek mythology. As if summoned by his thoughts, the boy's ghostly face appeared before Cope's torch.

"Thought you weren't going to make it," Cope said.

"It's not so easy sneaking out of camp with so many men around," Stillson said.

Cope suspected this might be a subtle criticism of his own severely understaffed operation, but he needed Stillson's help so he didn't complain.

"Can you see the top of that hill?" Stillson asked.

"Barely."

"It's at the base of it. They covered it up with a little bit of dirt and rock but it's still there."

Why didn't they take it? Cope wondered. If only a little bit of dirt separated him from what sounded like a fine specimen of mammoth skull, or even Titanothere, he would be out here with torches.

"Let's go."

They left the cover of the pines and crossed open ground. Cope kept the torch between them, which rendered it visible only from the sides, but also meant he got a face full of smoke.

"Here," Stillson said after a minute.

The hill loomed above them, the scrub grass on its top glowing in the moonlight like white fire. What Cope was after was in the shadows. Stillson had said the skull was under a thin layer of cover, so Cope hadn't brought his shovel, only his pick. He used its flat side to brush the rock chips away until it made a familiar sound and scraped across something hard. Mineralized bone. No other sound like it. Bone. He put down the pick and used his hands for the rest. Stillson held the torch. Its primitive light revealed something more primitive still, a bone helmet with two bone tusks. The tusks rolled away as soon as he brought the skull out. They had apparently been trapped in the rock and slowly split away from the head. A smattering of teeth fell away, too, and Cope carefully collected them off the ground while holding the battered skull in one hand.

"Alas, poor Yorick. I knew him, Horatio," he said under his breath.

Stillson laughed. Apparently the young man wasn't the ill-educated desert rat Cope took him to be. Edward decided he needed to know more about his young informant, but now was not the time, not when such a specimen waited to be examined. Dawn was arriving fast, and Marsh's pick monkeys would be at this thing again at first light, no doubt. Stillson held the torch out where he could see better, and Cope turned the skull this way and that in the flame's light.

The skull seemed to come to life under the nervous twitching of the flame. Most of its left side was gone, but its right appeared intact. A ridge of light flickering across its one good eye socket made it look as if it were raising an eyebrow, to show it was annoyed to be brought back to the surface world after such a long rest. Cope's fingers explored the skull. The rear portion of it lacked the distinctive saddle shape of the Uintathere, and it certainly wasn't large enough or wide enough to be a mammoth skull. If he didn't know better, he would say the skull came from a dinosaur, not a mammal, but then that wouldn't explain the tusks. He felt the line under what remained of the upper jaw. There was no tusk socket, no good growth of bone to serve as an anchor. That would mean they probably fit the lower jaw, but Marsh apparently hadn't found that piece.

"This makes no sense," Cope said.

"Why not?" Stillson asked.

"Why would these tusks, or tusk-like teeth, whatever, grow out of the lower jaw?"

"What's wrong with that?"

"Stillson, if I were to punch you in the face, right in

the mouth, which part of your face would hurt worse? Your upper lip, or your jaw?"

Stillson took a step back with the torch.

"I don't know."

"Come back here, lad, I'm not going to really hit you. If I did that, though, your lower jaw would hurt more. It might even get dislocated. Its purpose is flexibility, so that means it's also a little less sturdy, at least in most animals. Your upper jaw is molded into your skull, which is comparatively heavy. So why would you have your biggest digging devices or weapons attached to that lower jaw, where you're just asking for trouble? This species would have gone extinct from jaw dislocation alone."

"Oh."

"This must be a mistake. The bones of one creature have gotten mixed up with another. This skull looks like the side of a Hadrosaurus skull, with the tusks of a primitive elephant stuck on the front."

"Maybe they died while they were fighting," Stillson said.

"Not a bad theory, except neither one ate meat."

"Maybe they were fighting over some grass."

"They lived hundreds of thousands of years apart, or more."

"Maybe it's a mistake."

"That, I believe, is the best answer."

Cope examined the skull a minute longer and then stuck it back in its bed of shale. He rolled the tusks back where they were.

"Well, if it's a mistake, it will be Marsh's to make and not mine. I can hardly wait to read his description of this thing. Maybe he thinks he's dug up a dragon or something."

He stood and dusted his hands off, and took the torch back from Stillson. It was now nearly light enough that he could put it out.

"Stillson, thank you for letting me know about this. I believe my camp will be moving a little closer up this way."

"But you said it was a mistake."

"It is. But I'll be honest with you. Charles and I have not been having much luck lately. Actually, we haven't had hardly *any* luck lately. We have found virtually nothing in the last week, and before that we found nothing to write home about, quite literally. We found a few interesting things further down the river but nothing much. In the last week even that has dried up. A tooth here or there, but that's it. If I didn't know better I would say someone has been to our site ahead of us and cleaned everything out. So, mistake or not, this thing shows there are at least bones around here. That's good enough for me."

SIX

O.C. Marsh yawned and gave a luxurious stretch before remembering he should not be in a good mood.

Cope had fallen for his fake monster head, which lightened his spirits a little. He and his men had assembled an ad hoc beast out of spare fossils, after failing to find any good ones in the area. A partial Hadrosaur skull, truncated Titanothere tusks and assorted unfossilized teeth from cows and rodents had merged to form what the men dubbed "Old Whatchamacallit," the newest ancient beast to be discovered in Montana. Marsh had hoped Edward Cope would steal it outright, write a paper about it, and telegraph the news back east. The man at Fort Benton's telegraph office was standing by to copy any such messages for Marsh's viewing pleasure in just such an eventuality. So far, Old Whatchamacallit was still there, one of his men reported, but Cope had definitely had a look at it.

He would probably get so excited he would move his camp here, and that was fine. Fun and games could not conceal that the storied Judith River beds were not what Hayden had made them out to be. He had done well here, but so far that experience had not been duplicated. Marsh's men had spent less than a week in the field, true, but they could usually come up with something better than a wacky skull they made themselves. Any

41

halfway decent effort around here should turn up more than the exceedingly infrequent fossils they had found. Hayden had reported the inland sea was generous with its leftover bones, but one could not have told that from Marsh's first dig site. Less than a quarter cartful of fossilized bone was unearthed, and most of those specimens were shattered or decayed. In some places, the men reported what appeared to be signs of fresh pickwork, where the rock appeared to have been shaved away. But that couldn't be. No one was out here, no one but Cope, and he was no doubt busy with Old Whatchamacallit. Stillson said Cope was complaining about the dearth of bones, too, and he had been here since late August.

Stillson. Al Stillson, mystery boy with the dirty face. Cope's look at Old Whatchamacallit was proof enough that the unclean lad was a double agent. This angered Marsh a little. Was there no such thing as integrity in the young people anymore? Did loyalty extend only so far as there were dollars to back it up? On the other hand, this situation could be a boon. Before, he could only use Stillson to keep an eye on Cope, and that was meant sending a part-time lad to do a man's full-time job. Now he could do even better. He could use Stillson to steer Cope wrong, steer him into barren bonefields. This could completely obliterate whatever time advantage Cope once enjoyed by getting to the field earlier. Cope had done a fast one on him by stealing away that missionary's femur, but the beast it belonged to was still in the ground, still up for grabs.

It was still up for grabs, but why did he have to grab it personally? Why had he even come here? There was so much work to do back home. The Peabody Museum was under construction at Yale. It was just a building right now, and not even a finished one, but his job was to make it great. Boxes of fossils were arriving from all over the country, and even other parts of the world. There were so many bones to examine and catalogue and name. The thought of the monographs yet to be written was staggering. That was the best kind of work. Any brute could dig up bones, but it was the rare brute that could put them back together and chart out a connection between one ancient beast and another. Darwin had looked in the distance and seen the lay of the land; Marsh was finding all the steps that led from here to there. As if he didn't have enough to do there, his new home, too, was under construction. Good old Prospect Street. He would have plenty of room when it was finished, and it was likely to hold nearly as many fossils as the Peabody Museum.

All that to do and yet here he was, flat on his back on scratchy blankets on top of lumpy ground, and in the cold air to boot. But he had to come. The men were skittish about Sitting Bull, and no one could do better with the Sioux than he could. He had thought his expeditions with the Yale students would have been his last long field trips, given how much work remained to do. Yet here he was out here again, all because of the foolhardy Custer, and not even decent bones to show for it.

But where to look for them? Closer to the river? Further away? To go further east was to risk trouble with Sitting Bull, who was rumored to be heading this way. But going north had been a mistake, and there was little time to make mistakes. So east it was, redskins or no redskins.

One of the soldiers, a man named Dyson, parted the tent flap and looked tentatively inside. His eyes looked unfocused, as if he was just waking up. The soldiers were getting more sleep than anybody else in the camp.

"An Indian is here to see you, sir," Dyson said.

Marsh sat up and shoved his blanket aside. This was a fine way to start the morning.

"An Indian? Where is he?"

"By the north edge, sir. Blank is keeping a rifle on him."

"Sioux? Crow? Piegan?"

"Sioux."

"For God's sake, unless he's got a bloody hatchet in his hand, take the gun off of him. Tell him I will be right there."

Marsh struggled into his pants and boots and wool shirt, and grabbed his black jacket off the back of his reading chair. He wet his fingertips with his mouth and smoothed his moustache. He generally did not need to worry about the sad wisps of hair that clung to his head, soon to be as extinct as the dinosaurs themselves. Edward Cope had him bettered in the hair department, there could be little doubt about that.

He parted the flaps of his tent and walked briskly into the camp. Past the cooking tent he saw Jed Blank, the other soldier, standing nervously next to a tall man with dark skin and jet black hair. The man held the reins to a horse that looked too small for him. Blank and the Indian were not talking. Blank did not lean on his rifle but kept it dangling loosely at his side, his middle finger supporting the back of the trigger guard, his index finger dangling near the trigger. This proximity to death did not seem to bother the Indian in the slightest. He looked as relaxed as if he was waiting for breakfast. Marsh hoped he spoke English; he was not yet awake enough to try to muddle through in Sioux.

"Stillson!" Marsh shouted. "See to this man's horse."

Stillson scuttled up to the Indian and took the reins, but the Indian kept his eyes on Marsh.

"Greetings, sir," Marsh said, speaking slowly.

He extended a hand to the Indian. The Indian did

not smile, but his face seemed to lighten almost imperceptibly, and he gave Marsh's hand a couple of quick pumps. He had a good grip.

"Professor Marsh, I believe. You look well, sir. I recognize you from campus."

Marsh could not help but look surprised. The Indian's English was perfect, probably better than Blank's.

"You—you went to Yale?"

"Indeed I did, sir. I studied government and politics, which I regret kept me out of your classes. I heard nothing but good things about them, so it's no doubt my loss."

"I'm glad you heard good things, but I must confess this is a bit of a surprise."

Marsh turned to the soldier, whose eyes were firmly locked on the Indian, awaiting any sign of impending violence.

"Blank, I don't believe we will need you further. You don't happen to have a raiding party waiting to murder us, do you?"

"Indeed not."

"See there, Blank? Run along now."

He grasped the Indian gently by the arm and led him towards the middle of camp. The diggers gaped as they passed. If the Indian had looked like he was waiting for the morning meal, he might as well get it.

"Would you care to join us for breakfast, Mr.—"

"I have two names, sir, you may choose whichever you like. My name back east is George Burgess. My name out here is Sitting Lizard."

"I don't pretend to be on such good terms with Indians that I can bandy about their tribal names with ease, and I don't care to call you Mr. Lizard. May I call you Mr. Burgess, then?"

The Indian laughed, a healthy basso rumble.

"Please call me George. I would be delighted to eat breakfast with you."

They ate under a large tent, at another well-appointed oak table that would not have looked out of place in any New Haven restaurant. The cook, a man so wiry he never seemed to actually eat his own food, scowled as he served coffee and dried apples. He had no choice but to serve the Indian, but that did not mean he had to look happy while doing it. A few minutes later he came back with flapjacks, a special item Marsh requested for his surprise special guest. The cook's scowl had only intensified at the extra work required of him, since Marsh couldn't very well serve only the Indian the pancakes, so the cook had to make them up for everyone.

George Burgess was sitting close enough for Marsh to see him clearly, and he watched him carefully, although he tried to do it as surreptitiously as possible. Burgess was quite at home with eastern-style dining, despite his Indian garb. He had no problems with knife and fork, and even partially extended his little finger while sipping his coffee. When the men's eyes happened to meet, they exchanged delicate smiles and looked away.

"So," Marsh said, after the cook had graced them with his latest and best scowls while cleaning away their plates. "It is unusual for a man such as yourself to attend Yale. How did that come about?"

Marsh had taken care to phrase his question as inoffensively as possible, and had spent a good portion of his eating time fashioning it in his mind. He seemed to have done an adequate job. Burgess smiled.

"First off, I am a full-blooded Indian, of the Sioux tribe. My mother died soon after I was born, and my father was killed not long after in a skirmish with a Crow tribe. A traveling group of Methodist missionaries was passing through right about that time. I was having some health problems—I believe I had caught pneumonia—

and they persuaded the tribe to let them take me back east. Two of that group were named Burgess, a man and wife. They adopted me once I recovered. I grew up in Illinois. I was treated like anyone else, more or less. My parents had hopes that I might become a missionary as well, but I fell prey to a lower calling and studied politics and government at Yale. But somewhere, tugging at the back of my mind, was the thought I would need to return to my real people. I am not really a white Methodist, after all. I am a Sioux Indian, and I could not ignore the degradation of my people. These are hard times for the Sioux. After graduation I came back west, and here I am."

"And what is it you do, exactly, Mr. Burgess?"

"George, please sir. I serve as an emissary, although to be honest I am not particularly trusted by either the Sioux around here or the U.S. Army. I just do what I can."

Marsh stroked his moustache and sipped his coffee. He wondered if the newspapers in New Haven knew about this young man, and what he was doing. It would make a fine story.

"George, I have enjoyed meeting you and hearing your story, but I am not sure why you are here. I have no quarrel with the Sioux."

"I know. We all know what you did for Red Cloud. That's why I came to visit with you. To be honest, some of the Sioux here wanted to raid your camp and ask the questions on their terms. I reminded them of Red Cloud, and said we could just walk in and talk to Professor Othniel Marsh, and he would answer honestly."

"Call me O.C., please. What do you wish to know?"

"Why is there so much attention being paid to this area right now? You well know that previous searches for bones have been nothing but covers for gold hunts. I do not believe there is any gold here. Yet there is much sudden interest. Sitting Bull may come through here soon. Is this part of some plan to capture him?"

Few people could understand the desire to dig bones out of the ground. It was rarely assumed to be an activity carried out for its own sake, and Burgess was right—some fossil hunts were nothing but a cover for gold searches. But surely his modest operation could not give anyone that impression, and Cope's certainly couldn't. Cope had barely enough men to set up a camp, much less dig for gold.

"George, I assure you I am here because I received a significant sample of bone from this area. I am following up on that and nothing more."

"And the other gentleman? The one with the small camp down the river from you?"

"Much as I would like to tell you he is the vilest scoundrel imaginable, out to plunder any and all, I must confess that he is here for the same reason I am. We have both seen the bone sample, and are seeking the dinosaur it came from."

Burgess finished his coffee and set the cup on the table. He looked hard into Marsh's eyes.

"And the third gentleman? The one whose camp seems to shift all the time?"

Marsh sat back in surprise, causing the chair's legs to dig into the ground. He very nearly turned over, but managed to catch himself and only spilled a few drops of coffee across his clean shirt.

"*Third* man, did you say?"

"Yes. He travels fast, but I do not know how many horses he has."

Third man? Who could that be? Ferdinand Hayden was not in the field anymore, and neither was Joseph Leidy. Leidy had complained to anyone who would listen that he couldn't buy specimens like Cope and Marsh, and so he had opted out of paleontology altogether, contenting himself with creatures he could study under a microscope. It wasn't likely he was back out here. Who else could it be? Who else was there?

"Where is this third man?"

"So I take it by your words you're not familiar with him?" Burgess asked.

"No, I am not. Where is he?"

"I told you, he moves around. Not just his digging locations. He moves his *camp*. He moves it nearly every day. One day it may be a mile from where it was the day before, the next it could be ten miles away."

"Well, how big is it? Who's in it? You probably know every bush that my men relieve themselves on, so you must know something about this man."

Burgess leaned forward, resting his forearms on the table.

"Virtually nothing. A man of our tribe named Running Horse did manage to spy into the camp one day from a tall pine tree. He saw what looked like a big piles of bones scattered around the camp. He called them the bones of the Thunder Horse. Do you know what that is?"

"Yes," Marsh said. "I've heard the term."

Hayden had said some Indians thought the Thunder Horse came to the earth during storms to help them hunt buffalo. When he had dug up fossil bones the circumference of a man's waist, the Indians assumed he had stumbled across the remains of a Thunder Horse.

"That's all he could see. We do not know if he is digging up only bones or if he is after something else. He usually camps under large rock formations, so no one can see down into where he stays. Running Horse got lucky that day, but we have not been lucky since."

"Why not just sneak up on the camp?"

"Some of my tribespeople have attempted just that. They say it cannot be done. The camp is protected by a ghost wall."

"A ghost wall?"

"That's what they call it. It is a wall that simply keeps them from moving forward. It has no color, it cannot be seen, but no one can walk through it."

"And this is around his camp."

"Yes."

Marsh snorted and put his coffee cup down.

"Oh, come on, George. I'll bet that wall does have a color, and it's green. He's paying your men to shut up and protect him."

There was a flash of anger in Burgess' civilized eyes.

"That is not true. No one has spoken to him, and certainly no money has changed hands."

Marsh gazed absently at the tent flap. The cook brought fresh coffee, and Marsh hoped it would help him think.

"You keep talking about one man. How do you know there's only one? Surely he's not out here by himself. Has anyone seen him at all?"

"No. We have come across the remains of some of his camps. We have found only one set of boot tracks at each of them. He is a tall man, and his boots have ridges on the bottom."

"Ridges?"

"Like snake tracks."

"Have you found any horse tracks? Cart wheel tracks?"

"Nothing. That is why I do not know how many horses he has. There are his boot tracks, and not many of those. And nothing else."

Marsh lapsed into thought again.

"George, I don't know what to tell you. I don't know anything about this, and I certainly wish I did. Are your people keeping track of him every day?"

"As best we can. No offense intended, but we keep track of all white people, after Custer. There is much to do, and in fact I must go now. I thank you very much for the excellent breakfast. I will tell my people that you and the man with the small camp—"

"Edward Drinker Cope."

"I will tell them that you and Mr. Cope are after nothing more than bones, and will not be a threat. As for the other man, it seems that no one knows."

Marsh rose and shook hands with George Burgess, and courteously held the tent flap open for him.

"George, would you mind telling me where it was that Running Horse saw those Thunder Horse bones?"

"I would, but actually I don't know myself. I heard that story second hand. And I wouldn't bother trying to find it, if I were you. Running Horse said he went back the next day and the camp was gone, and so were the bones."

So at least *somebody* was getting bones out of the Judith beds.

"Will you be paying a visit to Mr. Cope? He might prefer a midnight raid to a nice breakfast visit."

Burgess paused, and looked strangely at Marsh.

"Come to think of it, I believe I heard something on campus about you and Mr. Cope. You are not friends. Is that correct?"

"That would be a very diplomatic way of putting it."

"Would you like for me to arrange for a raid of Mr. Cope's camp? I'm sure it can be done."

Marsh looked at him for a moment until his visitor's face broke out in a broad grin.

"George, don't tempt me like that unless you mean it. But are you going to speak to him?"

"I'm a little pressed for time. If you will guarantee he is only after bones, I will not bother him. Of course, if you don't want to do that, since you don't like him—"

Marsh patted his arm.

"Oh, no, no. I can guarantee that. Cope is my problem, he shouldn't be yours."

"Thank you. Good day, then, sir. It was nice to meet you."

"It was nice to meet you as well. I'll pass along your kind words of the pancakes to my cook, and they will no doubt put a smile on his face. And speaking of faces, the young man with the dirty one will have your horse waiting."

Burgess gave a small wave and began walking out of camp. Marsh noted that the soldiers kept their rifles handy, although they didn't raise them.

"Oh, George."

Marsh walked as fast as he could to catch up with the long-legged Indian.

"Let's not make this a one-time visit. Please drop back by—soon, if you can—and let me know what this fellow is up to. If you can find out."

George nodded.

"If I can find out, I will."

Marsh let him walk out this time, and stood looking after him until he was just a blurry shape on the horizon. So there was yet another team in the field, and a quick one at that. Maybe this could explain the fossil drought. The dinosaurs died, and their bones lay in the rock for millions of years, slowly turning to stone themselves. In time, skulls became separated from vertebrae, hands bade goodbye to arms, teeth scattered like pebbles. Above them the mammals grew more numerous and complicated, until one mammal rose on its hind legs until its brain grew large enough to comprehend the mysteries happening right under its feet. And then everything had to happen in a flash. If one big-brained mammal didn't get the bones out of the ground fast enough, another big-brained mammal would come along and dig them up, assign them a Latin name and write a paper about them, probably in so much haste he would get some of the particulars wrong. The slower big-brained mammal would like to investigate links and study as many big fossil fragments as possible in order to make a careful, definitive conclusion, but the first big-brained mammal had rendered that nearly impossible. And now yet another fast-moving big-brained mammal had come along, making the first two look sluggish indeed.

He watched the men get ready for the field, watched Al Stillson hook the four horses to the bone cart. Probably another fruitless day ahead, especially if they hit upon ground already covered by the new bone digger in the field. Then an idea occurred to him. His moustache slowly turned up into a smile. Edward Cope was a fast bone digger, and faster still to cable news of his findings to Philadelphia. But out here he was short handed, and as it turned out an even faster paleontologist had appeared on the scene. Only Cope didn't know he existed. So what would happen if a slow, methodical paleontologist from New Haven joined forces with a fast digger? Surely the stranger would see the sense in signing up with one of the premier scientists in the country. Surely he would see the sense in putting his speed in the service of Othniel Charles Marsh.

SEVEN

Al Stillson guided the horse down through the ravine, heading for the river. Walls of yellowish sandstone rose up on either side, their flanks dotted with shadows and dark pits of shale. These rocks seemed to be what were driving the paleontologists crazy. Othniel Marsh brooded in his tent, staring at the few tiny bones his men were able to find. At times he looked like an ancient seer, trying to divine the future with chicken bones, although his were fossilized. Edward Cope, being a man of action, preferred to rave along the rock faces. He never cursed, but he beseeched the Lord loudly, asking for more discoveries.

Stillson had not had much call lately to act as a double agent. There was not much to spy after, and he feared for his bankroll the longer the fossil drought continued. On his one trip to Cope's camp in recent days, Stillson had been badgered about what Marsh had done with the mysterious skull he dug up. Was he writing a paper on it? Stillson didn't know. He hadn't seen it again.

In the end, it was Marsh who asked him to run the errand to the trading post called Fort Clagett, to see if Cope had attempted to have a message delivered from there to the telegraph office back at Fort Benton. The Missouri River was too low for boats to make it back there, and Benton was too far a ride for such an unpromising mission, but Marsh thought Cope would get an overland delivery via the local trading post. Stillson had been puzzled by this. If anyone knew nothing was happening, it was Marsh. Cope was finding even less than he was. One of Marsh's assistants had told him that Marsh was as crazy for bones as Cope, but Stillson hadn't quite believed it. The man was Sam Sharp, who had a scruffy beard, a high forehead and usually a distant look in his eyes. In fact, he looked something like a younger version of Marsh. He wandered up one day while Stillson was preparing the horses.

"I hear you might be keeping tabs on Mr. Cope," he said.

Stillson tried to avoid meeting his eyes. Marsh had told him to keep quiet, and he didn't quite trust Sharp. Sharp looked like he was always into something.

"Could be," was all he could think to say.

"You better watch out," Sharp said. "I worked for Marsh for a while and then I worked for Cope. Now I work for Marsh again."

Stillson looked at him now. Sharp was staring straight at him, but it wasn't an intense gaze. He looked about half asleep, as usual. What was most unnerving about the look was it was deceiving. The other members of the camp said he was a sharp cardplayer and a crack shot with his rifle despite his dopey look.

"Why did you switch?"

"Never you mind. Just know that it's not a course of action I recommend. You don't just go back and forth between these two. That's like getting caught between two rocks. They'll grind you into flour. I advise you to pick one and stick with him. I'd go with Marsh, if I were you. He's raging ambitious."

"But Mr. Cope seems so much more—" Stillson said, and stopped, realizing he had already revealed too much.

"Energetic? Yes, he's that. But a slow fire sometimes burns longer, young Stillson. Don't forget that."

He hadn't. The slow fire that was Marsh was apparently heating up, and had sent him to check for any telegraph deliveries involving bones. Cope could not possibly have sent anything out, but Stillson wasn't going to argue because a trip to Fort Clagett was a nice break. It would mean seeing someone other than the surly men in camp, and the moody Marsh. He might even try to get a drink, since the men in camp didn't want to waste any of their whiskey on him and wouldn't surrender their bottles.

He was beginning to think he had not chosen the correct route. He thought this ravine continued on a broad path all the way to the river, but it was beginning to show troubling signs that it did not. There were more rocks in the path, and they were getting bigger, as if they were drawing strength from the nearing waters of the Judith. The horse was having to step lightly around them, a slow prance that was beginning to make Stillson feel a little nauseous. The sandstone began to close in on them, a giant tide flecked with the green of the scrubby pines that hung on the sides of the stone like nesting birds. Stillson thought he saw something flash to his left, up on the rocks, and for just an instant tugged on the reins as he looked up. At that same instant, the horse put one hoof directly on a large stone.

Stillson felt a rush of movement and a flash of light. He had the vague and unpleasant sensation that his feet were over his head, and he felt something warm and wet. Was he swimming? Had he taken a dive? There was a man reaching to help him, reaching to pull him out. He could not make him out clearly. It was like staring up at a giant from the bottom of a well. The man reached towards him and he saw another light, this one less intense than the light that had flung him in the water. His head felt even warmer, but no longer

felt wet. He felt hands moving over his head. The man
was looking at him strangely. He wore a long dark duster
but a hat that did not match it. The hat was the color
of straw, the color at the center of leaves at this time
of year in eastern Montana. Or was that his hair? The
man's hand moved in front of his face, and he closed
his eyes.

It was well past afternoon when Stillson opened them
again. The horse stood nearby, staring at him for lack
of anything else to do. Its reins were tied around one
of the better-rooted scrub pines, which held it in a
completely uninteresting part of the trail. There was
no grass for the horse to nibble, no rocks to kick at,
nothing but the pine tree itself, and even it was too
high to reach. The sun had already relinquished its
place at the top of the sky. This meant that he was
running very late. He had hoped to get to Fort Clagett
and back in one day, but now that was impossible.
Stillson moved to get up but found that harder than
he imagined. His arms and legs felt heavier than the
rocks around them. He heard the sound of horses'
hooves, approaching rapidly from the way he had come.
Stillson just managed to turn his head to look. His horse
looked that way, too, glad to have something happening.
There were a lot of horses and coming their way as
fast as they could without hitting the stones in the road.
From the sound, they were better at that particular
skill than Stillson and his horse had been.

Stillson tried to shout but couldn't find words in his
throat. He lay there instead, a large rag doll propped
up against a wall. It wasn't like they could miss him.
He heard the hoof beats begin to slow as the sandstone
walls closed around the intruders. The problem wasn't
that they wouldn't find him, it was that they might step
on him. Finally the hooves stopped thumping altogether
and he heard the sound of two human feet hitting the

ground. It was easier to roll his eyes than to move his head, so he just looked up. A tall man was striding towards him. He was an Indian, dressed in traditional garb except for his feet, which were shod in cowboy boots.

Stillson felt fingers against his face again, saw the Indian's face up close as he examined whatever the damage was.

"Are you all right?" the Indian said. "What's wrong with you?"

His English was perfect, betraying no pauses as the mind hunted for words. Stillson looked at him. Well, I was riding into Fort Clagett to see if we had intercepted any telegrams from a rival paleontologist, but I got distracted and my horse stepped on a rock accidentally and I fell and hit my head, and a strange man came along and then I passed out but now you're here. He thought all of that but none of it made it past his lips. The Indian looked at him a minute more and then walked back to his men, who were waiting on their horses at the point where the walls began to narrow. Stillson could not make out what they were saying, and was not even sure it was in English.

In a moment he returned, with two other Indians. Stillson had not done proper studying of his Indians, but he believed them to be Sioux. This was good, he thought. Professor Marsh seemed to have a soft spot for the Sioux, so maybe the feeling was mutual. He felt hands lifting him up, saw someone take his horse's reins off the pine tree. The Indians were quick. In no time at all they had stripped two small pine trees of their limbs and strapped them to his back, and then strapped the whole arrangement to one of the Indian horses. He had seen Indian children carried this way, tied to the back of a horse so tightly they couldn't fall off. It did not make him feel grown up to be carried in such a manner, but he couldn't even stand, let alone ride a horse. He hadn't been doing that so well when he was hale and hearty.

The tall Indian issued a stream of commands to his fellows. Apparently they were going to cease what they were doing and do something else, was all Stillson could make out from watching the Indian's hand gestures. It appeared that two of the Indians were to carry on in the direction they had been heading, but everyone else was going back the other way.

Stillson felt a surprisingly smooth hand on his cheek and looked up into the tall Indian's face. He felt ridiculous strapped to the horse.

"Don't worry, young miss," the Indian said. "We'll make you well."

Stillson swallowed and blinked. Had the dirt been knocked off his face in the accident, or did the Indian just have very discerning eyes? Whatever the reason, his secret was out.

EIGHT

"I'm sure you're used to coffee in the morning, but we don't have any."

"That's all right. Thank you, anyway."

It was an unusually chilly dawn, and Stillson stayed curled up in her blanket in the doorway of the conical Indian tent. What did they call them? Tipis. The women had undressed her in the night and wrapped her in some manner of rough gown. She felt sort of sorry. The Indians had prepared a healing ritual for her that was supposed to take most of the day, only when she woke up she felt fine, better than she could remember having felt in a long time. Maybe better than she had ever felt in her life. She felt cleansed and refreshed from the inside out. She actually didn't want any coffee, or any breakfast or anything. She felt great and needed no outside stimulation. If it weren't for the fact that some of the women were washing her clothes now, she would be up and gone, riding like the great wind across the plain.

The Indian squatted on his heels outside the flap door. She could see him much more clearly now. He was tall, and today had his long black hair tied in a pony tail in back. He was still in Sioux garb, but had a western-style jacket over his buckskin.

"My name is Sitting Lizard, or George Burgess, whichever you would like to use," he said.

"Which do you prefer?"

"Neither. I use Sitting Lizard out here and George Burgess back east."

"Since we are out west, I will call you Sitting Lizard. My name is Al Stillson. Alice Stillson, actually."

"It's very nice to meet you," Sitting Lizard said. "I looked at your hat and clothing after we brought you in. I've seen you before. I thought you were a man. You work for Professor Marsh, don't you? You took care of my horse."

Stillson smiled.

"Yes. Back when I was just Al Stillson. Although he may fire me now since I didn't make it to Fort Claggett."

"I will talk to him about that. I believe we can take care of that. If you tell me what you need, I will send someone in a hurry to Fort Claggett."

"I wouldn't think they would welcome the sight of an Indian approaching the fort in a hurry."

"Perhaps I will go myself. They will not be alarmed. I know many of the people there."

"Mr. Marsh wants to see if anyone has arranged to send a telegram up to Fort Benton. He wants to know if any messages are going out about bone discoveries by Mr. Edward Drinker Cope."

"Yes, Mr. Cope. I do not know him but I know who he is. Are you sure he's not looking for any discoveries from the other man as well?"

"What other man?"

Sitting Lizard laughed.

"This man has a very low profile, it seems. There is another man in the field. He appears to be digging up bones, but that is all we know about him. That is why I came to speak with Professor Marsh, to see if he knew anything. He doesn't. But he wishes to learn something."

I bet he does, Stillson thought. If Cope is enough to

make him crazy, having yet another competitor will drive him right over the edge. But why wouldn't he tell me about it?

"That is only one of the mysteries around here, young lady," Sitting Lizard said. "Another mystery is why you are running around pretending to be a man when you make a perfectly presentable young woman. A pretty young woman, I daresay."

Alice Stillson blushed.

"I have been told that I am not conventionally beautiful, but I am attractive. My cheeks are a bit broad, as you can see. If I wear a man's clothing and cut my hair, I can pass for a slightly effeminate young man. If I add a little dirt to my face I can pass for a regular young man."

"A pretty young man," Sitting Lizard said.

He had a big smile on his face. He was enjoying this.

"Yes, I guess so."

"Now we have the how, Miss Stillson, but we don't yet have the why."

"Would you like the long version or the short version?"

"As I suppose I am off to Fort Claggett today, I suppose the short will have to do."

She was from a wealthy family in St. Louis, although one that had already seen the peak of its fortune and was now sliding down the other way. Her father, desperate to maintain some sort of status, had promised to marry her to the son of an even wealthier neighbor, a neighbor whose fortunes were still on the rise. That would have been fine except Stanton was a dolt, a young man who was willfully dumb. He had, as far as Alice Stillson could tell, no real interest in anything, including her. He was content to be and to spend and anything beyond that was an obstacle too great to mount. Her father sensed this in Stanton, and at one point in his desperation (and after he had consumed a few too many) had even whispered the heresy that she could always take a more interesting lover if she desired.

She did not desire, but also did not know quite what to do. Her father's reach went a long way in St. Louis. Despairing of her predicament, she had escaped by reading trashy illustrated weekly accounts of the wild west. They were full of cowboy derring do, dastardly Indians and wide open spaces. She had taken to imagining herself as a cowboy and her unofficial betrothed as an Indian.

"I was always practical. So I thought, why not come out here and do some research and start writing those stories myself? The grammar is always terrible in those things. I figured I could do better, but I didn't want to come out here as a woman. I didn't want to be cowering at the wall while the hero saves the day. I also didn't want to be raped. So I disguised my looks and came out west. I went to California initially, just to see it, but it's hard to wander around dirty there so I came back this way. In Fort Benton I heard of a paleontologist who was looking to hire people. I had read stories about gunslingers but I had never read one about a paleontologist, so I hired up with Mr. Marsh."

"So you're going to write stories about the brave paleontologist."

"I hope to, although it looks like I'll have to make a lot of things up, since nothing seems to be happening. I think I may have to exaggerate a bit to make him into a wild west hero, too."

"You came out here to research these wild west stories."

"Yes."

Sitting Lizard started laughing, so that he nearly rocked back on his heels and fell over.

"What's so funny about that?"

"I'm sorry," he said as his laughs petered out. "It's just funny that you think anyone actually puts any work into those things. I've seen them. I even met somebody who wrote a few of them, once. They don't research them at all. Most of those writers have never been further west than St. Louis itself, and I doubt many of them have been that far. They sit in New York and Philadelphia and grind those things out, using second-hand stereotypes."

This could be a problem, she had to admit.

"Oh."

"Well, maybe your stories will be better than anyone else's."

"Maybe."

"Do you know anyone in publishing? Do you know anybody at the magazines?"

"No."

"So how are you going to get your stories published?"

"I just will."

She thought about her betrothed to be, and a quick series of images passed before her mind. Stanton escorting her to the theater, dressed up, slightly bored. Stanton dining with her at the home of a friend, slightly bored. A tiny little baby being born, and looking ever so much like Stanton, already ever so slightly bored.

"I just will," she said, and her green eyes met the brown eyes of Sitting Lizard full on.

He put out a hand to touch her face, so slowly and gently that she never even flinched. His arm moved like water. His fingers brushed her cheek. She kept her eyes on him but he looked at her face, her lips, her forehead. His fingers and knuckles were very soft, not what she expected.

"You fell from a horse but there's not a mark on you. Not a scratch."

Her eyes opened wider, showing more of the green.

"None? I thought you had washed me off. I felt blood running down my face, or I thought I did."

"No, when we came down the ravine we found you sitting up like a doll. Your clothes were dirty but your face was clean."

"Usually I manage to keep both pretty dirty. What were you doing in the ravines, anyway?"

He looked off in the distance, as if unsure what to tell her.

"You remember the man I mentioned? The other one digging up bones? We've been trying to keep an eye on his camp but he moves it around all the time. Someone thought they had seen it closer to the river, through that ravine. We were heading through there until we found you, but we hadn't found him. Two braves continued on looking for him, but they didn't find anything."

A picture flashed before her eyes of a man, reaching for her face. His hands were even smoother than the Indian who later found her.

"Sitting Lizard, I just remembered something. I saw a man. He found me before you did. I was really dazed and didn't get a good look at him. He was sort of looking me over and then I fell asleep."

"What did he look like?"

Sitting Lizard seemed very interested. He hunched even closer, nearly crawling inside the tipi with her. An Indian woman two tipis over gave him an odd look.

"It's hard to tell. I was dizzy and couldn't see straight. He looked big, but I'm not sure how tall he was. He had blonde hair. But it's—"

"What?" Sitting Lizard asked as her voice trailed off.

"It's hard to explain. I wasn't scared. I sort of felt this peace coming over me. I think he realized I'm a woman. I sort of felt a sense of surprise, but I never felt fear. And then I went to sleep."

"And when you woke up, you didn't even need the ceremony."

"Yes. I hope that's no trouble. I just felt so rested this morning. I feel great."

"A tall blonde man."

"Yes."

Sitting Lizard looked past the tipi flap. A woman walked their way, holding a folded pile of black cloth. She carried them like they were weights, and it occurred to Alice that the woman no doubt had more pressing things to attend to than washing her clothes.

"Here comes your clothing," Sitting Lizard said. "I'll let you change back into them."

"Tell her thank you for me," Stillson said when the woman handed her the shirt and trousers.

"You're welcome," the woman said, without looking at her.

"We're pretty good with English these days," Sitting Lizard said when the woman left. "That's another thing you won't read in those wild west stories of yours."

Stillson put the clothes on the ground inside the tipi, on a dry patch of grass. Sitting Lizard did not move, so she did not get ready to don them. He was still looking after the woman, but in a vacant way, as if looking far beyond her.

"I'm sorry," she said.

He turned back to her and gave her a smile so faint its warmth did not quite reach his eyes.

"Don't be sorry. I didn't mean to sound angry. It's just that there's a lot going on. Sitting Bull is heading this way, and I'm not sure what will happen when he gets here. We've been keeping the women and children here, but Sitting Bull is likely to go further north. I'm just not sure what will happen."

"Will you go with him?"

The already faint smile faded completely.

"That's one of the things I'm not sure about."

They sat in silence for a few moments, her green eyes looking into his brown ones.

"I'll let you get dressed," he said, and impulsively brushed her cheek again with his hand.

"Thank you. You have the softest hands in the west."

He stood and laughed.

"Oh, Lord. Please don't put that in your story."

"He had hands like iron," she said, pulling up her black shirt and fluffing it out.

"Steel. Hands like steel. Come find me when you're ready and we'll get you back on your horse and back to Professor Marsh. I'll go on to Fort Claggett and see if anyone has sought to send telegrams."

She began pulling the tent flap closed.

"I suppose this is the end of Alice Stillson," Sitting Lizard said.

"You don't like Al?" she asked, looking through the flap with one eye. "If you're nice Alice will come back."

"I hope she does," he said. "I hope she does."

NINE

And I thought I would be lonely out here! The scenery is fine, although harsh, but not harsh enough to keep bone diggers away. The professor of Copeology at Yale is here, although he is trying to keep things quiet. Mr. Marsh did not come out here with his usual fanfare. He probably does not want the Indians to bother him again so that he gets sucked into all those political matters like he did two years ago.

I am pleased to hear thee are doing well. Tell Julia to put that gopher in alcohol if she wants to keep it and I will help her draw it and describe it when I get home. I will leave it up to thee as to whether she can keep it in the house. Thee are probably doing better than I; I have seen more fossils in Philadelphia than I have out here. Marsh dug up some sort of skull and bones, although I think it was mixed up and he did not think much of it. I have been tempted to go dig it up myself if he left it there, so at least I would have something.

Our cook and guide seem worried about the Indians but I have come across only a few and all peaceable, so thee should not worry. The newspapers in Helena and elsewhere have published some cock and bull stories about Sitting Bull and the Sioux but nothing has happened here. Some Piegans came by one afternoon but they were pleasant and we have heard nothing more of them.

The landscape here makes one tend to think, especially in the absence of bones to dig or hostile Indians to avoid. I miss father; it is just about a year now since he left us. Did thee realize that? One year gone, and his physical presence is little more than the bones that I seek here, yet he lives on in my mind. If I came across his skull, would I revere it as his or ponder what it would mean for his brain size and eating habits? I do not mean to make morbid jokes, but I tell thee my devotion to both science and human feeling would require me to do both at the same time. That is my way of praising God to the fullest. I know it bothers some that I no longer go to the meetings, but I cannot abide that all men must teach religion or they are good for nothing. It is absurd to think this, and becomes more so when we consider the limited state of all mankind's knowledge. If my theories are true and if my findings are correct, atheism will receive its death blow. This would be hastened along if God would assist me in finding fossils here, but it is not in my ability to know His will.

If things continue as they are, we will not remain here much longer. We will first—

Edward Drinker Cope held the letter to the plank as a strong gust of wind roared through the camp, rattling Boston Mickle's pans. The camp was higher up from the Judith River than usual, which meant less of a ride to the bone-hunting grounds but also left it more open to the elements. A lone outcropping of sandstone rose behind the east side of the camp, but it was wide open for the other directions. The moon was nearly bright enough to allow him to write without hunching near the fire, but the cold made it necessary if he wanted to put down words without his hands shaking. Jenks Dart had seen a boat captain on the river who offered to take mail, so he decided to write to his wife to take his mind off the lack of activity in the field. It had only succeeded in focusing his mind on exactly that.

He looked up until the gust of wind had passed, and from the corner of his eye thought he saw something strange to the north of his camp. A green flash, out on the horizon, bright enough to leave an afterimage on his eyes when he blinked, but fast enough that he couldn't tell how far away it was. He had been out in the west numerous times and had never seen anything like that. In fact, he had never seen anything like that back east, except for perhaps once in Philadelphia when a fireworks show had gone awry, sending green-burning flares out low across the sky. He still decided this was unique; those green lights had lingered longer than this flash. Cope got up and folded his letter, nearly forgetting to sign it.

Cope folded the letter and tossed it in Dart's tent, pitching it atop his blanket so he would see it. The lanky outdoorsman tended to focus intently, but only on things that were directly in front of him. Even while signing the letter and throwing it in the tent, Cope didn't take his eyes off the horizon, hoping for a repeat. Charles Sternberg came out of his tent while Cope wandered by.

"Ho!" Sternberg said. "Are you sleepwalking now?"

"Did you see that green flash?"

"No."

"You're from out this way. Can you see the northern lights from here?"

Sternberg eyed him with bemused suspicion.

"Not usually."

"There was a green flash on the horizon, right over there."

Sternberg squinted, and then shook his head.

"Just moonlight out there now, it looks like to me. The northern lights last for a while, when you can see them. I've never heard them described as a flash."

"Well, it was there."

"I didn't say it wasn't."

There was a shout from the darkness around the camp. It sounded like Jenks Dart. Cope and Sternberg exchanged glances and then ran around the tents to see what it was. Neither one had a pistol, but Cope grabbed his pick on the way past the pickle-barrel table. It probably wouldn't do much good, but it was better than nothing. They ran as fast as they could in the dim moonlight until they got to a trail that ran past the north edge of the camp and eventually led to the river. There was a rolling sound, like water rushing. Dart was standing at the camp-side edge of the trail, yelling as horses shot past. Cope could not see the riders, could only make out man-shaped legs dark as shadows along the horses' white flanks.

"Slow down!" Dart said, holding his everpresent rifle by the middle and waving it like a flag pole. "Give somebody some warning!"

The riders did not hear him, or did not heed him if they did. They stormed down the road and out of sight, the horses' hooves sounding like distant drumming before fading entirely.

"Jenks!" Cope said once the horses were gone. "What's going on down here?"

"I almost got run over by those damned Indians!" Dart shouted. "They come barreling up the trail like it's broad daylight and everybody can see them!"

"What were they running from?" Sternberg asked. "Or were they chasing something?"

Dart was out of breath from shouting.

"I don't know," he said in a more normal voice,

although one ragged with little gasps. "I didn't see anything in front of them, so I guess they were running."

Sternberg looked down the trail.

"I don't see anything after them, either."

Cope peered off into the darkness. They were on lower ground now, and he couldn't see the murky horizon, could only see the road rising before them and the moon riding high above it.

"Which way does this trail run, Jenks?" he asked.

Dart pointed north. Cope looked in the direction of the long finger. It was where the glow had been. Maybe the Indians knew something he didn't. If they knew anything at all about it, they knew more than he did.

"Did you get a good look at them, Jenks? What sort of Indians were they?"

Dart was now back to normal, was once again the unflappable outdoorsman, ready to tangle with any man or beast.

"They looked like Crow to me."

"Do you know where they are camped?"

"Of course. There are a lot of them, hundreds. They're on the other side of the river, near Fort Claggett."

Fort Claggett sold some of the same supplies and foodstuff as Fort Benton, only it had half as much stock and sold it for about twice the price. Cope had bargained furiously for his horses and supplies in Fort Benton, and aimed to steer clear of Claggett as much as possible so as not to wipe out what savings he managed to achieve.

"Are they peaceful?"

"Except when they run up and down the road like maniacs," Dart said.

"I tell you what, Jenks. Go down there tomorrow and ask some of them to visit me. Ask them for some of the ones who were running on the trail tonight."

Dart did not look very happy about the assignment, but Cope ignored his sullen look.

"Maybe we'll get Boston to cook them up a little dinner," Cope continued. "And shoot something good if you can."

"If I *can*?" Dart said.

He looked slightly hurt.

TEN

He moved about as fast as the clouds that flirted with the moon above, and tried to mimic their silence. When his feet or hands had occasion to crack a twig, he would wait for minutes to pass before moving again. A real Sioux brave could do this at three times the speed, and with less noise, but he felt he wasn't doing too bad for a Yale graduate. He was near the camp, could hear the men sleeping. One of them made as much noise sleeping as two regular men did awake, but he had been warned to expect that. Two of his braves waited on horses three hundred yards back. They were there if trouble arose, but could not come closer without turning their presence into a self-fulfilling prophecy.

George Burgess crept around a patch of scrub pine and saw the fire and the tents. He heard regular snores—and, from the one tent, snorts and coughs—but didn't see any people. Professor Marsh at least kept up the pretense of having guards, but this camp was wide open. He had seen a crude map of the camp, drawn with the small index finger of Alice—or rather Al—Stillson. It showed the fossil storage tent to be on this side, which was fortunate. It was the side of camp bordered by the last hunches of a ravine and the beginnings of a meager pine wood. These benefited the campers by blocking the wind, and they benefited

74

an intruder by affording him places to hide. The cart used daily in the field was parked on the open side of the camp, near the sleeping tents. Getting to it would have been much more of a challenge, one he was glad not to have.

Burgess made it to the fossil tent by feel, keeping his rifle slung under his right shoulder. The moon was out, but it was keeping company with the party of clouds tonight and could not be bothered to assist him. The tent had been thrown over the wooden sides of a collection cart, but had not been cinched too tightly because the wind wasn't too bad here. He was able to slide under the tent side and stand up inside it. He leaned his rifle against the cart and let his fingers roam across the bottom of the cart bed. This was probably not such a good idea. Scorpions or other creepy crawlies could mistake the cart for a hotel made especially for them, what with its warm piles of folded rags. He hoped the eight-legged residents of the camp were sleeping as surely as the two-legged ones.

He came across tiny hard objects that felt like rocks. This was close, but wasn't exactly what he was pursuing. Finally he felt a long lump at the edge of the cart, wedged in the groove where the cart's side met the bed. It was nearly three feet long and knotted on both ends like a club, and was swaddled in rags like a baby. This had to be it. With agonizing slowness he drew the lump out and held it, marveling at its weight. Crazy Horse once said he believed his bones would turn to stone upon his death. This bone proved that could be true. He cradled the bone like an infant and slid out from under the tent flap, retrieving his rifle as he did so. Burgess almost laughed at the thought that he was a god of thunder; he had a thunder stick in one hand and the bone of a Thunder Horse in the other. His amusement lasted until he was back around the edge of the pines. He felt something cold on his neck, something cold and metallic and round.

"Turn around very, very slow," a voice said.

It was low and gravelly, the sort of voice he felt as well as heard. He obeyed. The moon obligingly peeked around a cloud just as he turned. It showed him a man as tall as he was, with stringy hair and a new beard. The man held his rifle in one huge hand, keeping its barrel in constant contact with Burgess' throat.

"Drop it or kiss your head goodbye," the man said.

Burgess let go of the bone, giving it a little nudge as he did so. One of its rounded ends thumped against the man's foot. His immobile face cracked into a grimace and he looked down in pain, just for one second. That was long enough for Burgess to swing his own rifle around, one handed, and knock the man's barrel aside. He had hoped to knock the gun clean out of his hands, but he had underestimated the man's grip. The man recovered instantly and brought the rifle barrel up to Burgess' lips. Burgess did the same with his own gun.

"I hope you didn't break that bone," the man said slowly.

He spoke slowly because he was watching the intruder carefully, waiting for the slightest opportunity to blow his head off. Burgess did not blink, but stared hard into the man's left eye. He dared not shift his gaze from one eye to the other; one would have to do. In the time it took his vision to shift across that mere inch, he could be dead. His arm was tired of holding up the rifle with no support, but he could not think of that now. The other man's rifle barrel was close enough to kiss, and he gave no indication of being weary of holding it.

"I have no quarrel with you," he said. "Give me the bone and let me go."

"What is your name?"

"Sitting Lizard. Of the Sioux. May I ask yours?"

Their conversation proceeded slowly, as if both men had trouble with English.

"Jenks Dart. I work for the man who owns that bone."

Burgess became aware that a large cloud was approaching the moon, which would drop the rifle-toting combatants back into darkness. He did not glance up at the moon to verify this, because had he done so he would have been instantly dispatched to a place where he wouldn't care at all about the weather. Either the Happy Hunting Ground, or Heaven or Hell, depending on whether the Sioux or the Methodists were correct. He could only sense the impending darkening of the moon, and knew then he wouldn't be able to look this Jenks Dart in the eye, and that was worrisome. That was when the trigger would have to be pulled, and he really didn't want to do that. He was sure Jenks Dart wouldn't mind.

"I will bring the bone back," he said. "The man who wants it only needs it for a little while."

"I don't think so. I'm afraid I'm going to have to kill you."

O.C. Marsh had a plan, but it was complicated to explain just at this moment. He had told Burgess about an earlier success with something he had called "Old Whatchamacallit," a slapped-together make-believe beast he had buried to fool the man who was even now snorting and kicking on the other side of the pines. Marsh was growing increasingly disgusted with his own inability to find bones, and with the inability of the Sioux to keep track of the speedy third bone hunter. Why not put together a bigger, more elaborate Old Whatchamacallit, and see if this mysterious scientist could be tricked into digging it up?

"Then I and my men will march in there and see about this ghost wall," Marsh said.

The problem was he didn't have enough bones to make a really attractive fossil find. He fetched his men to dig up the first Old Whatchamacallit, although he seemed angry it was still there. Then he decided he needed another bone, a leg bone he said would be in Cope's camp. He had seemed angry at Al Stillson for some reason, and had determined to send him on the errand. Burgess had thought about Alice Stillson's face, so soft without its covering of dirt, and had instead volunteered to do it himself.

"Stillson can give you a layout of the camp," Marsh had told him. "But don't tell him why you're going. He is not to be trusted."

So here he was, rifle in face, arm getting tired, no bone. Alice could probably have done a better job after all.

"I don't think you want to kill me," Burgess said.

"No? You're a Sioux who attacked a white man. I'd be doing General Custer a favor."

They stood in silence for a long moment. The clouds rolled in, and Burgess could almost feel the metallic rasp of Jenks Dart's trigger moving to ignite the blast.

"How long have you been out here, anyway?" Burgess asked.

"Long enough."

"I'll bet just since earlier this year. You're not one of the Army men from Fort Benton. I'll bet you came here with another Army, didn't you?"

Dart's left eye twitched. Burgess tightened his own finger's grip against his trigger.

"I'll bet you came here with a general you didn't like very much. I'll bet you got out while you could. I'll bet you looked back and were glad you got away before that general got killed by the Sioux."

The eye was very nearly a slit.

"Damn you," Dart said. "I'll pay you back for what you did to Custer."

"You don't care about him. You wouldn't have left if you did."

"I care about him more than I care about Sitting Bull. I'll leave your body for him to find."

"And that will be the last thing you do. Sitting Bull needs me. He will come here looking for me. When he doesn't find me he will be looking for you. He will be looking for any remnants of Custer's Army."

It was getting dark now, very dark. The clouds were upon the moon. Burgess' trigger was pulled nearly as far as it could go without firing. Jenks Dart's was no doubt at the same place. All his education and training, all for nothing, and he, a Yale graduate, to die at the hands of a dirty deserter over a dinosaur bone. He should have been a missionary after all.

"Might there be any money in this for me?" Dart said after a long pause.

Burgess couldn't help himself. He blinked for the first time.

"I'm sure that can be arranged."

" 'Cause I need money to get away from here. My pay has been a bit slow in coming."

"I guarantee you we can arrange something."

Just as the light of the moon dipped them both back into the night's darkness, Jenks Dart said, "I'm going to put my rifle down now. I suggest you do the same."

Burgess' arm trembled when he lowered the gun, from exertion spiked with fear. He managed to keep a steady grip when Jenks Dart shook his hand, and managed to keep his breath from rattling when he finally exhaled.

"Custer was a bastard," Dart said, and they both laughed.

"The bone is broken," Burgess said when he picked it up again.

It was split in two halves, nearly in the middle. He

was not surprised. Marsh had impressed upon him the fragility of even the sturdiest-looking bone, and had said they could break even when handled with great care. They were not likely to withstand being thrown on someone else's boot-clad foot.

"I'm sorry."

"It's done," Dart said. "They come back into camp happy about having a tooth or a scrap of anything, so I don't see why having a big bone in two pieces should matter. And anyway, they won't be looking at it for a while. They'll probably think the cart just broke it. You are going to bring it back, right?"

"Yes."

Dart helped him get the two pieces back as close together as they would fit, and then wrap them in the rags.

"Maybe Mr. Marsh will be happy with this," Dart said.

"How did you know Marsh is the one who wants this bone?"

"Who else is there?"

Sitting Lizard felt his way back through the ravine to the waiting braves, his Thunder Horse bone and thunder stick once more in hand. He had nearly made it when he felt the presence of someone else behind him. Burgess stopped and took a deep breath. He did not need another death-defying encounter this evening. Surely one had been enough.

"Who's there?" he asked quietly.

Turning around in the ravine at this point was difficult, and he didn't want to break the bone further. He felt something pushing past his leg, something big, and nearly yelped in fear. Then he felt hands patting his chest, rubbing across his face.

"Are you unharmed, Sitting Lizard?" Alice Stillson asked, her voice carrying a healthy trace of fear.

She was about the only one who thought of him as an Indian out here, it seemed. The Sioux gave him the name Sitting Lizard somewhat grudgingly, Marsh didn't use it, and even he thought of himself as Burgess. The moon would not cooperate and let him see the face of his only true believer, and he wished it would.

"I'm fine. I'm fine, Alice. What are you doing here?"

"I watched everything. I followed you from camp. I was in the pines back there. I was just about to blow Jenks Dart's head off."

He leaned his rifle against the ravine and wrapped her in the crook of his arm. She squirmed in next to the dinosaur bone. He could feel wetness on her cheeks when their faces touched. She would have to put some more dirt there.

"Hold on," he whispered, and set the bone down carefully. There was no need to break it into thirds.

His braves would be getting restless, but there was still time. He held Alice Stillson in his arms and kissed her face and kissed her mouth. Her hat fell off and she didn't move to retrieve it. The moon still didn't come out, but now he was glad.

ELEVEN

Boston Mickle had outdone himself this time, despite the fact that he seemed terrified of his guests. The meager plank table had been replaced with an actual rough wooden table, which had been intended for fossil examination and which, unfortunately, was not getting much use for that purpose. The pickle barrels and planks still remained, only now they were used as seats for the distinguished guests, who sat around the table in their buckskin finery. The table, intended as it was to be holding heavy fossils, was just barely up to the task of holding Mickle's output. Its surface was entirely taken up with hen, duck, fish, potatoes, rice, dried apples and succotash, all procured by the death-delivering rifle, fishing line and picking hands of Jenks Dart. Mickle had kept the fire going all day to get them ready, but they did appear worthy of anyone's appetite.

Charles Sternberg looked down the table and thought that was a good thing, for the man sitting at the end opposite Edward Cope did appear to possess sizable eating ability. He must have been nearly six and a half feet tall. He earned a pickle barrel all to himself, because he looked like he could snap the plank boards right in half. His name was Twobelly, chief of the Crows camped just across the Judith River.

"Twobelly!" Boston Mickle had repeated when told

the chief was coming to dinner. "He sounds like my kind of man!"

The chief sat stiffly upright like an adult at a child's table, his knees visible at the edge of the table. Two of his braves sat on one side of the table, one on the other. They were smaller than their chief, which just meant they were normally sized, but they had fierce names. The two across from Sternberg were Wolfbox and Enemy Hunter, and the one at his left elbow was Bearhead. Despite their names, they appeared jovial, laughing and joking in English that could use a little work but was perfectly understandable.

"We should be getting some snow fairly soon," Sternberg said to Bearhead, who smiled and nodded.

"I hope Sitting Bull comes through before we have to leave our camp," he said, his smile never wavering from his broad face. "I hope to kill a few of his braves."

Sternberg smiled back at him for a second until he realized what he had said, then he kept the smile on his face so as not to offend.

"The fish looks good, doesn't it?" he said, and Bearhead nodded again.

"Thank you all for joining us today," Cope said, and Sternberg was relieved to turn his attention to his friend. "I hope you are doing well."

"Thank you," Twobelly said in a deep voice that boomed up from somewhere deep inside his massive chest. "Where is the man who carried the invitation to us?"

"He wished me to express his regrets," Cope said. "He had some business elsewhere and could not be here."

Dart was becoming more solitary than ever these days. He was the camp's ghost guard, seemingly everpresent and ever absent at the same time. He had not seemed happy to have Indians in the camp, and nothing Cope

could say would convince him to eat with them. He
would be around if needed, was all he said.

"I am sorry he was busy, but we are happy to dine
with a white man who is learning more about nature,"
Twobelly said.

"Well, let's dine then, before we lose the light and
this gets cold," Cope said.

They heaped food on their plates and began chewing.
Sternberg ate several good bites quickly, because he
feared that Cope could not bear to eat in silence, and
would soon begin a conversation that would no doubt
result in his food getting cold. He had barely gotten
the fourth bite of hen swallowed when he thought his
fears were to be realized. Cope cleared his throat and
flicked his tongue around in his mouth, a sure sign
that he was already bored and ready to start talking.
Instead, he leaned his head to the right side and pulled
out his upper plate of false teeth.

"Got some hen caught in there," he said to Sternberg,
and tried to quietly slide the five false teeth under his
dinner plate.

Sternberg heard the clank of metal on metal, as the
Indians put their forks down on their plates and stared
at Cope in astonishment.

"You pulled your teeth out!" Twobelly said. "Can you
do that again?"

Cope had become fairly lax about dental care in the
course of his numerous field expeditions, a laxness
that had taken its toll in his mouth. Sternberg had
privately chuckled that Cope seemed to have a tooth
exchange going—for every few dinosaur choppers he
might dig up, he was willing to leave one of his own.
Cope laughed and wiped the plate on his napkin to
make sure he wasn't flinging bits of food. He covered
his mouth and slid the teeth back in and smiled at
the Indians. Then, with a flip of the tongue, he flipped

the teeth out again, showing the gaps in the smile. The Indians roared with laughter, looking at each other in amazement. Twobelly nearly upended his plate and fell off the pickle barrel.

"Can you remove any other body parts, Mr. Cope?" he asked when his laughter had subsided enough to let him talk.

"Well, there's this," Cope said, and put one hand around his right eye.

He squeezed his fist and a white orb shot out from his palm. The Indians, and even Sternberg, gasped until Wolfbox shot out a hand and grabbed it, revealing it to be a scoop of potato. Wolfbox tossed it into his mouth, chewed hurriedly and swallowed.

"You have to grow another eye, Mr. Cope!" Wolfbox said, and everyone laughed again.

"Why, I just did," Cope said, bringing his hand away to reveal his right eye, blinking and intact. "I am very fast."

Once the merriment settled back down, the paleontologists and their guests were able to finish the meal. Sternberg ate as fast as he could, but Cope seemed satisfied that he had amused his guests and did not move to speak until three apple pies were on the table. Their steam rose, spread its tantalizing aroma and disappeared into the twilight.

"This is as good a meal as I have had in a long time," Twobelly said, and Sternberg noticed he had lived up to his name during it.

Finally, once dinner was over, Cope settled down to business.

"I believe I saw some of your braves ride by here last night," Cope said. "They were coming from out there, where I saw a green flash of light. I have never seen anything like that. Can you tell me what it was?"

The braves looked at Twobelly, but he did not look

back at them. He spoke as a man used to making his own decisions.

"I do not see what harm there can be in telling you, because we do not know ourselves. There are some strange things going on around here."

His voice nearly rattled the plates on the table now that their burden of food had been lifted and redistributed amongst the surrounding stomachs.

"But you must have some idea," Cope said.

His eyes were focused on Twobelly like he was some sort of new skull that had been unearthed, and there was not much on the planet that could gather his attention like that.

"We have found some tracks in the hills. They are the tracks of a man's boot. We have found no more than that. But where we have found them, something has bothered the rocks."

"Bothered? Bothered how?"

"Bothered in the same way you leave the rocks. With chips and cracks and holes. Bothered like the way you left them at your camp lower down the river."

Twobelly did not sound angry when he said the rocks were bothered. Sternberg suspected the word he was looking for was "disturbed," but did not think it wise to volunteer this information. He was not sure whether he should be worried that the Crows had been investigating their old camps, but felt it best to also leave that alone.

"Sometimes at night we have seen a green light, and the next day we have found the boot prints and the bothered rocks. But that is all we know."

"So what do you think he's doing?"

"We thought he was doing the same as you and the other white man. Digging up things."

Now it was Cope's turn to nearly fall off the pickle barrel. Sternberg shared a long look with him, and could almost read his mind. Was Leidy back in the field? Did Marsh have two teams out here? What caused the green light? Did Marsh have a new technique?

"This could explain the lack of bones," Sternberg offered, and Cope was nodding before he was even finished talking.

"I have also heard that a Thunder Horse is walking the ground here."

"A Thunder Horse? A live dinosaur?"

"I do not know what is a dinosaur. I have only heard that some Piegans saw a Thunder Horse, but I have seen no tracks myself and do not believe it."

Cope snorted.

"Nor do I. Although that would be interesting."

Thomas Jefferson had thought as little as six decades before that giant mammoths and lions could possibly still be found in the west, which was one reason he wanted it explored. Lewis and Clark had not run across any and, Sternberg thought, it was unlikely that modern paleontologists would see a living Thunder Horse.

"I *do* know that the other white man is planning to try to get inside the stranger's camp," Twobelly said.

Cope sat up straighter and clenched his chin, which made the hair on his chin twitch. He looked like an animal put on the defensive.

"He is? When?"

"I do not know. Soon."

"What do you mean, get into his camp?"

"I do not know. I have just heard that he is going to try."

"Charley!" Cope said. "He can't get in there before us."

"I agree," Sternberg said.

"He is going to try."

"Chief Twobelly, will you help us try to get in, too?

Can you tell us where he is and then help us get into his camp?"

Twobelly gave him a long look, and then shook his massive head slowly.

"That I cannot do. The other white man is working with the Sioux. What you would be asking is for us to go to war."

"*War*? I just want to get into the man's camp."

"Being near the Sioux may be a small thing for you but it would not be so for us. There would be a war between us. I am sorry, but you do not seem to have horses or possessions enough to persuade me to change my mind."

Sternberg recognized the look on Cope's face. It was the look that appeared when there was an obstacle to be surmounted. He knew it only from the field, and had only seen it when a fossil proved to be wrapped in a particularly tough bit of rock, but he had heard from others who knew Cope back east that it could also appear in other circumstances, such as when other scientists resisted his choice of a Latin name for a freshly discovered extinct beast. He knew the look could propel Cope to fantastic feats of digging, and had heard it could also lead to fantastic feats of persuasion. That might be the case with some learned researcher in Philadelphia, or against some mute beast encased in rock; it did not seem to be the case here, with Chief Twobelly. He would not be swayed by scientific arguments, and his face appeared to be carved in a type of stone more solid than anything visited by a scientist's pick.

"Chief, as you wish. I do not seek to cause you to take up arms against your enemy. I only ask that you let me know if you learn when the Sioux might undertake this thing."

Chief Twobelly's massive head nodded slowly.

"I have heard it said that you should never miss a chance to cause trouble for your enemy," Twobelly said. "I do not want to have a war now, but I should obey this wise saying."

His face slowly cracked into a smile, and Sternberg realized he was joking. The braves laughed nearly as loudly as they had when they witnessed Cope's false teeth.

TWELVE

A few tiny clouds low in the sky glowed pink. The sun was just setting behind the eerie hills, but O.C. Marsh could see no evidence of a ghost wall. It was just a normal sunset. His men had constructed a new beast, one with Old Whatchamacallit's weird head and the purloined femur from Edward Drinker Cope's camp, plus some sun-bleached bovine bones and a few other odds and ends thrown in for good measure. The mysterious rogue paleontologist seemed to have taken the bait. George Burgess had come into the camp in the afternoon, saying the Sioux had spotted him near the Big-Legged Duckbill Cow, as the men had taken to calling their creation. Marsh had called in the men from yet another fruitless dig site. They had bigger quarry to hunt now.

"So where is this ghost wall?" Marsh asked George Burgess, who was conferring with several Sioux.

The twenty or so Sioux were dressed in full warpaint, even though soon it would be dark and difficult to see all their finery. Burgess, too, was in warpaint, his face marked with stripes and splashes, his buckskin shirt festooned with multicolored braids of horsehair. The other braves looked natural in their costume, but Marsh thought it looked a little odd on Burgess. He looked like the other Sioux, of course, but there was something about his carriage that made him seem less like an

Indian in warpaint than a man in costume. He's a Yale man, all right, Marsh thought. Even out here, dressed like that.

"Try to go forward," Burgess said.

This was easier said than done. The Big-Legged Duckbill Cow had been planted in some flat land, near a series of hills but not too close, to make it easier to see into the man's camp if he took the bait. Apparently he had quite literally done just that; he dug up the composite beast, every single speck of it, and then camped nearby, on the other side of the rocky outcropping, just at the base of where the sandstone began to rise precipitously. His camp was in a neat little valley, which made it impossible to see from where Marsh stood. The rock on the side of the most passable slope was brittle and granular, which made for slippery footing, even for good climbers. Marsh was not a good climber, so he motioned for Burgess to send two or three of the Sioux on ahead. He watched as they made their way up the sandstone face, their moccasins finding slots he would not have seen. They walked until their feet were a dozen feet or more above his head, and then they stopped in a ridiculous pose, their upper arms splayed as though resting on something.

"Why are you stopping?" Marsh called up.

He modulated his voice as best he could. He wanted the Sioux to hear him, but did not want to attract the paleontologist's attention.

The Sioux warriors only looked back, nodding at George Burgess. They were truly stealthy. They would make no noise.

"Ghost wall," Burgess said.

"There's nothing there!" Marsh said, his voice rising with annoyance. "They're just standing there!"

"It does look that way, doesn't it?" Burgess said.

He motioned for the Sioux to climb down. They lowered

their arms and picked their way back down, moving as swiftly and silently as if they were ghosts themselves.

"Let's go up ourselves," Burgess said. "It doesn't look too hard. I think we can make it, but we should try before we lose the light completely. I'll help you."

He took Marsh by the arm, but Marsh politely—but firmly—shook off his grasp.

"I can make it, thank you."

"Be careful," said a voice behind them.

It was Al Stillson. Marsh had thought twice about bringing Cope's little spy along, but thought it best to keep him where he could see him. Left in camp, Stillson might have reported to Cope, and Marsh wasn't ready to have that happen yet. Now he could see everything, but would have no one to tell.

"Don't worry," Burgess said, and gave Stillson a gruff tap on the shoulder.

Marsh and Burgess picked their way up the sandstone. Marsh tried to remember where the Sioux had put their feet. It actually wasn't that bad. The sandstone was flat in spots, places that made natural stair steps. Burgess moved ahead of him, picking out the steps. He had only to follow, putting his boots where Burgess' moccasins had been. The watching Sioux braves began to get smaller and smaller, but then Burgess stopped.

"Don't tell me," Marsh huffed in exasperation, his voice made husky by lack of breath.

"I can't go any farther," Burgess said. "There's something here."

Burgess was three feet ahead of him and two steps higher. He rested his hands on what looked like empty air. Marsh fumbled his glasses out of his pocket and strapped them over his ears. Burgess was pushing at the empty air, but his fingers seemed to be touching something; Marsh could see where the tips of his fingers moved as he pushed.

He began pounding on the air, an action which produced only muffled thumps. Marsh watched closely. Burgess' fist stopped at the same place each time, not one jot before or after. What was it they did in France? Mime? He did not think George Burgess knew mime, and if he did he could not be this adept at it.

"Let me try," Marsh said, and Burgess moved obligingly out of the way.

Marsh huffed his way up the steps and hit the ghost wall, stopping so suddenly that he nearly lost his balance. The Sioux were right. There was something here, although what it was he could not tell. He looked around. The grass and rocks on the other side of the ghost wall seemed as sharp as the grass and rocks on this side, or at least as sharp as his eyes and glasses would render them. He pushed at the wall. It was smooth to the touch and seemed to have no temperature. Marsh put the fingers of his left hand on it and peered intently. The skin beneath his nails blushed, but he could see nothing at all that was touching them. He pulled his fingers back. They left no mark.

"Excuse me," Marsh said, and made a grumbling sound in his throat.

He pulled his head back and sent a small whitish wad of spit flying as hard as he could. It spattered on the rocks on the other side, yet when he touched the air again, the ghost wall seemed as solid as before.

"What could this be?" Marsh said, not trying to hide his astonishment from Burgess, who appeared equally baffled. "It's obviously some kind of semi-permeable membrane, but that doesn't do it justice."

"Ghost wall is the best description I can think of," Burgess said, and Marsh had no choice but to agree.

They heard a scuffling noise behind them, and turned to see Al Stillson, picking his way slowly up the rock steps.

"Don't come up here," Marsh said. "You can't help."

"But I think I can," Stillson said. "I just noticed something while I was watching you. This ghost wall doesn't seem to go all the way to the ground."

He pointed at the ground to their left, where the smooth rock steps gave way to patchy scrub grass and loose gravel. A scorpion was crabbing its way up the hill. It shoved some small rocks aside and then passed where the limit of the ghost wall should have been, but clambered on its way unhindered. Small bits of dust and gravel fell further down the slope as it passed. They moved right underneath the wall.

"I'll be damned," Burgess said.

He walked down and around Marsh and over to the scorpion, which scurried faster when it saw his looming form. He dug in the path of the scorpion like a dog trying to get under a fence, which was not far from the situation. He put his hands in the small trench he had made and pushed them forward, palms up.

"The ghost wall is touching the base of my thumb," he said after a moment.

His fingers wiggled free on the other side.

"What does it feel like?" Marsh asked.

"I can't quite describe it."

He moved his palm along the bottom of the ghost wall. Marsh and Stillson could see the skin near his thumb moving, pushed down by an unseen force.

"I can feel a pressure. It's not a wide wall, but it's not sharp, either. It's just there. It seems sort of ragged on the bottom, because before it was touching the rocks. It didn't change when I moved them."

The scorpion had now made good on its escape, having scuttled under a lump of loose rocks on the other side.

"Good eye, Stillson," Marsh said, and Al Stillson smiled. "I guess we should start digging."

THIRTEEN

"What in the devil are they doing now?" Edward Cope sputtered.

He and Charles Sternberg hunched behind a copse of pine trees. Cope squatted at the base of one and peered around its trunk through his small field telescope, which was powerful enough to show him that something strange was going on two hundred yards away. Marsh and an Indian walked halfway up the side of one of the sandstone hills, only to bend down and start scrabbling at the ground. Then they came back down and waved for some of the assembled Sioux braves to start digging at the same spot. Then one of the Indians got on his back and scooted up the hill for about six feet before rising to stand again. He wandered off and quickly came back, pointing somewhere off to the right. Then someone shouted something about having found a better spot, and the whole gang wandered around the side of the hill and out of sight.

"What do you think they're doing, Charley?" Cope asked.

"I don't know," Sternberg replied, his voice a little clipped. "You won't give me the scope, so I can't see to tell you."

Cope lowered the telescope and folded it up.

"There's nothing to see now anyway. They're all gone

off and it's too dark. It's the oddest thing. They were digging frantically at the ground, but there's nothing there."

"There has to be something there. O.C. Marsh doesn't dig at the ground for nothing."

"Don't I know that? But they weren't digging like they were actually trying to dig something up. They were just digging a little bit, and then one of the Indians got down on the ground. It looked like he was scooting under a fence, but there isn't any fence there."

They sat and pondered that for a moment. It was now nearly completely dark, although a rising sliver moon brought the promise of its pale light. They had brought a lamp, but Cope was not inclined to light it, not with those warpainted Sioux around. They were being friendly with Marsh, but that did not mean they would be friendly with him; if anything, it meant they would probably be extremely unfriendly, especially if Marsh had any sway over them. They had just enough light left to get around or go home.

"Let's go to where they were," Cope said. "I want to see what they were doing on this side."

"I suspected as much," Sternberg said.

Boston Mickle had cooked up another fine feast, but the warning from Enemy Hunter of the Crow had come just before dinner. He said whatever the other white man and the Sioux were doing to get into the stranger's camp, they were doing it now. Cope and Sternberg had eaten nothing since breakfast, but Cope would starve for days before he would let O.C. Marsh get ahead of him. If Marsh was investigating this third man in the field, Cope would be there, too, empty stomach or no. He had hoped to have Jenks Dart join them, but Dart had vanished as soon as the Crow scout arrived with the news, and had not returned. He was getting awfully skittish around Indians these days.

Cope and Sternberg hustled over to the sandstone hill in a low crab walk. Marsh and all his Sioux were gone, but he could hear their voices from around the hill. They had gone up the sandstone steps, which he could now barely see.

"Come on."

He began walking up the steps, racing the fading light, Sternberg behind him. They got halfway up when suddenly he bumped headlong into something that felt hard as a tree. Cope pinwheeled his arms but couldn't help falling backwards into Sternberg. Cope hit the ground on his back, but Sternberg rolled down like a log, not stopping until he fell amongst the tufts of grass at the base of the hill. It was an amazingly quiet pratfall. Cope had the wind knocked out of him and couldn't make a sound, and Sternberg had released only a few grunting sounds on the way down. Cope lay on his back, trying to get his lungs working again. It felt like someone had taken an iron and flattened them out completely. When he finally managed to get them to refill, he sat up and saw Sternberg crawling back up the hill, his left cheek scuffed and bleeding.

"You don't seem to have your sea legs about you," Sternberg said when he got closer.

"I do, too. There's something here after all. Some kind of fence, although I didn't see it. It must be what they were digging under."

"I didn't see anything."

"I didn't either. That's what's strange. Is your leg okay?"

"No, but that happened a long time before this."

"Are you bleeding?"

"Yes."

"You should be more careful."

"Thank you. It would have been worse, but my face landed on this."

Sternberg held something round under Cope's hand. It felt like a basket.

"What is that?"

"Warpaint. Some of Marsh's Sioux must have left it behind."

Cope stood up and went bounding down the hill, nearly knocking Sternberg over again.

"Where are you going?"

"To the lamp. Come on, I need your help."

Ten minutes later, Cope stood in the copse of trees, stripped to the waist and shivering, but proudly wearing his very own warpaint.

"How does it look?" he asked.

Sternberg did his best to suppress a smile.

"About like you would think."

"But does it look like them?"

"Yes, if they were very pale and weren't wearing shirts. But they're dark and they're wearing buckskin. Also, they have shaved recently."

Cope grabbed some of the red powder from the basket and smeared it across his bristly beard and moustache.

"Well, I don't have time for all that, and besides it's dark. Maybe I can blend in long enough to see what's going on."

"No one can say you didn't try," Sternberg offered helpfully.

"I'll go back to where we just were, where that first Indian went under. You keep an eye out for—I don't know, for something. Just keep an eye out. And quit smiling at me. I need your help to dig."

"Yes, great chief," Sternberg said.

He blew out the lamp before he could see the look Cope gave him.

FOURTEEN

He had not seen so many Sioux in one place since—
since the battle. Since before the battle, because he
had left then and had not looked back. He had heard
the screams and the sounds. It was amazing how far
the sounds carried across the ground. If the earth had
been kind it would have absorbed them, drawn them
to itself, but it did not and he could hear everything.
He heard the screams of the men who had once been
his friends and he had heard his own breath loud in
his head as he strove to put great distance between
them.

Or maybe he had never heard the sounds at all, just
imagined he had, just heard them in dreams. The
ground was plain and flat and he was very far away
before anything happened. He left when he started
having bad dreams. He had not slept well ever since,
so his early escape had not brought him any peace,
just a longer life. Edward Cope did not sleep well either,
but he woke up refreshed each day. Jenks Dart did
not sleep well and woke up more tired than ever.

He dreamed about his friends. They used to sing
songs at night, when it seemed like being in the Army
was just a fun way to camp out. Sometimes women
would come out from the towns and give them water.
He heard that some women had witnessed the battle,

had been closer to it than he had. He dreamed of how Evan, the lanky one from Wyoming, had taken a piece of leather and tied a string to it. He could make it move just like it was a black snake, just by twitching his fingers. He had certainly stirred up Richard with it, Richard from Ohio. Richard did not know one snake from another but did not like the thought of any of them, and Evan had driven him near to insanity with the snake that always seemed to pursue Richard, but which Richard could never catch. The snake seemed most likely to come to him when he was writing letters home to his fiancee, and he would jerk the pen and leave ink blotches on the paper. The fiancee ended up breaking up with him because his letters made no sense and did not sufficiently express his love for her. That was the only day Jenks could remember that Evan put the snake away and did not bother Richard. Now they were both dead, Evan and Richard and Evan's snake. None of them moved anymore.

Cope kicked and bucked in his tent, but Dart sometimes screamed in his, so that he could not even sleep in the camp. He slept in the ravines or in the trees, and sometimes he put a stick in his mouth at night so he would not shriek along with the screams he heard in the night. He spent every day with the taste of wood in his mouth.

He was a very good shot, quick and accurate on the draw, blessed with a good eye and fast hands, but he doubted any of that would have been good enough to save him. He could have been the best shot on the field, the quickest man on the field, and he would probably even now be as dead as the worst wretch there. If he had stayed. Custer was nuts, but he looked good, he looked like he knew what he was doing. Up in that saddle, that proud nose leading the way, he looked like a god. He could ride a horse like no one else, but that particular skill wasn't enough to save him, either, no more than his fast hand could save Jenks Dart (had he remained there).

Dart squinted down the barrel of his gun. It was almost dark, and the barrel of his rifle was a pleasing dark purple as he held it over the sandstone ridge. The ridge overlooked a small valley that bore only a small copse of pine before another sandstone ridge rose up on the other side. The round form of Professor O.C. Marsh was at the edge of that ridge, gesticulating up at nothing. The assembled group of Sioux warriors followed his lead and looked up at nothing. In the dying light of the sun the horsehair dangling from their shoulders made them look like wraiths. It must have been terrifying at Little Big Horn. It was terrifying enough thinking about it without being there. He should hate them, he supposed, but he did not, not quite. He had not even hated the Indian he had seen the other night, the one who now owed him money, the one who had true guts and a strong arm and a purloined bone. It was hard to find fault with someone for killing people who were behaving stupidly.

Were they part of Sitting Bull's force moving through here? They were rumored to be coming this way, but that was not his fight anymore. That had never been his fight. He had gone away from that. It had taken until he was a cavalryman in the Army before he realized he was not enthusiastic about being in the Army and about killing Indians. He only liked to shoot things that had four legs, or flew. He was even something of a scientist now. Scientists seemed to like dead creatures, and those he was willing to provide.

Maybe he should just shoot anyway. Shooting a man could not be much different from shooting a sheep. He could get most of them. He would not shoot Marsh, of course, or the young boy he had caught slinking around in the ravines. They had not taken away his friends and his dreams, so they could live. He could start with the Indian who had been in the camp and had taken the bone, although he could not tell which of them he was. He should have shot that one when he had the chance, but that had been at quarters too close for comfort. He needed a little distance for his killing. Maybe he should start with the tallest Indian and work his way down. He could perhaps even have time to reload once or twice. The Indians might try to climb up the side of the hill, but that seemed to be difficult going after about the first dozen feet and they would be easy shots. Or maybe they would run for the trees, but that would take precious seconds, too. He would have time.

He squinted down the purple barrel, which was now deepening to black. He was losing the light entirely, and his chance. Dart saw a white flash off to the left. Something was going on in the pines. There were two white men there, kneeling before a flicker of light. One of them stood up and appeared to be halfway to wraith form himself. It looked almost like Professor Cope and Charley Sternberg, but one of them looked half Indian. He lowered his rifle and rested the barrel along his cheek. It was cold from the wind. Jenks Dart could not shoot if he couldn't even tell the difference anymore.

FIFTEEN

Tiny, sharp slivers of shale dug into his back. Edward
Cope pushed himself forward, under the wall he could
not see. He could feel its lower edge scrape across his
forehead, pushing his eyebrows, scuffing the tip of his
nose. He was looking straight up into a clear sky as he
went under. The night was wearing a thin crescent of
moon and pearls of stars for decoration.

He felt he had been here before, somehow. Not here,
of course; not painted up like a bad Indian, sliding up
a hill to get under a barrier that wasn't there. All of
that was too strange even for a man who made his living
describing fantastic creatures that had not lived since
long before man walked the earth. He had never been
here. But he could remember a time flat on his back,
sick, his back itching and freckled with pain.

He had been young then, and had just given up
farming as an occupation unsuitable for his talents and
interests. The growth of plants was interesting, but they
were invariably the same plants, year after year, no
variation. How much more interesting to see where
the plants came from, to find the plant that started it
all. How much more interesting to part the dim mists
of time to find the original plant, something no one
had seen, rather than to part the dawn's early mist in
Pennsylvania only to find the same plants over and over

again. People had seen those; people waited expectantly for those to be placed on their dinner tables. So he had given that up, finally with his father's blessing when Alfred Cope realized it would do no good to stand in his way.

Then his father surprised him. Alfred paid for a trip to send his son overseas, where he could meet the best minds in science and get his mind off of farming for a while. It was everything the young Edward Cope could have hoped for, so of course before going he became dreadfully ill, with welts on his chest and pain in his head and back. He had not wanted to be out of the farming business quite enough to want to end up on his deathbed so soon, but for a while it looked like that might be the case.

A strange feeling came over him as the due date for his voyage drew near. He had not had the feeling before, not while his life was so readily planned out. He would be a Quaker farmer, and that would be that. For some that would be a fine goal, but for him it was a goal to work against. Once he had conquered the possibility, he had the feeling he had not expected. As the ship drew nearer to the harbor, he realized his malady to be caused by fear. He was going off into the great unknown, with no one but himself to guide him. It was what he had always wanted, and he was afraid. And now he had that feeling once again, as his knees slid through and Charley Sternberg pushed against the bottom of his heels to help get him all the way into the other side. He had returned from Europe with his Quaker faith somewhat shaken, loosened, dislodged. What could be in store for him now?

Edward Cope quickly lost these thoughts when he heard the Indians muttering to themselves on the other side. They were not speaking English, and he could not understand the Sioux tongue, but he could sense the excitement in their words. He stood upright, brushed himself off as best he could, being somewhat careful not to dust off any of Sternberg's hastily applied warpaint, and waved to his companion.

"Are you all right?" Sternberg asked.

Charley stood all of six feet away, and Cope could see him and hear him just fine, but Sternberg could not walk through the wall of air. What man could have something like this? Cope had never heard of anything like it, anywhere. He would have to get something like this to keep Marsh and his cronies out of the best bone fields.

"I'll be back in a few minutes," Cope said. "Don't go anywhere."

He cautiously crept around the hill. Most of the Indians had come inside the man's camp, but Marsh was not to be seen. He probably could not be bothered to actually drag his bulk through the dirt, although the exercise would no doubt do him good. It would be his loss. Cope crept slowly up behind the rearmost group of Indians, who were facing away from him, towards what must be the center of the stranger's camp. The Indians were not looking at each other much, which was good for him, but as he drew closer he saw where their attention was diverted, and then he wasn't looking at them, either.

The stranger had the largest—and oddest looking— tent that Cope had ever seen. It was huge and shaped something like two dinner dishes put one atop the other. It seemed to almost glow in the moonlight, like it was made of a highly reflective metal. And it was definitely metal. The wind had picked up, ruffling his moustache and the horsehair braids of the Sioux, but the tent did not flap at all. The tent took up about one-fourth of the area of a small craterlike valley between the sandstone cliffs. Cope estimated it to be about seventy feet in diameter, maybe more; it was hard to tell, and he didn't dare risk running out ahead of the Sioux, who were creeping forward as if they were closing in on a large, dangerous animal. For all they knew, they were.

Cope fell in with four Sioux who headed off to the left side of the tent. They seemed to be moving a bit slower than the others, and he hoped they were the ones with the worst eyesight of the bunch. As they crept forward, he noticed a small green light in the middle of the open space in front of the tent. He squinted, and saw there were several of these points of light scattered about on the ground. The Sioux saw them too, and moved over as a group to investigate. They walked in a crouch, as if afraid to stand upright, and Cope crouched along with them, being careful not to get too close.

As they drew nearer he saw—bones! Arrayed near the small green light was the skeleton of a dinosaur, one that must have been nearly twenty feet long or more. It rose before them in the night like the remains of a funeral pyre, and indeed seemed to glow in the faint moonlight. When he shipped bones out of the field, they were still mostly packed in their dirt for protection, not to be cleaned for months later. These bones were so spick and span they looked like they had never been acquainted with dirt. In fact, they were so clean they looked like they had never been wrapped in skin and muscle. All the creature's parts seemed to be there. Cope could see a hump of spine next to the pickets of its ribcage. So this is where all the bones were. No wonder he and Marsh were having such a time. This man, with his huge metal tent, was getting them all!

The Sioux began an anxious mutter when they saw the remains of the beast. Cope longed to lunge at the animal and stash whatever he could under his arms, but he held back. A ferocious muttering ensued between the Sioux. One of them even turned to look back at him, but didn't give him a long look and didn't seem to be alarmed. One of the Sioux stuck out an arm and attempted to touch the bones, but apparently encountered the same sort of invisible wall that surrounded the camp. I absolutely must get one of these, Cope thought.

Suddenly a green light emanated from the center of the tent, and a booming sound rebounded through the camp. It sounded almost like a language, but not one Cope had ever heard. One of the Sioux took several steps back in a hurry, moving so fast he bumped into Cope and sent him sprawling over a knee-high mound of sandstone. Cope's heel tucked into it and he went down hard on his back. The group of Sioux let out a simultaneous warcry, which was quickly picked up by the other warriors. It echoed around the camp just as loudly as had the sound from the stranger's tent.

Cope had barely noticed that the Sioux warriors were packing bows and arrows, but he heard the rhythmic twang of arrows being loosed. He jerked his neck up to see what was going on, but couldn't get a clear view through the rapidly pumping legs of the Sioux. For just an instant, it looked like the Sioux were firing at a tiny little man who stood by the dinosaur. The little man appeared to be as black as shale. Odder still, he seemed to have glowing red eyes, but that couldn't be. Cope sat up on his elbows and looked around. The Sioux had demonstrated their bravery and were now retreating in high style, and at great speed. By the time he regained his feet, they had gone.

The green light from the stranger's tent had vanished as well. Cope stepped cautiously around the sandstone mound and back into the center of the small valley. The green lights that marked the dinosaur bones still glowed in the night, but there was no sign of a tiny black man with red eyes, and for that Cope was glad. Sometimes his imagination outstripped his eyes, and he was grateful when his rational mind could get things back to normal. He stepped around the rocky ground in front of the tent with care, now that he had no other Indians to stand with him.

He rested his hands at the small of his back and peered upwards at the nearest dinosaur skeleton. He was chilled from lack of a shirt, and from a goodly dose of fear, but the sight of the unmoving beast warmed him. It looked like a standard sort of early Cretaceous herbivore, with one exception. Around the creature's neck rose a magnificent bony frill, which sloped to a rhinoceros-like nose that bore a single long horn. Cope stared at the creature's skull. He doubted he could encompass it even with his arms outstretched. He could not see much detail on the bony shield, but dared not explore it with his hands for fear of setting off the green light from the tent again. What manner of beast was the bony shield meant to defeat? The Allosaurus?

Latin words floated into his mind. Cope did not care to leave a fossil find like this long unnamed, even if it had been found by someone else. *Monoclonius*, his mind said. One horned. He thought about the name, which had flung itself hurriedly out of the back of his mind. It did not do much to describe the great swelling frill, but actually the frill, as interesting as it was to the modern mind, was not the most salient feature of this dinosaur. The horn was perhaps not so interesting to someone familiar with the rhinoceros of Africa or even the domesticated bull, but no horned dinosaurs had yet been discovered. Monoclonius was perhaps the right name after all.

Having dispensed with the naming of that creature, he walked quietly but quickly over to where another

of the green lights glowed. Everything was strange in
this camp. There were invisible walls, and now these
green lights. He stopped and squinted at the next one,
which stood level with his chest. Perhaps it was some
type of flame encased in a small glass lamp, but when
he touched it there was no heat, and no smoke was
coming from the top. The light did not flicker, even
when he tapped the small yellowish pole that held it
up into the night. Likewise, the light that had shone
from inside the giant metal tent had been a steady beam.
That would certainly be helpful at night. Whoever this
scientist was, he had very fine equipment.

The beast at the next green sentry light was a
Trachodon, a duckbilled dinosaur of the sort that once
congregated around the ancient inland sea like giant
reptilian gulls. Its bones were piled up like those of
the Monoclonius, and Cope wondered why the man
didn't just put them inside the tent. Surely there was
room enough. The duckbill's skeleton was nearly
complete, but no better than some specimens Cope
had seen back East. He was glad that even the mystery
paleontologist, with all his tools, could not find every
bone.

He was familiar with the Trachodon, but the next
pile of bones brought a further surprise. It was
something he had never seen, something even stranger
than the horned dinosaur. Its head appeared to be that
of another type of duckbill, a Hadrosaur, but the rest
of its body didn't match. The teeth scattered around
its skull in the dust looked variously like those of a
herbivore and a carnivore, all together at once. The
sharp incisors seemed to glow up at him reproachfully
in the moonlight, as if inviting him to touch their points.
This creature was even less together than the Trachodon.
The only other bones visible were some cracked ones
he couldn't immediately identify, and a long femur that

looked suspiciously familiar, and suspiciously out of place.

Cope headed around the beast for a further look, but failed to keep his eyes on the ground. The toe of his right boot caught a rock and he fell, palms out. His hands came to rest on the invisible wall around the odd skeleton. He jerked them away as fast as he could. When the Sioux had touched the one around the horned lizard, a great racket had emanated from the tent, and Cope looked that way nervously to see a repeat performance. Nothing happened. He cautiously reached out a hand again, and tapped the invisible glass with one finger. Nothing. Perhaps the man had gone to bed, or perhaps there had been no connection between the Indian's touch and the ensuing commotion.

He moved to continue around the bone collection and saw a flash of red, and then found himself sprawled on the ground again. A tiny man dressed in a jet-black costume advanced on him, muttering something in what sounded like German. The man could barely have stood above his knees, but he strode with purpose straight at Cope. He could see nothing of the man's face, only an inky blackness punctuated by two glowing red dots.

"Charley!" Cope shouted, turning his head to the left. He could only hope he was facing Sternberg's one good ear. "Charley!"

He realized that Sternberg could be of no help. He readied his foot to kick the tiny creature, but when he turned his face back around the little man was gone, vanished into the night. Cope stared at the place he had been, his foot still raised to deliver a blow to the little fellow's midsection. The little man was gone, but something big was moving around behind the unidentified skeletal remains. It was a big man with long hair, walking fast. He approached so rapidly that Cope had no time to take note of his clothes. All he

saw was the man's broad, long face, and an expanse
of hair that hung around darkly around it, like seaweed
around a rock. The man seemed to walk as fast as a
normal man would run, and he was towering over the
prone Cope before Cope could move.

"Why are you here?" the man said, in a deep voice,
almost a growl.

Cope surely imagined it—could only have imagined
it—but green light escaped between the man's teeth
and curled around the edges of his eyes. A steady green
light, without flicker. Imagination or no, the next thing
he realized, Cope was running at full speed for the
place he had dug under the invisible wall. He misjudged
it, it being hard to account for something you can't
see, and ended up slamming headlong into the wall,
which threw him hard on his back for the third time
of the night. The sharp rocks dug into his back but he
kept moving and slid underneath and about halfway
down the hill before he realized he was clear and
regained his feet.

"They found us, Ed," Charles Sternberg said.

He stood on the flat land at the bottom of the
sandstone hill, in the middle of a semicircle of angry-
looking Sioux. At the end of the semicircle was an angry-
looking Othniel Marsh. Marsh held his torch tightly
and advanced until he was nearly nose to nose with
the panting Cope. The two paleontologists had not seen
each other since 1868, eight years before, but Marsh
did not seem in the mood to discuss the past.

"What did you see in there, Edward?" Marsh
demanded.

"Nothing," Cope said, when he had caught his breath.

SIXTEEN

"It's a beautiful night," Alice Stillson said, and she could feel Sitting Lizard's long hair moving against her rough-cut bob as he nodded.

It was actually a cold night, but the space under his arm was warm. His back was up against a sandstone wall, the same wall that had surrounded the stranger's camp last night. There was no trace of the camp tonight. Getting to the small valley where he had been was as easy as walking up the sandstone steps. There was no ghost wall, no piles of bones. The stranger had moved his huge tent so completely it was as if he had never been there. Tonight, there was only Sitting Lizard and Alice Stillson, a sickle moon and every star in the universe.

"I'm glad you could come out tonight," he said.

"I can pretty much come out every night. Mr. Marsh isn't giving me much to do anymore. He doesn't trust me anymore."

"You told things to the other one, didn't you?"

"Cope? Yes, I did. I didn't think I would get caught. I didn't know how crazy they both are."

"Everyone is crazy in that camp. You should steer clear of that other man."

"Jenks Dart?"

"Yes. The deserter. I do not like the looks of him."

"I don't either."

"Is the other one crazy, too?"

"The cook? I don't think so. He just cooks all the time."

"Then he's probably crazy. You should stay away from that camp."

"Mr. Cope hasn't paid me yet."

"Stay away."

He gave her a quick hug to show he was serious. She hugged him back and snuggled closer, although if she got much closer she would be wearing his shirt.

"Why do you like Mr. Marsh so much? Why do the Sioux help him?"

"He helped them first. Have you ever heard of Red Cloud?"

"No."

"He is a great chief, the head of the Oglala Sioux. He surrendered to the Army and moved into the reservation land in the Black Hills. But the Army was giving him and his men terrible food. They were starving. Professor Marsh came through there on some sort of fossil hunt, and Red Cloud told him the story and showed him the bad food. Then Professor Marsh went back east to show his findings."

"On the fossils?"

"Yes. But he also took what Red Cloud had showed him, and he told everybody. It was in the newspapers. He wrote to President Grant himself. The Secretary of the Interior ended up resigning."

"I had no idea he had done that."

"You didn't, but the Sioux did and they haven't forgotten."

She had not quite pictured Marsh as being heroic.

"He is apparently something of a wild man when he is in the field. I didn't hear this directly, because I didn't have any classes with him, but someone I know said he once told a story about shooting three buffalo while riding his horse alongside a stampede."

Alice Stillson definitely could not picture the bulbous, nearsighted Marsh doing anything like that. Cope, maybe, Jenks Dart, definitely, but not Othniel Marsh. Maybe he was just getting older.

"His house in New Haven is famous for all the mementos he has there, like animal heads hanging on the wall."

That she could picture, although she didn't want to think about dead animals just now. Sitting Lizard's arms felt good around her, like tree limbs. The way his hair hung down reminded her of the weeping willow in her front yard in Missouri. She used to sit in the crook of the tree in the summer and the slender leaves would drift over her face, like his hair was doing now. She was a long way from Missouri. Her family probably missed her. Her throat tightened as she thought of her mother, at home, crying, thinking her daughter was dead. But she was here now. She didn't want to think about Marsh's dead animals or home. She forced herself to live in the moment, to feel Sitting Lizard's arms and his breath and his hair. She was not in Missouri. She was in Montana, and she would write a book about it.

Her notebook had not been used much of late, except to record Edward Cope's discovery of the strange fossil head, which she later found out was planted by Marsh. That particular entry had required a little rewriting to make her sound less gullible.

"What did you think about my writing?" she asked.

He handed her back the few pages she had ripped from the notebook to loan him. They weren't particularly good, and she really shouldn't have shown anyone anything just yet, but for some reason she wanted him to read them.

"I liked it. Your punctuation needs some work, though."

"I'm not using it right now, to save ink. I'll fix all that later."

"Oh. Then I liked it. I thought it was funny that you compare Marsh to a badger. I really did like it."

The notebook had less about Sitting Lizard, and she would never show him that. Writing about the others was easy. She could just record what they looked like and what they did. But how to describe him? She could not leave him a cipher. She sensed there was so much more there, but she could not put it into words and consequently there was less in the notebook about him than about anyone else, and he was the best one of them all. She folded the pages into her jacket and leaned her head against him.

"You are very quiet," he said.

She turned her face up to his and kissed him, an impulse kiss that lasted a long time. When it was done she looked up at the shadowy tower of sandstone that rose above them.

"What did your Sioux say was in there, in that man's camp?"

There had been so much confusion last night after Cope and Sternberg left that she had not gotten a satisfactory answer.

"They said there was a giant tent, and piles of bones all around, under their own ghost walls. And there were little men with glowing red eyes."

"Oh."

She was not sure she could use that in her book.

"Why didn't you go up there? Under the ghost wall?"

"I wanted to, but I'm not sure the Sioux completely trust me yet. They didn't want me to go. They wanted me to stay with the white man."

"I'm glad you stayed with the white man, because that meant you stayed with me," she said, and kissed him again.

She felt something stiff pushing against her ribs, and smiled. She reached to touch him in that most intimate spot, but found her hands closing on something metallic and cold.

"I see you found my telescope," he said with a chuckle. "Hang on, let me untie it."

He produced a small golden telescope from under his buckskin shirt and extended it with a series of clicks.

"Why do you have a telescope?" she asked.

"Look up there," he said, pointing at the sky. "I have it because once, long ago, I thought I might study astronomy. My parents bought it for me. They thought it would show me God's glorious handiwork. Then I changed my focus to something considerably less glorious. Politics. But I never could bear to part with my little telescope. It's really a pretty good one. Sometimes I just sit and look at the stars."

Stillson saw something through the scope, a bright series of stars that she knew had to be a constellation. She handed him the scope.

"What is that constellation?" she asked, trying to point it out for him. "It looks sort of like a bucket."

He stared through the scope for a moment and then handed it back, shaking his head.

"I don't know. I told you I didn't study long."

She soon grew more interested in things down to earth, too, and put aside her star gazing to give him a kiss. The stars were all still there when their lips parted again, and the moon. Was it her imagination or had it moved a little in its course?

"I wish we could stay here forever."

"I do too," he said. "But I have to go tomorrow."

She twitched in surprise and felt the telescope shrinking in her hands.

"What do you mean?"

He gently took the telescope away from her and hid it back in its pouch.

"Sitting Bull is near here. He is going further north, and the Army is after him. The Sioux that are camped here plan to join him. I have to go with them."

She turned to fully face him, which took no small amount of twisting and turning in his arms.

"So let them go. You stay here."

She could barely see his eyes. She could only see the white parts, and the rest were lost in the night.

"You know I can't do that. This is exactly the sort of thing I came out west to do. These are my people."

"And what am I?"

He closed his eyes and she saw nothing at all for a long time.

"I'm sorry. I have no choice. I have to go."

"Where will you go?"

"I don't know. Just further north, is all I know. There isn't much north left, so maybe into Canada."

"Will you come back?"

"Alice, I—"

"Will you come back?"

"Alice, I could get hurt. The Army is not playing. You heard about Little Bighorn. Sitting Bull and his men killed General Custer. They are nearly the last wild Indians left out here, and the Army is out for revenge. I have to be there to do what I can for Sitting Bull. I just don't know what is going to happen."

"It's not what is going to happen, it's what you make happen. You make a promise. A promise means that you have to keep it. You promise me that you will come back here and that means you will have to come back here. I don't care if you have a leg shot off. I don't care if you have an arm shot off—"

She had meant to keep going but her throat tightened again and she was crying. She nearly cried when she thought about home, and now she was crying when she tried to live in the moment. This night had started off so well.

The third kiss was the longest yet. Empires could have risen and fallen in the course of it. She felt her black shirt loosen under his fingers, felt the moon's icy caress on the tops of her breasts. She tugged at Sitting Lizard's buckskin shirt, but it would not move so he had to sit back and pull it off himself. She pulled her pants off and tossed them away, not caring if they fell halfway down the hill. Alice exposed her white body to the cold night, but it did not take long for Sitting Lizard to take the place of the sun and warm her. He kept his clothes with him, and put them on his back to form a makeshift blanket, although one that had plenty of gaps for the icy wind. Neither one complained.

Alice was not sure what to expect from sex. She had certainly not expected her back to be against sharp rocks, had not expected to be lying on a hillside in Montana at midnight with an Indian she barely knew. She had also not expected the pain she felt when he pushed himself inside her, and had not expected to have to hold on to clumps of scrub grass with her left hand to keep from pitching down the hillside as their hips thrust together. She had not expected the pain in her hips to shift to such subtle pleasure as Sitting Lizard spread his warmth inside her, but she was glad it did.

None of those were what she had pictured for herself, but as Sitting Lizard covered her face with his hair and her mouth with messy kisses, she had to admit these things were not at all bad. She pictured the milky face of Stanton, her father's idea of the man she should reward with her virginity. Were she with Stanton, she would probably be in a four poster bed, in a nice heated

room, in a nice house. Here she had the rocks and the
scorpions and the moon and the stars and Sitting Lizard.
Her choice was so much better.

"You promise," she said in a whisper.

"I promise," Sitting Lizard said, his voice a husky
rasp. "I will come back."

SEVENTEEN

Edward Cope's hands flew through the rags in the bone cart, flipping them up into the morning air. They hovered for a second like dusty ghosts and then fluttered to the ground. Cope had not yet washed, or done anything save get up out of his tent and hustle over to the bone cart. His face still bore faint traces of the red warpaint from last night, although he had wiped at his face with a dry towel until he had nearly pulled his beard out of his chin. He had been too exhausted after that to check on his prize, but after a short night filled with more tossing and turning than usual he was up early. Charles Sternberg stood groggily behind him, running the fingers of one hand over the stubble on his chin. Cope had made enough racket getting up to wake him through his one good ear. He was interested in what Cope might or might not find, although he made sure to give Cope plenty of room for any tantrums that might arise.

"I knew it!" Cope said as a floating rag brushed his face on its way to the ground. "The femur that priest sent me is gone!"

It was bad enough to spend weeks in Montana without finding much of anything, but quite beyond endurance to lose even the one good bone they had brought with them. This disturbed even the laconic Sternberg, who frowned and squinted around in frustration.

"How could that stranger have gotten his hands on it?" Sternberg asked.

"I wish I knew. But now it has ended up in his hands, and God knows *he* has enough bones already."

Cope had hastily pulled the old tent off the bone cart, and now stood amidst its folds, resting his fists on the cart's wooden edge.

"Ahh!" he grunted in frustration, and pounded his fists on the cart until he got a splinter and stopped. His face was pink, but Sternberg couldn't tell if it was just from the leftover warpaint or anger.

"You know, Charley, it reminds me of the story of David and Bathsheba's husband. Are you familiar with that one?"

"I believe I have heard of it."

"Well, it seems that King David, who had everything, conspired to get his hands on Bathsheba, the joy of her poor husband's life. So he arranged to have this man killed and then he slept with Bathsheba. That's the way this strange bone hunter is. It is not enough that he has corralled every dinosaur bone in Montana, but he has to take mine, too."

Sternberg leaned his back on the empty cart and continued looking around the camp, as if he expected to spot the femur in Boston Mickle's stew pot or holding up one of the tent corners. Sternberg was relaxed most of the time, although Cope could tell by the furrowing of his brow that he didn't like the loss of this bone, either.

"At least the man has not had you killed," Sternberg said finally.

"What?"

"You said David had the other man killed. This man has not killed you, he has just taken your bone."

Cope wished to pound his fists more, but he had just managed to extract the splinter and didn't want any additional pain.

"Well, it's a bad analogy. Forget it."

"I just wish I had gone with you under that invisible wall to see those bones."

"You shouldn't wish that, really," Cope said. "It was a very strange place. I've never seen any sort of camp like it. Something very strange is going on here. How did that man get my bone? Where was Jenks Dart? He can catch that boy Stillson but he can't catch this tall man wandering in here and getting my bone? Have you seen Jenks today?"

"I haven't."

Jenks Dart had never been one to socialize much, let alone eat with them or even sleep in a nearby tent, but he would at least show his face once in a while. He had virtually vanished lately, wandering by only to pitch a few dead animals to Boston Mickle before departing again. That was basically all Cope was paying him for at this point, but it would be nice to have him around more often, if for no other reason than to keep thieving hands off the pitiful fossil collection Cope and Sternberg had amassed.

Cope really didn't know much about Jenks Dart. He had spent more time in Fort Benton negotiating for a cheap team of horses than he had trying to select a good team of human beings. He had just met Charles Sternberg, true, but Sternberg had eagerly begged for a place in the party. Boston Mickle had been a true gem fished out of the mudhole, and for what he did Jenks Dart had worked out well, but there was something in his recent manner that worried Cope. Cope had originally thought he could get by without a scout at all, but one of the horse traders said he knew a good man looking for scout work. Dart had not come to them until they were outside Fort Benton, which at the time had not bothered Cope, but it worried him now.

He had heard that there were a few Army deserters roaming the west, people who were glad to be away from Custer's command. It had not seriously crossed his mind that Dart might be one of them. He kept his hair long and his clothes just this side of filthy. He did not strike Cope as the sort of man who would join the Army and then leave it; he struck him as the sort who would never go near the Army in the first place.

"So what should we do?" Sternberg asked.

"About what?"

"About the stolen bone."

Cope's mind was busy hypothesizing about Jenks Dart's character, and had nearly forgotten about the purloined femur. Once reminded, his anger returned.

"I would like to march in there and take it back, and maybe get a few of *his* bone piles while I'm at it."

"That would mean you were stealing, then."

"Humor me, please, Charley."

Boston Mickle was fussing over his pots at the other edge of camp. It appeared it was nearly time for breakfast, so they should wash up in the river and make themselves presentable for another day of fruitless fossil hunting. Or maybe they should skip that altogether, given how hopeless it seemed. Maybe they should hang around camp all day, eating. That would make Boston Mickle happy, and at the end of the day they'd probably have just as many fossils to show for it.

Cope rubbed his eyes and began walking to the tent for his towel when Sternberg's voice stopped him.

"It appears someone is coming for a visit," Sternberg said, pointing to the pine trees beyond the cart. "He's a tall fellow."

Cope turned and nearly cried out. The approaching visitor was the same man who had towered over him just hours before at the strange boneyard. It was the unknown paleontologist, the one with all the bones of the field. Cope squinted as the man approached at a steady walk. No green light seemed to emanate anywhere from his person. He definitely wasn't Joseph Leidy, or any scientist known to Cope, but he looked like a normal enough man. Cope had not been able to tell his hair color in the faint moonlight, but now could see the visitor had long blonde hair bright enough to rival Custer's famous golden locks. He wore nondescript black pants that were streaked with dust and a tan shirt under a long black jacket. Now would be a good time to have Jenks Dart and his rifle around, but maybe there was no need. Cope saw no visible weapon at the stranger's side or sign of anger on his long face. If the man was upset about last night's after-hours visit, he gave no sign as he approached. He wore the serene expression of a neighbor popping over for breakfast.

"Greetings," the man said once he arrived at the other side of the bone cart.

"Hello," Cope and Sternberg said in tandem.

"I wondered if we might talk alone for a moment," the stranger said to Cope, as if they met every day.

"Mr. Sternberg may hear anything I hear," Cope said. "Please come into the camp with us."

The large table that had served for the feast with the River Crows was now put away in favor of the more comfortable pickle barrel table. It did not look large enough for the visitor, but it would have to do on short notice.

"A guest?" Mickle asked when he spotted the tall stranger. "I have plenty."

"I do not care to eat, thank you," the man said.

He spoke stiffly, as if unfamiliar with English, although his words carried no identifiable accent.

"Very well," Mickle said, a little bit miffed.

"Please sit down," Cope said, indicating the largest

barrel. "I apologize. You have caught us before we have washed."

"It is I who should apologize, then," the stranger said, with an awkward smile on his face.

Cope started to say he was sorry for breaking into the man's camp, but then it occurred to him that the stranger might not recognize him. He was in reality not particularly sorry about having done it, so he would wait and see if an apology was actually necessary before issuing one.

"You seem interested in what I am doing out here," the man said to Cope. "I did not mean to scare you last evening."

So much for that.

"I am sorry about that," Cope said, but the man waved the apology away.

"Think no more of it. Please let me introduce myself. My name is Swenson. Alf Swenson."

"Swenson? Is that a Swedish name?"

"Swedish, yes. I am from Sweden. But I am currently working here."

"I am Edward Drinker Cope, and this is my associate, Charles Sternberg," Cope said, and there was polite head nodding all around. "Tell me, Mr. Swenson, where did you get your fabulous equipment? That metal tent is astounding, and your invisible wall is very near to being unbelievable. Where on earth did you get them?"

"Why, in Sweden," Alf Swenson said.

Cope leaned forward on his pickle barrel, facing Swenson with such evident interest that the visitor leaned back a bit on his own barrel.

"I have been to Europe, and I have met with top scientists here, but I have never even heard of such a thing as an invisible wall, Mr. Swenson. How does it work? Does it modify the air particles somehow?"

Swenson maintained his persistent smile, which

revealed an impressive row of long, perfectly level white teeth, the polar opposite of the straggly fragments that survived in Cope's head.

"I cannot reveal that to you, I'm sorry," Swenson said. "It is a Swedish invention."

Cope threw out his hands.

"So?"

"I am not supposed to reveal its operation."

"Well, then, don't," Cope said. "Just tell me where I can procure one myself. Are they expensive?"

"In Sweden, and yes."

"You are not very helpful, Mr. Swenson."

The smile did not go away.

"I am sorry for that. But that is not what I—"

"Tell me, what survey are you with? Hayden? Wheeler? Powell? Because I have been funded by both the Hayden Survey and the Wheeler Survey, so if you are working for one of them we are working together."

Sternberg managed to stifle a chuckle, but the visitor seemed puzzled by the question.

"Survey? I am not sure."

Cope and Sternberg exchanged quick glances. There were several geological surveys working the west, and Swenson had to be associated with one of them unless he was independently wealthy and working on his own. Marsh was independently wealthy, but even he worked under the authorization of the Powell Survey.

"You're not sure?"

"It is complicated and I don't recall. I am working for Hayden, I believe."

"Why, that's fine, then. So am I. That means you can share your findings with me with the utmost confidence."

Ferdinand Hayden did not care for Edward Cope, but Cope felt the stranger did not need to learn this fact just now. The stranger did not nod his head. He only smiled politely.

"As it happens, that is what I wished to speak to you about. I was hoping to do my work here without bothering anyone, but I seem to have attracted a great deal of attention lately. The people of this place seem very interested in keeping an eye on me. Some of the people are pale-skinned, like us, while some have a darker hue. I am sure you know of them."

Cope looked at Sternberg, who discreetly cocked an eyebrow.

"Did you grow up in Sweden, Mr. Swenson?"

"I did."

"So you are not very familiar with Indians, I gather."

"Indians?"

"Those with the dark-hued skin."

The stranger's smile seemed a bit forced now, but never left his face entirely.

"Oh. Yes, of course I have heard of them. Anyway, I do not wish to be the center of attention. I wish only to get my work done in the shortest span of time possible."

"I see. And what exactly is your work, Mr. Swenson?"

"Extricating fossilized bone from the surrounding mineral cover. The same thing you are doing, I believe."

"You seem to be having much better luck than I am," Cope said.

Swenson did not reply, only nodded and continued to smile at Cope and Sternberg.

"You seem to be interested in the specimens I have collected, and you have displayed some resourcefulness. I would like to offer you a deal. If you will keep everyone away from me, I will give you half of what I have collected."

Cope could not keep the surprise from his face, and he noted that Sternberg could not, either.

"Half of what you have collected? Have you already written up your findings?"

"I have not done anything. You can have half of what I have, and can do with them as you please."

"Where are you sending your bones? Won't they care if you give half your bones away?"

"That should not be your concern."

Cope rocked on his pickle barrel, using one booted foot on the ground to move back and forth.

"But I'm just interested in knowing whose secondhand bones I'm getting. The Museum of Natural History? The British Museum? The Peabody Museum at Yale?"

He gave a quick laugh at his own joke. The Peabody Museum was Marsh's undertaking; Cope could not be so lucky as to intercept bones meant for New Haven.

"I am not at liberty to say," Swenson said.

He kept smiling, but Cope was not.

"Won't you tell me anything?"

"No. I have offered you a deal. You keep everyone away from me and you can have half of what I collect. I will even improve the deal. If you help me I will give you a map that will show you where other bones are available in other parts of this land."

Cope snorted.

"A map? Like a treasure map? And where did you get this from? Don't tell me."

"Sweden," the man said.

"I knew it."

"That is my offer."

Cope ran his fingers over his moustache, which was tilted up on the left side from the buffeting it had received during Cope's restless sleep the night before.

"Excuse us for one moment, please."

"Certainly."

Cope beckoned to Sternberg, and they hopped off their barrels and wandered away to discuss the offer. Cope draped an arm around Sternberg's shoulder, which was difficult because Sternberg was an inch taller. In his excitement, Cope walked too fast, which made it hard for the crouching Sternberg to catch up. Sternberg did not complain, but limped along as fast as he could.

"This is very peculiar," Cope said, and Sternberg could only agree to that.

"But he does have the bones. You said so. You saw them."

"That's true."

Cope was working on the other side of his moustache now, furiously battening it down while he pondered. They walked around in a broad circle while the stranger sat on his pickle barrel and waited, the ghostly smile still on his face.

"Yes, he does have the bones. He has piles of them, maybe complete skeletons. How many bones have we collected ourselves?" Cope asked.

"Let me put it this way," Sternberg replied. "I used to find more fossils back on the ranch in Kansas, and I wasn't even looking for them then."

Cope unloosed his arm from Sternberg's neck, allowing the younger man to stand fully upright.

"That's not good."

"Plus now we've lost the only good bone we had, that femur we brought out here."

"Thank you."

"I'm just telling you the situation."

"You want me to help him, don't you?" Cope asked.

He looked up at Sternberg with slightly narrowed eyes. Sternberg swallowed and looked away.

"Not so much for the bones he will give us. But I would like to see his map."

"Hmmm. You really do like digging up fossils, don't you, Charley?"

Sternberg nodded. He was a shy young man, but there was real steel in him, no doubt about that.

"Yes. I do."

"I'm glad I sent you that money."

"I'm glad you did too, sir."

"No sirs out here, Charley."

Cope patted his young charge on the back.

"Come on, let's go talk to our Swedish guest."

Boston Mickle had approached again, offering his wares, but he scrambled back to his tent as Cope and Sternberg approached.

"Mr. Swenson, we would be glad to help you," Cope said when they regained their barrels.

"I am glad to hear it."

"There's just one thing. In order to keep the other pale man away, I will need some of your bones."

"I am not ready to part with them. I am not sure which ones I can give you."

"You won't have to part with them. I just need them for a little while."

"And the dark—the Indians?"

"If I keep the paleface away, the Indians will stay away, too."

"Very well. You will have your bones. Which ones do you need?"

"The skeleton with the bony frill around its neck, and the one I was looking at when you walked up to me. I am not sure what that one is."

"I am not sure either, but I know the one you mean," Swenson said. "I will need to look them over again, but I believe I can do that. Just keep your part of the bargain. I should be finished with my work shortly and you will have your bones and your map."

"Do you need to borrow my horses to bring the bones? Charley and I can go with you."

Swenson rose to go.

"There's no need. They'll be here by the morning."

He walked off in the way he had come, around the cart and through the pines.

"I had no idea the Swedes were so advanced," Sternberg said when the man had gone.

"Nor did I," Cope said.

"Are you really going to give the bones back? What will you do with them?"

"I'm not really sure what I'm going to do with them yet, Charley. But I think right now I'll go wash up. I think we're going to have some interesting days ahead of us."

EIGHTEEN

For two days after the encounter at the mysterious
stranger's tent, O.C. Marsh had been relatively happy.
The Indians who had been inside provided a most
unsatisfactory account of what they saw there, one that
George Burgess had been utterly unable to translate
into anything useful. Marsh learned only that there were
bones inside, but the rest of it was taken up with vague
descriptions of some large shape and talk of spirit men
and the sound of a Thunder Horse. And then Edward
Drinker Cope, of all people, had come charging out,
painted up like an easterner's idea of an Indian. The
Sioux had considered killing him, Burgess told Marsh
the next day. The idea had floated around in their Sioux
mutterings, but never reached Marsh's ears. He was
not really sure how he would have voted on that.

The next day had passed without incident, and with
little consciousness; Marsh was tired from staying up
so late and had given the men the day off, although
he did send one to Fort Claggett to inquire again after
the telegraph operator. Al Stillson had gone the last
time, and nearly been injured, to no avail. Digger Phelps
had not minded the errand, despite the poor health
example set by Stillson, because it meant a break from
his sweaty companions and a chance to perhaps set
eyes on an actual woman. Another man was sent to

132

see if the mysterious prospector was still around. This proved an easier errand, and the man was back quickly, saying there was no trace of him.

Marsh and his crew returned to work the next day. Marsh felt refreshed but was not expecting much. He lost his Sioux help, for one thing. George Burgess had come to see him and to say he was taking off with Sitting Bull. Marsh had mixed feelings about this. He found it both stupid and admirable at the same time, although previously he had not thought himself capable of admiring anything stupid.

"I hate to see a Yale man get killed unnecessarily," Marsh had said to Burgess while shaking his hand goodbye. "The War between the States did enough damage."

Burgess had appeared withdrawn and sullen as he shook hands.

"That was nothing to what will happen to the Indians," he said, and Marsh could not argue.

Burgess then left with the Sioux. The men were ready to get back to another fruitless day, except for Stillson, who appeared angry about something and was not much good. He did not give the horses enough food, which made them cranky.

With all of that going on, Marsh had not expected to find much, but as it turned out one of his men uncovered a tiny bone, a fragile tube nearly as light as air. Marsh recognized it as the bone of a Pterosaur, a primitive flying lizard. He had found several such creatures before, and more of them, but this was a bone for a new type. So after all the drama there was something to write home about after all, and as the evening neared he set about cleaning the bone and writing a full description of it. He put on his glasses to get a better look at it, and occasionally paused to stroke his beard and think. Doing this was what he liked doing best in all the world, so given his recent luck he was not terribly surprised to be interrupted right when he was enjoying himself the most.

"I'm back," Digger Phelps said as he walked under the tent flap.

Phelps, as was his wont, had apparently had some sort of run-in with a whiskey bottle while in Fort Claggett. He held the side of his head with one hand as if afraid it would fall off, and from the looks of him it might. The lamp flame flickered as he walked to the table. Marsh hoped Phelps's breath would not ignite.

"Did our man at the telegraph have anything?" Marsh asked, a bit nonchalantly as Phelps did not appear to have anything in his hand.

Marsh expected a slow nodding of the pain-ridden head, but didn't get it. He felt a twinge of fear as Phelps stuck one hand in his shoulder bag and produced several telegrams. Phelps extended them with a shaking hand, and Marsh fairly snatched them away.

Have discovered new dinosaur stop. Named Monoclonius after single horn at tip of skull stop. Also possesses bony frill around neck to ward off predators stop. Unknown what predators frill was for stop. Cretaceous period stop. Skeleton mostly complete stop. Specimen eighteen feet long stop. More to come stop.

Marsh let out an angry shout, which sent Digger Phelps from the room, clutching his ears lest his head explode like an egg. Marsh nearly hurled the Pterosaur bone across the tent, until he remembered that it was among the few fossils he had found in Montana. Humble or not, it need not come to harm. More to come! Here he was holding a bone no larger than a piece of straw and Edward Cope was telegraphing news of an entire skeleton, and one of a new type of dinosaur to boot. His mood was darkening as surely as was the Montana sky outside the tent. It was intolerable enough that he had found little, but beyond endurance that Cope had found much. Time for some drastic action.

"Stillson!" he shouted. He stuck his head outside the tent flap and repeated the shout. "Stillson!"

He intended to send the little double agent out to perform more spycraft, with the promise of more money than both he and Cope had previously promised, put together. As it turned out, Stillson was walking towards the tent with a stranger in tow. The hunched stranger was a thin, dark-haired man, as best Marsh could tell. In the lengthening evening shadow, as he was, he could almost pass for the father of the short, mousy Stillson.

"Sir? This gentleman wants to see you, sir."

It was not usual to receive visitors in the middle of nowhere, especially at night. Marsh cautiously shook the man's proffered hand.

"Did you want to talk to me about something, sir?" Stillson asked.

He had kept largely to himself of late, which probably meant he had realized Marsh had discovered his traitorous nature. Marsh was not sure if this made him less useful or more useful, but it was not something he cared to discuss in front of a stranger. The man could be affiliated with Cope, for all he knew, and Cope had advantage enough already.

"I do, but we'll take it up another time," Marsh said. "Just don't go wandering off."

There was really nowhere to wander, but Stillson nodded and walked away.

"Please, sir, come in my tent," Marsh said. "I believe there's another chair over there in the corner, if you'd be so kind as to pull it up."

The short stranger walked under the extended tent flap without having to duck his head. Some advantages to being of small stature, Marsh thought. Less bending and flexing of the skeleton. His own bone structure was getting bent and folded all too often out here in the west. While the man found the chair, Marsh carefully wrapped up his Pterosaur bone and put it in one of the table's small drawers. If the man was an emissary from Edward Cope, there was no need for him to see any of the meager bone collection Marsh possessed.

"I am sorry to bother you," the man said. "I believe we share a common problem, and I have come to offer my help."

"And what problem might that be, sir?"

"The man who is digging up all the bones around here."

That got Marsh's attention. He crooked his elbows on the table and leaned forward. His visitor sat straight up in the chair, far enough away from the table that the lamp light created interesting shadows under his eye sockets and nose.

"And what do you know about him?"

"He is my adversary. I know that he intends to dig up the best bones and leave you and me with nothing. I have been watching you for some time. I know that you are competing with another gentleman for these bones. Did you know that your adversary and my adversary have now teamed up to work together?"

He spoke dispassionately, but the words hit Marsh like cold water. No wonder Cope was able to telegraph word of a new finding! He hadn't found anything at all, not by himself. Marsh was a little relieved that it required two paleontologists working together to best him, but he did not like to lose even with those odds.

"How do you know this?"

"I just do."

The man moved as few parts of his face as possible when he talked, and his voice rarely wavered with inflection. In the lamplight, he looked like a ghost, drained of all his earthly cares, come from beyond to impart news.

"I cannot place your accent," Marsh said. "Who are you, and where are you from?"

"I am sorry for not introducing myself earlier. I must have forgotten my manners. My name is Thornton Grieg. I am from Iceland."

"Iceland? I have never met anyone from Iceland, but it sounds like an interesting place. Is it? Tell me a little bit about it."

Grieg seemed to grimace a little. So he could move the muscles in his face after all.

"I really did not come here to discuss Iceland. You may read about it at your leisure in any number of books—"

O.C. Marsh did not care to have his reading dictated by a stranger. As a professor at Yale, he was perfectly aware that he could read about Iceland until his eyes fell out of his head, but as a scientist he was also aware that first-hand observation can be invaluable.

"Sir. Tell me about Iceland or you shall have to leave my camp."

Grieg glowered at him for a moment, or at least Marsh took the subtle bunching of the eyebrows as a glower.

"I tell you, there is no—"

"Tell me something about Iceland."

A long moment passed.

"It is cold."

"I believe I could have deduced that from the name alone. More, please."

"There is a variety of interesting flora and fauna."

Marsh had begun the questioning out of curiosity, and continued it from anger. Now he was getting annoyed about the lack of information it was providing.

"An example?"

Grieg did not soften his glower, faint as it was. It did not seem to please him to discuss his home.

"There are herbivorous quadrupeds and small ferns."

"What sort of ferns?"

"Green ferns. Beyond that I do not know."

"Surely you must—"

The stranger rose to go. He leaned in over the table, which put him on eye level with Marsh, and which gave Marsh his first good look at him. The stranger's skin was as smooth as ice on a pond. Up close, he looked like a porcelain doll.

"I do not have long to visit. I only came to tell you about how you might obtain more bones than you could possibly want. If you are more interested in discussing Iceland, then I have the wrong man."

Marsh's annoyance faded and his temper cooled. If fossils were the payoff, then his pride could be reined. He did not want to beg, but he was willing to get pretty close to it.

"Please, sir, I was merely curious. Please sit back down."

Grieg's gravelly face faded back out of the lamplight. He sat back in his chair and regathered his dignity by immobilizing his already tight face. No trace of anger was left in his stoic features.

"How may I find these fossils?" Marsh asked when decorum was restored.

"You *won't* find them, not if you don't help me. The man whose camp you surrounded the other night has acquired most of the bones in this area. He intends to acquire even more, and will take them away from here for purposes I consider immoral. I would like to take them away from him. I am willing to give you some of them if you will help me."

Marsh stroked his beard. It occurred to him that the man must be insane, some sort of desert wanderer.

He had probably watched Cope and Marsh search for bones, and it had triggered bizarre fantasies. Such a man could become violent, and Marsh regretted upsetting him earlier.

"Why come to me? Why not do it yourself?"

"Because you have the most men of anyone out here. You have seven men in your camp, two of whom have weapons. I am out here by myself."

"But if I help you, I would only get some of the bones."

"I realize this is not what you wanted to hear. But you must know that would still be many more bones than you are finding on your own."

The man must have been watching the camp very closely. Marsh cursed himself for being so lax with the soldiers. They spent more time playing cards than working, but he had let it pass. Now he realized he had more than the Indians to fear out here. The soldiers could let their poker skills get a little rusty for a while.

"Mr. Grieg, I am not usually in the habit of stealing bones from other people. I would prefer to dig them up myself. I am afraid what you are advocating is little more than theft, and you must realize my position would not allow me to do that."

"You do not seem to understand," Grieg said. "The man is taking the bones away improperly. He does not intend to—to leave them for anyone. He will take them very far away."

"You mean he's going to take them to a foreign country?"

Surely Cope would not be a party to that, but Grieg nodded his head vigorously.

"Well, why didn't you say so? That does make things quite different."

While it was true that America as a whole was not always appreciative of the great scientific finds that lay within its borders, it was not so cavalier as to blindly ship things off to other countries. Things might be borrowed among scientists, of course, but they were always returned.

"Where is the man going to take the bones?"

"Far away."

Grieg was maddening.

"Overseas?"

"Yes."

"Canada?"

"I do not know. Far away."

So his topographical knowledge was as spotty as his knowledge of ferns in his own country. Grieg was beginning to look as annoyed as Marsh, although his immobile face made it hard to tell.

"What country is this man from, and what is his name? You must know that, if you know so much about his activities."

Grieg seemed to shiver slightly. Darkness had fallen outside, and the temperature had gone south with the sun. Still, for a man wearing what appeared to be a reasonable jacket, it shouldn't be that cold. Marsh himself was quite comfortable, and was dressed in nothing more than what he might wear out for a fall evening in New Haven.

"I cannot discuss this further right now. I will come to you again tomorrow. Perhaps a bit earlier in the day."

"I don't see why—"

Grieg stood up, nearly knocking the chair over. He picked it up and walked it back to the corner of the tent. When he neared the lamp again he seemed to be hugging himself. Whoever he was, he was not used to the cold. Marsh assumed a native of Iceland would be a bit more cold-blooded.

"Please, I will come to you tomorrow. You should not bother to dig, you won't find anything. Will you agree to work with me?"

Marsh stood up and held out his hands in supplication.

"Sir, you give me so little information I do not know what to say. If what you tell me is true, I am disturbed that this man is taking our fossils to foreign soil. I would have thought that a European would be more respectful of our property, if indeed this man is European, but again you've given me so little information I do not know what to think."

Grieg moved to go. Marsh could not just let him leave like that, but the little man appeared increasingly agitated so he didn't know what else to do but to extend his hand. Grieg gave it a quick shake and then headed for the tent flap.

"Until tomorrow, then," Grieg said as Marsh again held the flap for him.

Marsh sat back down and pondered for a moment after the man left. There was obviously something terribly wrong with him, but his strange silent intensity was unnerving. What if he was right? What if Edward Cope was stupidly cooperating with some sort of foreign fossil grab?

"That would be the end of *that*," he thought, and was surprised to find he had spoken it out loud.

Yes, that would be the end of that. Cope had already ruffled enough nerves among the survey heads back in Washington. If true, the odd little man's news would be a disgrace to Cope. Marsh would no longer have to race into the field to try to keep up with Cope's frantic, sloppy pace. He would no longer have to rush his papers into print to try to get the truth out before Cope's half-baked summaries and monographs. There would be time enough for good science, time enough at last.

But who was this Grieg? Why was someone from Iceland wandering Montana, apparently alone, and why did he care what Cope and the other man did with the bones? Might he be thinking of trying to pull off a similar stunt himself? Then Marsh might be the one caught in a scandal, and that would never do. The Peabody Museum must be built, and he must build it.

He needed to know more about this man, but he could not be sure that Grieg was not dangerous. He should have one of the soldiers follow him, but that would be hard. The soldiers did not seem quite up to the call of stealth, and neither did any of the men, least of all Digger Phelps. He would probably fall off a mountain if sent out tonight. Marsh could not attempt it himself, especially with his eyes the way they were. That left only one person. Al Stillson. Small and quiet, certainly, but also untrustworthy. What a fix to be in. The persons he could trust were not up to the task; the one he did not was small and dark and stealthy and eminently suitable.

"Desperate times call for desperate measures," he muttered to himself as he reached for the tent flap to call Stillson again.

He seemed to be relying on a lot of desperate measures lately.

Perhaps, for the past was long and dark. For decades
in captivity... It reveled in the wanderings, bright as
no light. ...ory and what was waiting on... She...
he stranger and blink. His mind was... but Cope later
had reminded beside to mention...
...faintly confused...
"Alice, will go," ...cturing out ...
he only reason he was good at sitting rocks and measuring...

NINETEEN

So this is how it was now—Marsh was trying to kill her. Alice Stillson had been summoned and ordered to follow the weird little man, a complete stranger, out into the Montana wilderness without so much as a match to light her way. Marsh had said he knew she had spied for Edward Cope, but he would forgive her and pay her more if she would help him now. Marsh had explained that any illumination could give her away, and who knew what the man would do if he found he was being followed. He explained this hastily, and it had not seemed to occur to him that this did not exactly put Stillson in the mood to perform the mission at hand, higher pay or no. His sense of chivalry must have completely shriveled out here, but then again, he had no reason to think he should be chivalrous.

Stillson was actually less worried about the man than she was about the flora she was having to pick her way across in the dark. She had taken the precaution of listening in at the side of Marsh's tent as he spoke to the stranger, even before Marsh called her into action. The Army soldiers were busy losing their money back and forth to each other, and the men were working their way to the bottom of a whiskey bottle Digger Phelps had brought back with him. It was probably the only useful extraction they would perform all week.

Phelps, for his part, was lying on his cot, praying for
an early death. It seemed like a good time to put an
ear to the ground to see what was going on. What had
the stranger told Marsh his name was? Grieg. Grieg
had not sounded harmful so much as just odd, and even
a little confused.

Alice missed Sitting Lizard. Following Grieg would
be something he was good at. Sitting Lizard was quiet,
he was quick, but he was also gone. Actually, following
Grieg was turning out to be not so hard. After they
cleared the rough scrub that surrounded the camp,
there seemed to be nothing much on the ground to
trip her. It also meant there was nothing to hide behind,
but she was wearing her usual black, and the moon
seemed to be taking it easy tonight, putting out as little
light as possible.

Grieg was dressed in black, too, but she could follow
the small torch he carried. She hadn't noticed that he
was carrying one when he came to the camp, but he
had it when he left. It seemed to be a very small flame,
and it didn't flicker much, but it put out enough light
for her to find him. Now and then he turned his face
to the left or the right and she also caught a flash of
his pale skin in the moonlight. The lunar beams seemed
to love his skin. He practically glowed whenever the
moon could touch him, leaving a flashing trail for her
to follow in addition to that blazed by the faint light
of his torch.

Despite the light he carried, he did not seem
especially suited for this countryside. Maybe it was easier
to walk in Iceland, because he was certainly having a
time of it in Montana. Even with the illumination of
the torch he nearly fell several times, which slowed
down the chase considerably. Each time he paused
Stillson would crouch down and wait for him to start
moving again, which sometimes took a minute or two.

Once he did fall and then got up without her seeing him, and she didn't move until she saw the light of his torch further down the way.

Grieg also seemed gripped by the chills. Now and then she saw the reflection of the moon on his hands, not just his face. He seemed to be hugging himself. It was not warm out, but it wasn't all that cold, either, and for God's sake the man even had a torch. His flame did not seem to put out much heat, but Stillson would have been glad to have it. Grieg did not seem to think it was doing much good. She could hear him grunt in frustration as he made his way along. He was not having a good night.

At one point he turned to the right and made his way up a small hill. He had his back turned to her and she could not see him for a long time, until finally he turned toward the moon again and its beams glistened on his pale face. He must never go out in the sun at all, Stillson thought as she crouched down behind an outcropping of sandstone. Even back in the city of St. Louis she had never seen anyone as pale as that. Even Stanton, bless him, looked hale and tanned and hearty compared to this ghostly man, and he showed his face to the sun as little as he could.

Grieg sat on the hill for quite a while, looking out at nothing. Finally he gave what sounded like the offspring of a grunt and a sigh, and hugged himself again. The cold appeared to be getting to him, and he headed back down the hill, or tried to. His small torch seemed insufficient for lighting the way, and Stillson heard him cry out in surprise as he began to make his descent down the hillside in a rapid, if undignified, head-over-heels manner. He was silent as a stone when he finally came to a stop.

Stealth would dictate that Stillson should leave him where he lay and head back to camp. But what if he were dead? Surely O.C. Marsh would want to know that. What if he were dead and had letters from Edward Cope in his pocket, telling him what to do? Marsh would have her head if this turned out to be the case. He had already called her a two-timing weasel when he sent her out on this mission. Finding out who this man was would surely put her in a better light to Marsh, and after all he was again in the position of paying her the most money.

She uncurled herself from behind the rock and crept slowly down the hill, being careful not to slip and end up in the same prone position as the ghostly Grieg. He was most definitely unconscious, she found when she got to him. He was sprawled on his back on the ground, his left shoulder raised by a tuft of grass, his head dipping into a depression into the dirt. He looked like a porcelain doll, broken and abandoned, tossed down by an uncaring child. Stillson crept toward him on all fours, making as little noise as possible. Sitting Lizard had said that some of the Sioux could move silently as clouds, but she did not possess this skill. She tried only to make less noise than a buffalo, and thought herself to be succeeding in that modest goal.

She held a hand before Grieg's small mouth, which was opened only a slit. So he was breathing; that was something. What should she do now? If she moved him she might wake him, but he looked terribly uncomfortable the way he was lying. What if he had broken his neck, or his back? The wild west tales she had read never had anyone dying that way out here. It was always from a gunshot wound administered by a saintly sheriff, or a knife wound perpetrated by a cowardly villain, or an arrow wound caused by an uncivilized Indian. Maybe, just maybe, a broken neck could be caused by falling off a speeding wagon while shooting it out with marauding Indians, but it would certainly not result from taking a tumble off a mountain. She decided to take the chance and shift him around at least a little bit. It would not be terribly humane to ascertain that he was still living and them leave him in an uncomfortable position, only to have him die on the chilly rocks. Surely he would prefer to have his head resting on that tuft of grass rather than halfway under it.

He was deceptively heavy for such a slight man, as she discovered when she tried to shift his torso. He appeared to be as light as a feather but weighed as much as a horse, or so it seemed to her own thin arms. No wonder he had made such a racket when he went cartwheeling off the hillside. She pulled her hands out from under him and tried to work a different angle, when her fingers touched something metallic and cold. It was a round metal stick, about a foot long. She would have thought it was his torch, but metal didn't burn and it didn't have a mark on it. What was it, some kind of club? She turned it around in her hands, getting to know its shape by feel. There was a small bump towards the bottom. She pushed it, and the top of the tube lit up. Stillson almost fell over in surprise, and dropped the tube. The light promptly went out. She sat up again and grabbed the tube again. So it was his torch, only she had never seen one that worked like that. Its light really wasn't very bright. No wonder the poor man had been staggering around. She pushed the bump and the light came on again. She waved it around. She pointed it at a patch of scrub, and when she did so the light seemed to intensify, until she could see every veiny blade of grass. So maybe the light wasn't so bad after all. Why did Grieg have such trouble with it?

The magical torch was also deceptive about its weight, but in the opposite way to Grieg. It was lighter than it looked. Stillson hefted it in her hand. You could walk

around with it all day without any discomfort. This would
be a great thing to have. But, then again, Grieg wasn't
dead, so it was technically still his. That was the law
of the wild west, as her stories had told her. She had
almost forgotten Grieg as she played with his torch,
so she put it down with its light still shining and went
to move him. Stillson put her hands under his back
closer to his shoulders, hoping that would give her better
leverage.

She had just gotten him moving slightly when his
hand moved. It swooped towards her like a white bat
and sought her face. His cold fingers touched her head,
right above her ear. Stillson froze in place, hunched
over Grieg like a monkey, unable to move. She felt
like her brain was exploding.

Pictures flashed into her mind. She saw what must
have been a city, with tall buildings, taller than anything
in St. Louis. They reached for the sky. There was no
brick, just the same sort of shiny metal as Grieg's torch.
Metallic things flew overhead, like balloons, only faster.
People walked past each other, hundreds of people,
maybe thousands; it was hard to tell. And they weren't
people. They were lizards. Her eyes seemed to get up
close to them and she could see the bumpy skin, but
the lizards were shaped like humans. Two arms, two
legs, no tails. Their noses were shorter and their eyes
were bigger, but other than that they looked almost
the same as people. They seemed to be talking to each
other in what sounded like a whistling sort of language,
but she could make out nothing.

Then the pictures changed and she was inside one
of the buildings. This one was dark on the inside, and
there were lizard people sitting all around her. It seemed
to be a quiet place. It reminded her of a church. Another
image was flashing in her mind now—a vista of what
looked like an ocean, of all things. There were no lizard

people here, but tall reptiles, ones that stood on two legs and four legs and looked nothing at all like people. These looked more like Marsh's drawings of dinosaurs that she had seen. She seemed to be staring down on them from the side of a hill, such as the one Grieg had been standing on before he took his tumble. It looked like it was nighttime, but she could somehow see, although just barely. The ocean stretched out into the darkness before her. It seemed to go on forever. She could hear quiet whistling words coming from her own mouth, but didn't know what they were. She also felt an overwhelming sense of sorrow, one that made her eyes mist over and nearly made her knees buckle. It came almost in waves, sorrow crashing into her as inexorably as waves on the beach. Then everything seemed to go black.

Grieg's fingers moved from her head, and Stillson jerked away. The pictures stopped. She was left only with the night and the odd shining torch and the prone body of Grieg, which emitted a groan. Dying or not, Stillson leaped to her feet and ran away. She had made a good hundred yards when the image of a frowning Marsh came to her mind. It was not like she could just go back to camp and go to bed. Marsh would be waiting, expecting some kind of report. She did not care to say that the strange visitor fell off a hill and then she hallucinated about lizard-men and left him lying there with a torch that emitted light without a flame. He would surely expect a little bit more than that.

Stillson turned back. When she drew closer to Grieg, she saw that he had apparently gotten up and resumed his trek. She could again see the occasional flash of his torch and the reflection of the moon across his face. He kept looking to the left, where that vast sea seemed to have been located in the vision in her head. Had not Edward Cope mentioned that there was once an inland sea here, with dinosaurs around it? She seemed to recall something like that, but surely that was not what she had seen. That sea must have been gone for thousands of years. And why had the picture come to mind in the first place? It almost made her head hurt to think about it.

The ground was sloping down now, as they seemed to be nearing the river. She had not realized they had come this far. This trek was well worth what Marsh would be paying her. If Grieg had a camp here, Stillson saw no sign of it. There was a dark copse of trees near the riverbank, and the grass was now more even and plentiful, but aside from that there was nothing else around. She could hear the gurgle of the water. Was this the Judith or the Missouri? Probably the Judith. Whatever it was, it was no match for the sea that Stillson had seen in her head.

Grieg picked his way right down to the edge of the water. The light from his torch was now nowhere in evidence. He turned his face towards the moon one more time and then she saw nothing of him. She heard a splash. Had he jumped into the river? Surely not. Anyone walking around trying to fend off the cold in the air would not make himself warmer by jumping in the Judith River, especially not in late October. Maybe he had just thrown his torch into the water, although that didn't make much more sense.

Stillson hunched close to the ground and kept as quiet as she could, breathing only in long, slow gulps. She could hear nothing but the wind and the river, and saw nothing but the moon and the dark lumpy shapes around her. After nearly five minutes she stood up and walked closer to the water. It whispered as it swept past the bank. She could see the water only by the moon's reflection in it. She didn't see a man thrashing around in the water, and nothing seemed to be moving on the opposite bank, some forty feet across. So he must have really done it. Having failed to brain himself by falling off the hill, the mysterious Mr. Grieg had thrown himself in the river to drown.

This brought a sense of finality. Maybe this was something, strange as it was, that she could report to Marsh—perhaps minus the parts about the lizard-man city and the inland sea. Alice Stillson pulled her black hat further down on her head and headed back for camp, wishing all the while that Grieg had left his torch on the bank of the Judith River.

TWENTY

Cope had moved camp yet again, at Swenson's request, to a patch of flat land two miles further south of where the Judith met the Missouri. Charles Sternberg was still glad to see it, meager and poor though it was. Fort Claggett did not excite him, and the trip there by himself had been boring. Edward Cope could be counted on to deliver a running patter about anything that happened to be along the roadside, whether it was the history of the rocks that lined the road or speculation about what the flora under them might have been like hundreds of thousands, or millions, of years ago. He could make the trip interesting, but he had remained behind with the Monoclonius skeleton while Charles was dispatched to send its description to Fort Benton, from where it would be wired to Philadelphia and the waiting world.

He steered the horse up the broad ravine to the camp, where an odd sight met his eyes. When he had left the day before, the curiously cleaned skeleton had been splayed about the camp, its bones arranged into the approximate places where they belonged in life. Now he could see no bones at all, just half a dozen clumps of white sheets arrayed like parts of a dismembered snowman.

"Mr. Cope!" he shouted as he got down off the horse. "Where are you? What are you doing?"

Cope's bewhiskered face appeared from the other side of one of the white clumps, which stood several feet tall. He stood and walked towards Sternberg, trailing a length of white cloth behind him.

"Charley! Glad you're back. That didn't take long. You didn't see any of Marsh's boys around there, did you?"

Sternberg would not have known what they looked like if he did, but he shook his head no.

"What are you doing with the Monoclonius? I thought you were going to study it more."

Cope looked back at the white clumps.

"I am, Charley, I just decided to do that back in Philadelphia."

Sternberg turned a surprised eye to his boss. Cope just smiled.

"But Mr. Swenson said these bones were just on loan for now," Sternberg said. "You promised you'd give them back."

Cope patted him on the back.

"Oh, I'm sure Mr. Swenson doesn't want this one, or he wouldn't have given it to me, even on a loan. But there's something else. I was looking over this other pile of bones and I found something interesting."

He pointed to a pile of fossils off by itself near Boston Mickle's kitchen tent, and motioned for Sternberg to follow. Sternberg saw what at first glance looked like another fantastic skeleton, but on second glance appeared more like something a person would come across at a bone rummage sale. It had a cracked half skull with two tusks that didn't seem to belong, a smattering of teeth and one femur that was broken in two. Cope gently held up one end of the femur.

"Do you recognize this, Charley?"

Sternberg squinted at the bone.

"It looks like the femur you brought out here with you. The one now missing from our fossil cart."

"My boy, you win the cigar," Cope said. "This is the very same bone that was stolen from our camp. I told you he had it."

"So you think because he stole from you that you can steal from him? The Bible doesn't say that, Edward."

Cope's eyes darkened.

"Please don't quote scripture back to me. I know very well what the Bible says and what it doesn't. I'm not finished. Do you remember a while back that I went out one night with young Mr. Stillson, Marsh's spy?"

Of course Charley remembered that. Cope had spotted a skull that had him raving all the next day, and which prompted him to move the camp so Marsh wouldn't get all the bones.

"This is that same skull," Cope said, pointing to what looked like half of a Hadrosaurus skull. "Marsh insulted my intelligence by trying to stick tusks on it to fool me. But the other night I saw that it was in Mr. Swenson's camp, alongside the femur that I had brought all the way out here."

"So you think Swenson is working together with Marsh?"

"What else should I think? They must be in cahoots. Swenson said he wanted me to come out here to distract Marsh, but instead I think he just wanted me to move here to be out of the way so he and Marsh can dig everything up."

"But why would he give you a perfectly cleaned skeleton of an undiscovered dinosaur?"

Cope began pacing as he talked, although he was careful not to go anywhere near the bundles of rags.

"That had me confused for a while, too, my friend. But perhaps Othniel knew that I could not be persuaded to move out here without giving me something good. Othniel maybe got me to move once with that pile of bones, but he must have known that to get me to do it again would require something better, so he got Swenson to provide it."

"But do you think Marsh would actually give you a cleaned skeleton of something he hadn't even discovered? It seems like he would just give you another duckbill and be done with it."

"Maybe Marsh wouldn't, but maybe Swenson would. Maybe he doesn't know what he's doing. He didn't even know what survey he was supposed to work for."

"And so Marsh standing around with all those Indians the other night was just a ruse."

"A very complicated one, but a ruse, yes. That's exactly the word. They knew they would have to do something elaborate to get me to fall for it."

Sternberg thought back to that night. It hadn't seemed like a ruse at the time. Marsh's surprise on seeing Cope dash out of Swenson's camp seemed real enough, but then he hadn't had any prior experience competing with Marsh, and Cope obviously had. Perhaps the world of professional paleontology was a lot more complicated than he had been led to believe.

"What's the matter, Charley?" Cope asked after Sternberg had remained silent for a long while.

"Nothing."

Cope walked up to him and put a hand on his shoulder.

"I think there is something."

Sternberg did not want to meet his boss's intense eyes, and instead looked at one of the rag-covered piles.

"It's just that this is not what I wanted to do. I enjoy digging up the bones, finding them in the rock. I like discovering something buried and then bringing it up to the light. I don't like just having a completely cleaned skeleton delivered to camp overnight. That's not why I wanted to get into fossil hunting."

That was something else that bothered Sternberg

about Cope's conspiracy theory. The skeleton of the Monoclonius had appeared outside of camp the day after they met with Swenson. It was just there, on top of the ground, like it had been there all the time. Sternberg had not heard so much as a twig snap the night before, and Jenks Dart said he hadn't, either. Swenson managed to drop off the complete skeleton of a dinosaur that was nearly twenty feet long without waking anybody. It seemed like a lot of work just to fool Edward Cope, but again maybe that's the way things were done out here.

"Charley," Cope said, and put his other hand on Sternberg's other shoulder.

His voice was avuncular, and Sternberg had no choice but to look him in the eye.

"Charley, I would like nothing better than for you to find more dinosaur bones than you could dig up with a team of forty men. But we have so far come up with virtually nothing, and this trip has not been cheap. I have got to go back east with something, and now I have that something. Now, you have done a good job for me and I want to work with you in the future. But there won't be a future if I can't make my field trips fruitful. With this skeleton, this trip has suddenly become fruitful. Very fruitful. Swenson probably does not even know what this thing is, and he won't care if I take it."

Sternberg nodded glumly, and blinked. Cope did not blink at all.

"If Othniel is dumb enough to think he can fool me, then I am smart enough to take a chance when I get one."

"I'm with you," Sternberg said, and Cope released his shoulders and turned back to the mummified skeleton of the Monoclonius.

"Now. What we need to do here is get this beast

wrapped up and transported to the river. I saw a boat coming down that way this morning, and the man said some Army equipment is being shipped on the river tomorrow. The boat may have room for these bones, and I want to make sure they're ready when it comes through."

Charles had hoped to rest a while upon returning from Fort Claggett, but Cope was far too agitated and energized to permit any such indolence. Sternberg quickly found himself helping to wrap the bones and load them onto the cart, which groaned, for the first time of this trip, under the weight of a sizable amount of mineralized bone. By early afternoon the load was ready, and Sternberg and Cope fastened long ropes to the cart to aid in its downhill progress to the river. If the horses were left alone to carry the bones, the cart would quickly put itself before them and the whole shebang would go crashing down the sandstone and shale. By letting the horses walk down but aiding them with the rope, Cope hoped to keep the whole package relatively intact, and was glad to finally have the opportunity to move something big.

Cope and Sternberg wrapped the ropes around a tall but slender sandstone outcropping, so they could gradually let out the rope as the horses wended their way down. Boston Mickle was busy behind his tent, where he was preparing dinner. Jenks Dart was nowhere to be found, and Sternberg had nearly forgotten that he was ever part of the camp. This dig was increasingly becoming a two-man event. The snorting horses had made it maybe halfway down the treacherous hill when a particularly sharp bit of sandstone cut through Sternberg's rope. The fossil cart tipped precariously onto one wheel, and Cope began shouting at the horses to stop. They did, suddenly, and the cart crashed back onto the other wheel with a sickening crunch. Cope looked as if he had lost a dear member of his family as he tied up his rope and ran to check on the cart.

"Charley, we broke a couple," he shouted back to Sternberg, who held the broken end of his rope. "The frill didn't break, but the horn did on the front of the skull."

"I'm sorry," Sternberg shouted back.

"Don't be. Not your fault."

Sternberg's attention was distracted by Mickle, who came stomping around from behind his tent, walking faster than Charles had ever seen him move before. His chubby cheeks shook in anger as he carried a huge pot of rice to the middle of camp and set it down on the ground with a dull thump. Mickle had to be strong to carry a pot of rice that big, Sternberg thought. It would be nice to have his help with the cart, but it would also be nice to have some dinner once the cart was on the flat land near the river.

"Damn it!" Mickle said. "I got started watching you and forgot about my rice, and now it's too sticky to eat."

He jammed a finger into the pot and brought it up to show a glutinous mass that dripped from his fingers as slowly as molasses.

"Now we just have some hen, and nothing else."

Cope had shouted something at Sternberg, but Sternberg was listening to Mickle and had apparently turned his deaf ear to Cope. In a minute Cope had walked back up the camp, puffing from the exertion.

"What is going on up here? Charley, I told you to come help me try to wrap these bones a little better. Boston, why is the rice pot in the middle of camp?"

"Look at it," Mickle said, his chin extended in childish pique.

He looked a little bit like a large child, albeit a child with massive arms and an equally massive belly.

Cope examined the rice, and stuck a tentative finger into the pot. A smile crept slowly across his face.

"Say, Boston, what were you going to do with this?"

"I don't know. Throw it out, I guess."

"I don't think so. Can you make more?"

"More sticky rice?"

"Yes. Maybe two or three pots more?"

Mickle looked stunned, as if Cope had asked him to burn the hen for dinner.

"I suppose I could."

"Good. Charley, come with me."

Cope picked up one side of the rice pot, but he couldn't carry the whole thing without Sternberg's help.

"What are we doing?" Charles asked as they stumbled their way down the hill toward the cart.

"I think Boston has figured out a way to help us pack these bones without breaking them. We just need a lot of sticky rice, and we'll make that Army boat yet."

TWENTY ONE

Digger Phelps felt the unusual weight of the pistol in his palm. He had rarely held a gun before, preferring usually to equip that space with a bottle of some sort, but drinking would not help this night. There were stranger things out in this desert than anything he had seen after a long night of working his way through a bottle of joy juice.

It was nearly pitch black outside. The moon had retired its face and the sun had yet to awaken, so Marsh said they had a little time. The world seemed to be asleep, but Digger could hear things scuttling around his feet. He did not particularly wish to know what they were. His job was to stay close to the soldiers, who were actually going under the thing that everyone had now taken to referring to as the ghost wall. They had complained mightily, preferring to stick to cards, but Marsh had insisted they earn their pay and undertake this possibly hazardous mission at night. Marsh had said there would not be much time left; the man always made his move at first daylight.

Phelps was a lookout, for what ever good that did. He couldn't see a finger in front of his face, couldn't even see the silver of his pistol barrel, and yet Marsh had forbidden them to use any sort of light. This paleontology was much more secretive than he had imagined it to be.

"Where are you?" he whispered to Jed Blank, the Army man who had been told to try to crawl under the west side of the ghost wall. "Jed? Where are you?"

All he heard was the shuffling of dirt. Blank must have gotten to the other side. Marsh had told the men that sound could travel through the ghost wall, but maybe that was a mistake because Phelps wasn't hearing much of anything right now.

"Jed!" he said, his voice a little louder and sharper.

He didn't like not being able to hear or see, either, and only the feel of the sharp rocks under his leg let him know he could still feel. It was nippy out, and the gun had gone cold in his hand.

"Jed!"

"Shut up!" Blank's whispered voice came back.

There was a long silent pause, and then something right out of the Bible appeared. Phelps had once read the Bible a good bit, although he had gotten a bit rusty at it in recent years. The Bible was full of things like bolts of lightning and strange beams of light, not to mention demons from Hell, and that's just what this had to be. Right before him, not three feet away, stood a tiny man who seemed made entirely of brimstone. He was black as the night and would have disappeared into it entirely were it not for the solid white lance of light that shone from his forehead and played over the prone form of Jed Blank, who waved his arms around as if blinded. One of his waving arms held a pistol.

"Shoot him!" Phelps shouted.

"You shoot him!" Blank yelled back. "I can't even see him!"

Phelps remembered that he, too, had a pistol in his hand. He raised his right arm and aimed carefully at the center of the little demon's head, where the light was emanating. The demon was short; Phelps was sitting, but they were just about on eye level, or at least

eye-to-beam level. Phelps squeezed off two shots at
nearly point blank range. He heard a shout in the
background, and then what sounded like someone
falling down the side of a hill. Who was behind him?
Sam Sharp? No, he was on the east side, with the other
soldier, Tom Dyson. Was it Rick, one of the men Marsh
had hired for the digging? Rick had big muscles but a
high-pitched voice, and that shout had sounded a lot
like Rick. But why was Rick yelling?

At just about the instant that Phelps figured that the
ghost wall was apparently bulletproof, he went blind.
The demon must have turned its face to him. He saw
nothing now, nothing but white and the little veins inside
his eyelids. Phelps screamed and covered his eyes with
his hands, dropping his pistol in the process. His hands
did not seem to help much. He was surprised he could
not see his own thoughts, the light was so bright.

He heard another pistol shot, one that rang in his
ears. Now he would be deaf and blind, for real. Jed
must have got off a shot, but it didn't sound like it did
any good, because shortly after the shot rang out he
uttered a surprised grunt and then he didn't make
anymore sound at all. Phelps knelt in the rocks, panting
and covering his eyes. Now he would be blind forever.
He might end up a beggar like those guys he had seen
in New York, if he even lived to get back east at all.
For a long minute he could hear nothing but the sound
of his own breathing, but then he heard the crunching
of gravel behind him. Before he could think of the
futility of it, he turned to look.

It was a brimstone demon, maybe the same one,
coming up behind him, working its way laboriously
across the slope. He looked to where Jed Blank and
his demon had been, but they were both gone. This
must be the same one. He wondered at first how it
could get through the ghost wall, until it occurred to

him that it was a demon and must have had some sort of pass. It still had a light coming from its head, but it wasn't blinding this time. It shone at about the level of a torch, and this time he could see two tiny red lights burning behind it. The things must burn hellfire for eyes.

He fumbled on the ground for his pistol, but the thing seemed to anticipate the move. It shot out another beam of light from its head. He closed his eyes in a panic but this beam was smaller and much less bright, and green. It was almost soothing. In fact, it was too soothing. He had managed to pick up his pistol but had it only halfway to a firing position when the beam caught him right in the gun, sending a green sunburst skittering off his hand and across the rocks. He dropped the pistol again. His hand was numb where the beam had touched it, more numb than even the cold had made it.

The demon kept advancing. He could almost see its face now, except that it didn't seem to have a face, just a rounded blank slate broken only by two glowing red dots. He would have thought demons had fangs, but these were sort of understated as demons went. He saw no mouth, no fangs, no muscles visible on the short arms. They looked more like walking black dolls than infernal demons, although they did seem to be able to breathe some sort of fire. The demon appeared to be just about to blast another green bolt at him when it took a wrong step and went skittering on the rocks, nearly falling. The beam shot up into the sky, disappearing into the low clouds before the demon righted itself and shut the beam off. It was advancing on him again when a large bird plummeted from the sky and hit it directly on top of the head, sending the little demon pinwheeling down the side of the hill, its light seeming to wink on and off as it rolled.

Phelps couldn't tell what kind of bird it was, but it must have been heavy because the demon went down like it was being tugged with a rope. He didn't stay to worry about the bird or the demon. The hole that he and Blank had dug was still there, and he intended to go through it. They had dug under the ghost wall, leaving dirt on top of the hole just like that weird little man had told them to do. If you leave dirt at the top of the hole the ghost wall won't go all the way to the ground, he had said, and so far he had been right, except he had failed to mention the existence of demons from Hell. That was a pretty big oversight.

He felt his way to where the hole was and pushed himself through, blinking his eyes against the dirt. He knew that the ghost wall was invisible, but he still somehow felt that there should be something on the other side that he hadn't been seeing before. He sort of expected to bump into Jed Blank, but the Army man was nowhere to be found. There was nothing on the other side of the wall, or at least nothing more than the darkness he was familiar with on the outside. He pulled himself to his feet and set off, although he wasn't sure where he was going.

After a few steps, he became aware of a green glow off to his left. He clenched his right hand into a fist and wished he still had his pistol, although it had not proven to be much help so far. There was a rise of sandstone he couldn't see before. He could only see it now because the green glow revealed its edge. He crept up to it and found Jed Blank after all.

Blank was hovering in the air, a foot off the ground, glowing green from every pore. His eyes were wide open and he stared back at Phelps, who gave an involuntary yelp upon seeing him. Blank's eyes didn't move. His mouth was open just a crack. He looked more like a wax dummy than a man, and a frightened wax dummy at that. This wasn't where he had been when the demon first saw him. The demon must have brought him here and hung him up in the air like an old shirt.

"Jed?" Phelps asked tentatively.

He walked closer to the soldier, but he didn't want to get too close. He was afraid Blank would suddenly lash out and drag him up into that green goo with him.

"Jed, can you hear me?"

If Blank could hear, he gave no sign. The green glow seemed to pulse around his body. Phelps looked at Blanks' outstretched right arm. Blank had managed to draw his pistol after all, but it hadn't done much good. The pistol floated in the air, too, an inch or so away from Blank's open palm. He looked like he was either reaching for the gun or throwing it away. Phelps could almost swear that there was a whiff of smoke coming from the barrel, frozen in place by the green glow.

He heard the familiar crunching coming from his left. The demon must have worked its way back up and was heading around the sandstone. He would no doubt like to hang Digger Phelps up there next to Blank, to complete his collection. Phelps wouldn't give him the chance. The green glow coming from Blank lit the ground for about five or six feet, and that was all the light Phelps needed to get a good running start into the middle of the stranger's camp.

O.C. Marsh squinted at the lights that shot out at odd times from the hill where the mysterious paleontologist had made his new camp. All he could see were glowing flashes of white and occasional bits of green.

"So much for the element of surprise," he said to Thornton Grieg, who sat next to him with an unreadable expression on his smooth face. "Things do not seem to be going well."

Marsh and Grieg were ensconced at what Digger Phelps had jokingly referred to as the bunker, which was really just a table set up under a nearby collection of scraggly pine trees. Marsh hated to take the table out for that purpose, but Grieg wanted it so and they managed to find a relatively flat spot for it so he had agreed. It was his specimen examination table and he didn't want to bang it up, although it had not seen many specimens lately.

Marsh brought along a small telescope, which was generally useless for observing what was actually happening at the stranger's camp. All it really did was bring the darkness—and the occasional flashes of light— slightly closer. Marsh still couldn't make out much of anything. Grieg had armed himself with what looked like a more serious piece of hardware. It was a squarish box topped with what looked like two oversized goggles. The odd little man refused to let Marsh look into the eyepieces, but he peered as closely at them as he could when he got the chance. They did not appear to have any thick lenses on the front of them, but whenever Grieg looked through he let on as if he could see everything that was happening as if it were occurring in daytime. His explanations did not do likewise for Marsh's imagination.

"I see he brought the _____," Grieg said at one point, shortly before Marsh heard shouting and gunshots. "And not the new ones, either. Those are nearly antiques."

His voice fairly dripped with contempt, although Marsh could not imagine why, or even understand what he was talking about. The word Grieg used had sounded smooth, almost musical, but Marsh could not imagine trying to replicate the sound with his own mouth.

"What is that? I suppose it's an Icelandic word."

"Of course," Grieg said as he stared into his goggles. "It means something like helper. Or assistant. Something like that."

"So there are more people in there, not just the one man?"

Grieg turned to face him. He had not wanted to allow a light near their bunker table, but Marsh hated to sit in total darkness so Grieg allowed him to put one on the ground at his side, as long as he kept the wick turned low. In the vague lamp light, Grieg's face appeared as smooth as a billiard ball. It looked like he sanded it each morning to make sure it would shine.

"Something like that."

"Well."

Marsh's men were armed, as were the two soldiers, so having a couple of extra men around shouldn't matter too much. But if this man was smuggling bones out of the country illegally, he might be desperate, and it would be better to deal with only one desperate man, not a whole group of desperate men.

"How many of them are there?"

"I see only one."

The shots cracked a moment later, followed by an eerie green beam that poked its thin finger into the sky.

"What the hell is that? What is going on? Who shot what?"

"Your man Phelps shot at a _____, and then it fell down the hill."

"Digger hit something?"

"I'm not sure, but it fell down the hill."

The sides of the hills around here were slippery and treacherous, as Marsh well knew himself. Anybody could fall if they weren't careful. Marsh had seen Phelps miss his aim with a pickaxe, so he wasn't sure he could hit anything with a gun.

"Where is Digger now?"

"He is going under the wall now and into the camp. The _____ is coming up after him."

"Can you tell about anything else?"

"No."

They sat in silence. Marsh listened for more sounds, but couldn't hear anything on this side and Sam Sharp and his men would be too far away for him to hear unless they loosed a truly spectacular barrage of gunshots.

"Can I ask you a question, Mr. Grieg?"

Grieg turned his moon face to Marsh.

"Why do you refer to that thing you say as an *it* instead of a *he*?"

Grieg stared impassively at him, as if Marsh had suddenly begun speaking Spanish.

"In the pronoun sense," Marsh went on, a little flustered. "Usually when you talk about a person without naming them, you call that person a *he*, not an *it*."

"It was an oversight," Grieg said after a long pause, during which he met Marsh's troubled eyes with a placid look. "Perhaps I meant to say he."

He returned his gaze to his goggles.

"Or perhaps you said it because these things of yours are its," Marsh said, annoyed that the little man could get under his skin.

"Perhaps," Grieg said. "Please be quiet, we may hear something more soon."

Marsh had once gone to a fortuneteller as a joke. She was a tired old woman who had a limited bag of tricks, but Marsh probably got more useful information out of her than he would from his odd ally. Maybe Ed Cope had the right idea. Hooking up with a paleontological gangster was dumb, but at least the man seemed to be doing something.

Al Stillson had not had much luck trailing Grieg

back to his camp. He had a boat stashed at the Judith River and Stillson had lost him there, but did not have much else to report. The man did not like the cold and was not all that good at navigating at night, but beyond that Stillson hadn't found out much. It seemed a bit odd that a man who hated the cold would be up to night boating on the Judith River, but Stillson said that's how it was. Stillson had speculated that maybe the man's visit was a prank, and that having got in his boat he would float down the river and not come back, but Marsh attributed that to wishful thinking the next evening when Grieg returned, dressed in a thicker jacket and carrying a blanket and a heavy valise.

Marsh invited him to eat. Grieg said he had already had dinner, and Marsh barely needed any after he heard what the shiny little man had to say. The rogue collector would be near their camp and it would be a prime opportunity to subvert his plan to make off with the bones, Grieg said. Marsh had gathered the entire camp into his tent for a strategy session. It was hard to come by a strategy because it was sometimes difficult to figure out what Grieg was talking about, a task he made more difficult by mumbling and keeping much of his face hidden by his coat. It occurred again to Marsh that Grieg must be completely insane, but if he could lead them to bones then surely a little madness could be tolerated. He was not sure if the others in the camp felt the same way. Digger Phelps and Sam Sharp seemed more interested in calculating how much larger Marsh's tent was compared to theirs.

"I will need a utensil for creating shapes and a surface for expressing them," Grieg said.

Marsh had expected Stillson to go fetch them, since he was the smallest and quickest and knew where the paper was kept, unlike most everyone else, who knew where the cards were kept. Stillson didn't move, didn't seem to understand the request.

"Paper and pen," Marsh whispered, and Stillson scurried off.

Marsh barely understood what the man wanted himself. No wonder that no major writers had come from Iceland.

Grieg spread the paper out on the table and the camp gathered around. Marsh rubbed his eyes, trying to wake up. He had trouble sleeping the night before, thinking about what Grieg had said. He was a little sorry to lose some of his paper, which he had planned to use for sketches, but seeing as how there was precious little to sketch he figured it was probably not a bad trade, especially if he got some bones out of it.

"Here is the camp," Grieg said, drawing a irregular line surrounding a circular object. "This line is the edge of the hills. This is the man's _____."

"His what?" Sam Sharp asked, his confusion mirrored in the faces of everyone at the table, Marsh's included.

"His . . . ship. His . . . tent. His tent."

"Oh."

"Now, the last time you got into the camp, how did you dig down to the . . . the barrier . . . the—"

"The ghost wall?" Marsh asked. He was no longer abashed to say the name.

"Ghost wall, yes. How did you dig down to it?"

"We dug until we could feel the bottom edge, and then went under it."

"Ah. So I thought. You might as well have sent him a note saying you were dropping by to visit. He will have recalibrated the wall now to maintain contact with the ground, so your way won't work. I will show you another way."

He had continued on at some length about that, and then, his inscrutable face half eclipsed by his hat, shoved the paper to one side and began drawing a complex set of lines that looked like an architect's plan for a circular house. He drew a dotted line at one end of a large circle and then moved the paper again and began drawing a small square with numerous tiny circles in the middle of it.

"I would advise you not to look at anything here, here and here," he said, pulling the paper back and forth as he pointed. "It will just confuse you and you won't understand it. But when you get to here, you should see this switch. It is very simple. There may be some lights on it but ignore them. If you push this button you will open his tent wide open."

"Sounds easy," Sam Sharp said. "Let's go try it."

The little bastards had got Tom Dyson good. He floated in the air in a green haze, his eyes wide open. He looked like a cross between a ghost and some kind of dessert. Sam Sharp had not even seen the creature appear, but suddenly there he was, blasting a light out of his forehead like he was some kind of human torch.

Sharp regretted having made it under the ghost wall, because now the only place to run was closer to the mystery man's tent, and he was pretty sure that was a bad idea. If this man had this kind of reinforcements at the border of his camp, he might have some real doozies waiting closer to the wings. The other men were outside, and he had heard some yelling and seen some light blasts, so he was pretty sure he was alone.

"Come on, show yourselves," he muttered, but he wasn't really sure he wanted them to.

In his youth, he had the opportunity to become a gunslinger. It had seemed less of an opportunity than a pitfall, so he had actually applied himself to his studies in Nebraska and then headed a little further west, not to shoot people but to make a living however he could.

He had worked on the railroad and on the river, and then discovered that men were actually paying to dig up bones. That seemed like the finest occupation of all. He was generally a peace-loving soul, but there were many men working and riding on the railroad who weren't, and that went double for the river. He had definitely learned to keep himself out of trouble. And now this.

Dyson had not even had a chance to draw his pistol. It was still in its holster as he hovered there in the air. Sharp had a gun in each hand. He was ready. He heard a crunching sound just before him, and in the glow of the green light coming from the floating Dyson he could see one of the little critters approaching. It was a tiny little guy, no taller than some of the Indian children that used to play around these parts. What if it was a child? Sharp glanced back up at Dyson. No child could do that.

He took a step back as the little man approached, trying to get in the best position for a clean shot to the arm or leg, whatever would slow the little guy down. The head shot would only come if the man attacked. While preparing, he managed to do the worst possible thing. He bumped into something and fell over backwards. Another one was right behind him, and he hadn't heard a thing. Sharp landed flat on his back, the blow knocking the air from his lungs and the pistols from his hands. Some gunfighter he would make.

The little man that had incapacitated Dyson clomped closer. Its tiny red pinprick eyes seemed to glow brighter. It was preparing to blast him with that white light, or, even worse, that green beam that would lift him into the air and put him out of his misery, at least for a while. Sharp was not yet ready to be put out of his misery. He had hoped to enjoy the misery a little more, or at least until Professor Marsh paid him the rest of his wages. Sharp felt around for his guns, but his fingers found only rocks and the little man he had tripped over, who was squirming around under his legs. The advancing little man now had clear room for a shot. If he couldn't have a modern weapon like a pistol, he could at least have a shield.

He leaned up, his lungs gasping for air, grabbed the prone little man and hoisted him into the air. The little guy was heavier than he had expected. It felt like he was carved entirely from metal, but Sharp held him up just the same, arms quivering. The white light came first, and the man in his arms let out a high-pitched shriek, more shrill than any kid could make. Then came the green. Sharp tossed the little man into the air, and the green blast caught him and jiggled him like a marionette. Within the green glow that now enveloped the little man, Sharp could see sparks popping from his black head. He had never known a head to do that. The green beam cut off as abruptly as it had begun, and the tiny figure crashed to the ground. If the other figure had any remorse about blasting one of his own, he didn't show it. Sharp could barely make him out in the darkness, but the sparks coming from the other little man's head lit him intermittently, and they showed him advancing towards Sharp again, the sparking light giving him a menacing jerky look.

Well, he had made a principled stand, but Sam Sharp knew when it was time to chuck it all and run away, and now seemed to be about that time. This other little monster wouldn't fall for the same trick twice, and Sharp was all out of tricks. Then again, maybe the other little monster wouldn't blast him again if he had a hostage. He grabbed up the motionless little man—whose head was still emitting enough sparks to make him worry about catching his hair on fire—and backed up until he felt the eerie push of the ghost wall at his back. So far, could be worse. He kicked out with his left leg until he nearly fell down the hole leading to the other side, and then slipped through on his belly, holding the little man as a barrier.

He wasn't fast enough. The other little man could pass right through the ghost wall, and was almost touching him by the time he got out the other.

"All right, hit me with the green light, damn you," Sharp muttered.

The little man stood and looked at him, although Sharp could only see the two little red eyes glowing. Then the man turned away, the lights of his eyes suddenly vanishing. A great rumbling sound came from somewhere inside the camp, and the ground began to shake.

"I feel that perhaps you have not been telling me everything I need to know," Marsh said to Grieg, who sat stiff and still because he had been tied to his chair.

It had been a long night. Elsewhere in the camp, Marsh could hear the sounds of the men packing up. He was losing his crew, and his promises of extra pay fell on deaf ears. They had reconvened back back at the camp after the miniature earthquake had occurred, which happened at the same time the stranger's camp had mysteriously, and rapidly, vanished altogether. The ghost wall was gone, and with it the mysterious paleontologist and most everything else—everything but the sparking little man that Sam Sharp had dragged off the hill and a few fossil bones that were partially dug out of the earth. Marsh had wanted to investigate those bones further, but he couldn't very well finish digging them up himself and the men were too busy gathering their belongings and cursing his name. Digger Phelps had already disappeared, and Marsh could not honestly guarantee that more might fall the next time around.

Even Jed Blank and Tom Dyson, Army officers officially assigned to him, were calling it quits. They did not seem any the worse for wear for their experience of glowing and hovering, but they were still angry about it. Marsh and the other men had found them, blinking and sputtering, once the mysterious paleontologist had gone. Flying in the air while glowing green was not something the Army had trained them to do, and they were not bearing the experience gracefully. Like the others, they were leaving.

"I am sorry," Grieg said. "I had not realized it would be so difficult."

"Difficult! Look at this thing," Marsh said, pointing at the motionless little man. "Don't tell me this is something you have in Iceland."

The little man, on closer inspection, turned out to be made from metal and a softer substance that looked like metal but wasn't. It was almost like leather but it was shinier than any leather that Marsh had ever seen. Stranger still, small wires stuck out from the little man's neck like wayward hair. They appeared to conduct electricity.

"No one has yet managed to create a usable electric light bulb, so I fail to understand how the geniuses in Iceland have created an artificial man who seems to run entirely on electricity."

"He doesn't run entirely on electricity," Grieg rejoindered lamely, but it was not enough to mollify Marsh.

Marsh tried to be respectful to fellow scientists, and he was usually willing to overlook odd personal quirks, having run across many people with those during the course of his academic career. Yale was practically crawling with oddballs, and in fact anyone without strange quirks there would be the exception, not the rule. But this weird little man had pushed him too far, and he wanted answers. He had been somewhat surprised to find himself leaping up and tying Grieg to the chair, but his surprise had not caused him to tie loose knots. He did not want this man going anywhere, not until he had the truth.

"Where are you really from?"

Grieg looked defeated. He did not struggle against his bonds, not that it would have done him any good, judging from his skinny arms. Marsh's entire hand had wrapped around his lower arm, with room to spare, and Grieg had barely resisted him.

"I will tell you," Grieg said, looking up with his strangely smooth face. "Although it may not do any good."

Marsh had put the lamp very near Grieg this time, and he was struck again with how oddly smooth the man's skin was, like it had no pores at all, let alone bumps or blemishes.

"What do you mean? Have we scared the man away?"

"I do not think so. He must not have everything he wants, or he would likely have left before now. But I doubt we have many tries left to get his bones. One more assault like tonight and he will probably leave."

"That's just the problem," Marsh said angrily. "I cannot mount one more assault like tonight. In case you don't know it, my men are all leaving me."

"I am sorry."

"Your sorry does not help," Marsh said, turning his round face to Grieg.

It was a face that had terrified hundreds of students at Yale, particularly the ones who had not prepared for their assignments. It was a face that brooked no funny business.

"Tell."

An hour later he walked out of the tent into a camp that had grown silent except for the pawing of the cart horses. At some point in Grieg's story, the men must have rode off into the dawn, but he hadn't even heard them. Even the cook had gone, damn him. Marsh nearly fell back into the tent when a small dark figure approached him. It was another little man with red eyes, he thought, until the figure got closer and he saw it was only Al Stillson. Al Stillson the spy.

"My god, you frightened me," Marsh said, putting one hand on his chest. "Come for your extra pay, have you?"

Stillson blinked up at him.

"No, sir. I thought I would stay with you, if that's all right."

So his little spy was the only faithful member of his camp after all. Marsh looked down on him and gave a weak smile, and resisted the urge to doff Stillson's hat and rumple his hair. The boy was probably too old for that.

"What's the matter, sir?"

"Stillson, at this point it would be better to ask what *isn't* the matter. I have no men to help me, just when I need them the most. I have you, and for that I am grateful, but you and I won't do. I need more men, and they are not aplenty out here."

"No."

Then a thought suddenly struck him, one so absurd it almost made him laugh.

"Mr. Stillson, I don't suppose you know where Mr. Cope is currently camped."

Stillson averted his eyes.

"No sir."

"I don't suppose you could find out?"

"Sir?"

"See if the wretched cook left any food. Get a bit to eat and take one of the cart horses. Find Mr. Cope for me, and come back as soon as you can."

"Yes, sir."

"What are you waiting for?"

"I'm just a little surprised."

Marsh laughed.

"Not half as surprised as Ed Cope will be."

TWENTY TWO

Cope blinked into wakefulness at daybreak, to the sound of footsteps and an odd dragging noise. He flipped over on his stomach just in time to see Alf Swenson come stomping into camp, pulling the apparently senseless body of Jenks Dart along by the scruff of his collar. Even in unconsciousness Dart held onto his rifle, which left a long snake trail in the dust. Charles Sternberg blinked and rolled over in his tent only after Swenson banged on one of Boston Mickle's pot lids, which was still not enough to rouse the snoring Mickle, who would probably sleep through the end of the world. Swenson came to a stop when he saw that Cope was awake.

"I believe this is yours," Swenson said, and dropped Dart's head onto the ground. "He is a little too quick to point his weapon at visitors."

Cope got angrily to his feet. Having slept in his clothes, complete with boots, he was already prepared for the whole day, whatever it might bring, although he had not been expecting this. Sternberg looked a little too sleepy to be angry just yet.

"Well, this is a fine way to say good morning," Cope said, walking into the center of the camp to face Swenson, who stood with his arms crossed over his chest, the beatific smile of his last visit long gone from his

179

face. Cope stepped over Dart, who would not notice the indignity, and stood right in front of the big man. He crossed his arms, too.

"March in dragging a man's scout like that."

"He will be fine," Swenson said. "But you have greatly disappointed me."

"What do you mean? I have not had time to do anything, much less get around to disappointing anyone."

"You were supposed to draw attention away from me and my work in exchange for fossils, if I need to remind you."

"I did the best I could. Has something happened?"

"That is putting it in a mild way. Last night my camp was assaulted by the other man out here and his helpers. I was forced to abandon it before I was finished working."

Marsh! Cope's mind roiled. It didn't sound like they were in cahoots after all, if Marsh was raiding Swenson's camp. Maybe Swenson was on the level. The thought that they weren't a team was comforting, but the fact that Marsh had not taken the Monoclonius bait, and instead had gone after Swenson, was disturbing. He must know something I don't, Cope thought. That bothered him more than any threats this large Swede could make.

"Did—did they get away with anything?"

Swenson frowned.

"They appeared to have gotten a piece of my equipment, one of my helping units. They also nearly got some bones I had acquired but not yet processed."

"Bones!" Cope said.

That would the worst news of all. He did not much care if Marsh made off with the man's equipment, unless it was something really good, but if he had gotten bones as well then they were even on that score.

"What sort of bones were they?"

"I am not sure. I had not finished processing them. The men distracted me and I had to leave. But don't worry, I took the bones with me."

"So you didn't actually leave them there?"

"No."

"Well, that's a relief."

Swenson gestured quickly with his right hand, and for just an instant Cope thought the man was going to strike him.

"This is not why I came to see you, to discuss what I have done and what I have not done. I told you to keep those men away from my camp, and you didn't do it. If you cannot do it, just tell me and I will figure out some other way."

Cope glared at Swenson, although the tall man did not seem to notice his anger. Or maybe he noticed but he did not care.

"I can do it. I will need some more bones, though. And good ones. A complete skeleton. A predator, if you have one."

"Very well. It will be here by nightfall, although I cannot guarantee you a meat-eating creature. I will give you the best I can spare. In the meantime, I need you to return the two skeletons I have already loaned you."

This would be a problem. Cope shot a quick glance at Charles Sternberg, who shrugged. They had made the boat in good time, with the bones securely wrapped in Mickle's accidental rice paste discovery. The frilled dinosaur was on a long trip back east, and there would be no way to recover it.

"I have one of them. It's not very good. I think it was a decoy intended to fool me. You can have it back and keep it. I will need the other one for a little while longer."

"I don't think so. I have not finished cataloguing it. It appears to be a key part of my work here and I need it back."

Cope started to step back, and nearly tripped over the still-slumbering form of Jenks Dart.

"Well, that could be difficult. I didn't really think you would want it back."

He took a couple more steps backward, but the big Swede followed him. Dart slept through it all, and Sternberg began looking on with evident concern.

"Of course I want it back. You said you needed the bones for just a little while. Give me back both skeletons, please."

Cope stopped backing up.

"I can't do that. I have mailed one of them to Philadelphia. It's gone."

He was not sure what Swenson would do, but Swenson surprised him by doing nothing. He just stood there like a carving of a large Swedish man. No veins stood out on his forehead in anger, no muscles twitched in his arms. He did not even frown. He looked as though Cope had just told him breakfast had been delayed.

"I see," he said at last. "Then my business with you is at an end. I will take the other skeleton and leave you alone, and I ask you to do the same for me."

Cope felt a wave of relief, because he had not wanted to get into a fight with a man so much larger than himself, what with Dart unconscious, Mickle still snoring and Sternberg not much good for a fight with his bum leg. As Swenson turned to leave, he felt another wave of feeling, this one of panic. This meant no more bones, and no map of bones. This man was holding all the cards, and Cope had just dealt himself out of the game.

"Wait!" he said. "Give me another chance. I'll get the skeleton back to you. It can't have gone very far."

"I do not have time," Swenson said. "I cannot wait for you to return stolen goods."

"I can keep Marsh and his men away, I promise," Cope said, although he had no real ideas on how to do that. "There's no one else out here to help you."

Swenson stopped walking, so Cope had apparently hit on the truth.

"Without me stopping them, they'll raid you again and again until they get what they want," Cope said.

Swenson was listening, so he kept on.

"I've also heard that there may be someone else out here looking for those bones, so things may be worse than you thought," Cope said.

This was the Thunder Horse that the Crows had mentioned. This was pure poppycock, but Swenson did not need to know that.

That definitely got his attention. Swenson stomped back to Cope, stepping right on Dart's back as he did so. Dart gave a groan but didn't get up. Swenson moved on Cope so fast he didn't have time to react. Nearly before he could move, Swenson had hoisted him in the air by his collar.

"Who is it? What have you heard?"

"I—"

"Who did you hear it from?"

"The Indians. The Crows."

"And what did they say?"

"They said they have heard of a Thunder Horse walking around. They think some kind of dinosaur is out here."

He tried to utter a carefree laugh, but Swenson was cutting his air off and it sounded more like a gurgle.

"Put him down," Sternberg said.

He had dropped into a sort of boxer stance, like he was ready to take Swenson on in a fair fight, although any man who could lift another man with just one arm

was not someone to challenge lightly. Sternberg had
guts, and it worked—Swenson put Cope back down.

"If you work with him, you are already a dead man,"
Swenson said.

"You actually think there's a dinosaur out here?" Cope
asked, rubbing his neck where the collar had bit into
it. The raw skin would sting if he got any sweat in it.

Swenson was silent for a long moment. Cope coughed,
and Sternberg stayed in boxing stance, waiting for action.

"Of course not," Swenson said finally. Sternberg
relaxed. "Please forgive what I said. There is more
competition here than I expected. I am a little bit—I
do not know how to say it."

"On edge," Cope contributed.

"That would describe it. I do need some help."

"I'm your man."

"I see."

"I am."

"But you stole one of my skeletons, before I had even
catalogued it."

"It was a misunderstanding. It will not happen again."

Swenson seemed to stop to think about something.

"That may be. But you do not mind if I take a
precaution to protect myself, surely? My time here is
getting short, and I cannot afford to lose any more
specimens."

"What do you have in mind?"

"You will see."

A few minutes later a small man came walking out
from the copse of pine trees near the camp. He
appeared to be some sort of black midget with terrible
eye problems, not to mention a sizable hole right in
the middle of his forehead.

"This is my assistant," Swenson said, motioning to
the little man. "He is wearing some special equipment,
which is why he looks this way. He will make sure you

do not accidentally appropriate some of my bones. I will leave you a skeleton near camp later today. Do with it what you will, but do not take it. I will expect you to use it to lure the other bone hunters this way, and away from me. Do not fail me this time."

Boston Mickle suddenly stopped snoring, and peeked out from his tent flap.

"More guests?" he asked tentatively.

Cope stared at the little man, whose head came only up to his own belly button. This was the same little creature he thought he had seen in Swenson's camp that night. His arms seemed to have no musculature, nor his legs. His eyes showed no whites at all. He took a step toward the little man, and suddenly the hole in his forehead glowed, brighter than even an arc light in downtown Philadelphia.

"What is this?" Cope asked. "This man doesn't even look human at all. Don't tell me this is what your children look like in Sweden."

Swenson studied him for a long time, staring deeply into his eyes. Sternberg, thinking another physical confrontation was beginning, clenched his fists again.

"I cannot tell you," Swenson said. "But perhaps there is no rule against showing you, if it will convince you to do all you can to help me. I am traveling with a minimum of defensive equipment and I cannot keep being assaulted in this way."

He slowly extended his right arm again.

"I am not going to hit you," he said. "I need to touch you on the side of the head."

"Watch it," Sternberg said.

"Charley, it's okay," Cope said. "I think."

Swenson's rough fingers pushed their way through his hair to the side of his head. Then the camp went away, Montana territory went away, the dinosaur bones went away, Boston Mickle's queries about breakfast went away, it all went away. His head was flooded with images of vast cities, rising into the sky. The cities were taller than Philadelphia could ever grow, the tops of the buildings seemed to reach into the very heavens. He saw silvery vehicles flying through the air, he saw silvery vehicles flying beyond the air and into the blackness outside it. He saw them flying through space itself.

He saw another image of a city, this one burnt and smoking, its proud spires in ruins. He saw people, at least they looked like people, running and screaming in terror. He saw the silvery ships raining down brilliant plumes of fire. The pictures changed again. He saw a fantastic panoply of creatures gathered together, poring over images and charts of fantastic complexity, that would make a schematic drawing of all the species on earth look like a child's drawing. He heard the buzz of what seemed like thousands of different languages. A single voice cut through the din.

"Who all is having breakfast? Answer me!" Boston Mickle said.

The images stopped. Cope's mind returned to the camp, to the stranger's fingers on the side of his head.

"What was that?" he asked, but Swenson only removed his hand and turned to walk away.

"I cannot tell you. Let it be sufficient to say that I must have the bones."

"The images," Cope said. "I saw smoke and fire, coming from some sort of ships floating in the air. Was there some kind of war? Is there some kind of war going on?"

Swenson frowned.

"There is always a war. I can tell you nothing else. You can think of what you have seen and decide what it means for yourself. But you must help me. If you help me, I will help you. My assistant will keep an eye on you. Rest assured that whatever he sees, I will see.

Do not attempt to make off with any more of my bones. You will get everything you want if you will help me."

He began walking toward the edge of camp.

"Does your assistant have a name?" Cope called after him.

"He does not. And do not attempt to come close to him. He will not allow himself to be touched."

The little dwarf stared at them impassively, its red eyes seeming to glow in the morning light.

"What on earth was all that about?" Sternberg said at last, after Swenson was out of sight.

"I'm not sure, Charley," Cope said. "But I was wrong about our Mr. Swenson teaming up with Marsh. And I'm beginning to doubt he's really from Sweden."

TWENTY THREE

Clouds massed in the east, just above the hills. The ones on top were almost pure white, but the ones lower down were an ominous gray. To Sitting Lizard, the clouds just meant rain. To George Burgess, who had minored in English, they carried threatening symbolism.

George Burgess had been riding with Sitting Bull for two days before he ever spoke with him directly. There was not much chatting as the column of Sioux moved northward in a roundabout pattern, and much of the chief's time was spent catching up on the latest news and tending to tribal affairs. Word had come from the east just yesterday that Red Cloud had been completely disarmed by the Army. He was already living in the Black Hills reservation but now the Army, angered about the death of Custer, had stripped him and his braves of all weapons, and said they no longer considered him the leader of all Sioux.

Crazy Horse was still alive and on the loose, and so was Sitting Bull, but it was clear that the symbolic clouds on the horizon meant much more than rain. Sitting Bull never looked like a particularly friendly man, but when Burgess captured glimpses of him now he looked so withdrawn and distant as to be almost unworldly. He took care of tribal business as best he could, but increasingly there was less tribe to worry about. The

Army would stay on his tail forever, and would be more tenacious than any rain cloud could ever be.

Hundreds of Sioux spread out behind Sitting Bull, who rode toward the front of the column, behind a phalanx of scouts. Burgess was somewhere in the middle of the pack. He had hoped to make himself useful to Sitting Bull, but so far his language skills had not come into play. Sitting Bull did not speak much English, but he knew the ways of the white man and the Army—at least as far as they were practiced out west—better than Sitting Lizard could ever hope to. Burgess had fancied himself a bit of a horseman back at Yale, and was indeed locally renowned for his equestrian skills, but out here he might as well be riding a velocipede for all the progress he was making. He had never ridden this far, this long. He had certainly never done so without a saddle, but now here he was, his whole lower body aching while his horse struggled to keep pace without any meaningful directions from him. Indian women and children moved past him as if they had been born riding horses, while he struggled to keep from falling back even further. He wanted to think of himself as Sitting Lizard out here, but he felt more and more like George Burgess, political science major, member of the chess club.

At night, when his aching back kept him from sleeping, he reminisced about New Haven. He missed his bath tub. He missed his warm room. He even missed his dormitory room at Yale, that was how bad it had gotten. He also missed Alice Stillson. He could sometimes hear contented squeaks or cries from surrounding tipis. Even among the harsh reality of the Sioux escape from the Army, there was time for love. Then the dirty face of Alice would come back to him as if in a dream. Alice. She had come all the way out here for a dream she didn't even really understand.

Thinking of her made him feel better, but her image could still never quite make the pain in his back go away.

It was on the third day, in the morning, that the brave rode back from the front of the column to say that Sitting Bull wished to see him. A groggy Burgess quickly dressed in his best buckskin and horsehair. He contemplated putting them on over an eastern-style dress vest, to show his versatility, but decided that the image of a humiliated Red Cloud might be too fresh in Sitting Bull's mind, and that it would be best to play down his ties to the white man. At least for today.

He was nervous as he rode to meet Sitting Bull, much more nervous than he had been in going to meet Professor Marsh, but the effort of trying to keep pace with the messenger brave pushed the nervousness from his mind. It would not do to fall off his mount while riding to meet the leader, and so he kept a close eye on the path and followed as fast as he dared. It was not fast enough, and the brave had dismounted and was waiting impatiently as he approached. He dismounted and handed the reins to the brave, who looked at him without expression. Burgess was full-blooded Sioux, but when he looked in the flat eyes of the brave he felt like an outsider. He averted his gaze quickly, to try to cut the feeling off at the pass. The brave held the tipi flap for him but he brushed the man's hand away and pushed it open himself.

Sitting Bull sat alone. He wore a simple buckskin shirt under a blanket pulled over his round shoulders. He could have worn numerous feathers in his hair, Burgess knew, both white ones and red ones. White ones for physically touching an enemy during battle; red ones for being wounded himself. Sitting Bull wore only a single white feather. But for his famous face he could pass for the lowliest brave in the camp. As Burgess sat before Sitting Bull, he changed that thought. There was something in Sitting Bull's rounded face that set him apart. He was a leader, and up close he could not be mistaken for anything else.

"I am Setty Bool," he said, and with that he had very nearly exhausted his English and continued in Sioux.

"Several of my warriors have recommended that you be killed. You are no better than a white man, they said. In fact you are worse than a white man because you are born a Sioux but you have gone over to their ways. Are they correct? Should I kill you?"

It took Burgess a few seconds to mentally translate everything Sitting Bull said. Before he even had time to be afraid, much less fashion a response and put it into the language Sitting Bull would understand, Sitting Bull spoke again.

"I see you do not care what they say. That is the right way to think."

Burgess was not sure how to respond. Sitting Bull seemed to like the silent approach, which happened to work best for him as well. He kept silent.

"Do you know where we are going, one they call Sitting Lizard?"

"North," he responded, in his halting Sioux. "To Canada."

"And do you know why?"

"The Army is after you."

Sitting Bull nodded slowly. He was not a large man— Burgess had a good head on him—but his motions seemed to carry a ponderous slowness, as if he was not a living man at all, but a figure carved from granite.

"And do you know why they are after me?"

"Because of the death of General Custer."

Sitting Bull's head shook side to side now. Burgess knew that with all the questions coming his way, he was bound to get one of them wrong.

"They are after me because they want this land. The white man wants all of this land, every bit of it, and he will get it."

"But—the Black Hills reservation in Dakota territory—"

Sitting Bull motioned with his hand, and Burgess fell silent.

"It means nothing. They give it now, they will take it later. I heard that you grew up in the east. Is that right?"

Burgess nodded that it was.

"Chief Red Cloud has been east. Did you know that? He visited the place called New Jersey. He saw roads and bridges and the things called factories. He said the white man will do whatever the white man sets his mind to do. This is from Chief Red Cloud. He is afraid of nothing. He has pinned his enemies to trees but he said there will be no final victory over the white man. Back east, he said, they have conquered everything. They do not fear the rain or the snow or anything at all."

Sitting Bull seemed to be staring behind him, beyond him.

"He said they fly in the air and they float in the sea."

Burgess thought of the balloons he had watched fly over New Haven, and of the huge boats he had seen in the harbor. He suddenly thought that he would like to see them again, with Alice Stillson on his arm. He would like to fly in a balloon with Alice Stillson. He would like to fly in a balloon with Alice Stillson and with their son. The thoughts came flooding in so suddenly that he had almost forgotten where he was. Wherever he was, he wanted to be with Alice Stillson, and they would have a child that was a half-breed, and eventually that child would marry and produce a quarter breed, and eventually the Indian would completely disappear.

"Tell me," Sitting Bull said, bringing his eyes back to his visitor. "Is it true?"

It was impossible to lie. Burgess realized that Red Cloud was right. He had seen it all back east but it took until this moment, in the middle of nowhere, Montana Territory, for him to realize the truth. The white man had conquered every single thing, including his own heart.

"It is true."

Sitting Bull nodded. He knew it was true. He sat in silence for a moment, his face as impassive as the moon.

"But I have heard something else. I heard that you have seen a man who has a magical shield. The Sioux who traveled with you said they have witnessed a ghost wall."

Burgess had tried for days to think of a better way to describe the invisible wall that had surrounded the mystery scientist's camp, but there really was not one.

"Yes."

"And he has small magical men that will not die when hit with arrows."

"I did not see them myself, but yes, I heard of them."

"And he has flame that does not flicker and is not warm."

"I heard about that, too."

"He can also make noises like thunder and move like the wind."

"It seems so, yes."

Sitting Bull lapsed back into silence, saved from total immobility only by the slow nodding of his head.

"I also heard that a white man was there, one of the bone diggers."

"Yes. Professor Othniel Charles Marsh, of Yale University. In Connecticut."

Sitting Bull raised an eyebrow.

"Professor Marsh? Yes, I have heard Red Cloud speak of him. He helped get better food at the Red Cloud Agency."

"Yes."

"Professor Marsh is probably happy with that, and content to forget about the red man now and get back to his bones. Tell me, Sitting Lizard, what did this Professor Marsh think about the ghost wall and these other magical things."

"I don't believe he saw anything except the ghost wall. Well, you couldn't see that, but he felt of it."

"And what did he say about it? Did it surprise him at all?"

"He was shocked. Stunned. Amazed."

Sitting Bull fell back to his nodding.

"And this Professor Marsh is well acquainted with the modern ways of the white man."

"Oh, yes. He is one of the foremost scientists of the— of the white man."

Sitting Bull was quiet for a long time.

"Sitting Lizard, do you think you could find this man and his magical camp again?"

George Burgess sat back in surprise.

"I don't know. He was very hard to find the first time. I do not know."

Sitting Bull's eyes narrowed, an expression that frightened Burgess. How many men had seem him look this way up close, and lived to tell about it?

"If he can be found, the Hunkpapa Sioux can find him," Sitting Bull said. "I want you to show me where he is."

"But—"

"The women and children and many warriors will continue on into Canada. The best warriors will return to find this man. I will lead them, and you will show us where to go."

Burgess was not sure if Sitting Bull had ever told a joke, and certainly he did not appear to be joking now. His eyes had widened, but only slightly.

"And what will we do if we find him?"

"I will tell him I want his ghost wall and his flame that does not flicker and his men that cannot die and his thunder noise. These are weapons that can frighten even the famous Professor Marsh."

"I don't know if he was *frightened*," Burgess said, not wanting to paint Marsh in an unnecessarily bad light. "He was more amazed, really. And shocked."

"It does not matter. These are apparently things that are beyond what the other white men out here possess. I do not know where this man got these things, but I want them."

"The Army is looking everywhere for you."

"Yes. But what if they found me and I had a ghost wall? They could not touch me. You have witnessed the ghost wall yourself. Could they touch me with their guns if I had one?"

Burgess had to admit that they could not.

"But it will be very hard to get these things from him. What if we fail?"

Sitting Bull's eyes glared afresh.

"What if we fail? What if we do not try? How can I ignore this chance? Red Cloud is defeated. Crazy Horse is running. I am running. The white man spreads from one end of the world to the other, and puts us in reservations, and then changes his mind and moves us again. I was not born to accept crumbs from a white man's table. You are soft, Sitting Lizard, this means nothing to you. The Great Spirit may be bringing this man here with his magical weapons just so that I may take them and defeat the white man. How do you know this is not true? And how will we know if we do not try?"

Burgess could not argue with him. He looked at his knees in shame.

"We begin tomorrow," Sitting Bull said. "Look at me.

We leave tomorrow. It will be a small band of warriors. And you. You lead us to where the man can be found, and we will find him. This may change the world, Sitting Lizard."

Burgess nodded. It could change the world, all right, or at least their world. It could get them all killed. He would hate to think what his adopted parents would think, their young Methodist son shot as a marauding Indian, wasting that good Yale degree. But if going back had its pitfalls, it also had its delights. Alice Stillson was there. He had promised her to return, and he could keep that promise while it was still warm on his lips.

"This could change the world," Sitting Bull said again. "Yes."

TWENTY FOUR

Marsh had to admit it; he was nervous.

"You wait here," he said to Al Stillson, who looked disappointed to be left with Grieg and the horses.

Marsh needed to go in alone. He had spent eight years fighting Ed Cope through the scientific establishment and building him up in his own head to be a monster in need of vanquishing, but now he needed to go see Cope as a man. Their face-to-face meeting outside the stranger's camp had been too rushed to be a real reunion, and the two old combatants needed to talk.

"I'll yell if I need something. Grieg, you just behave."

Grieg sat miserably on the back of Stillson's horse. The combined weight of the two of them was not much of a burden on the beast, which flicked its tail impatiently. Marsh handed Stillson the reins of his own horse, and noted ruefully that carrying just him seemed to have made the horse weary. He was not getting any thinner these days, so maybe it was just as well that his cook had departed. He adjusted his jacket lapels as best he could. He resisted the temptation to ask the boy how he looked.

Stillson had located the camp while it was still fairly early in the afternoon. Nothing much seemed to be going on there. He said the only activity seemed to revolve around the scout, who seemed to have had some kind

of accident and was laid out in the middle of the camp.
So Cope wasn't hunched over some skeleton new to
science, ready to send a description of the particulars
back east. That, at least, was comforting to Marsh. It
was bad enough having to go see Cope. It would be worse
to walk in on him in the throes of some major discovery.

The camp was small, as he saw when he made his
way around the trees and down a slight incline. It was
just Cope and three other men, Stillson had said, back
when this expedition was still young, and before it had
taken so many odd twists and turns. He walked slowly
and saw no one at first. Then he walked around a cart
and saw a tall, thin man sitting on an overturned pickle
barrel, drinking something out of a tin mug. The man
had a bandage on his head as big as a turban, and had
a long rifle slung across his lap. This must be the injured
scout. Upon seeing Marsh, the man dropped the mug
and swung the rifle right at his chest.

"Don't move," the man said, his voice a growl that
would do justice to a bear. "Nobody will get the drop
on me again. I will shoot."

Othniel Charles Marsh, esteemed professor of
paleontology at Yale University, stood with his hands
raised like a common horse thief.

"I am not getting a drop on anyone," Marsh said. "I
came to see Edward Cope."

He heard a loud voice coming from around the other
side of the tents.

"Jenks!" a vaguely familiar voice shouted. "What is
going on out there? Who is here now?"

And there he came, marching around the tent, the
look on his face just as intent as it ever was. Edward
Drinker Cope, minus the wild Indian warpaint he had
worn the other night.

"Hello, Doctor Cope," Marsh said. "May I lower my
hands now?"

Cope stood still, stunned into an unusual silence.

"Othniel?" he asked after a long moment.

"Call me O.C., please."

"Is it really you, come to pay me a proper visit?"

"None other. May I lower my hands?"

Cope let out an explosive laugh and marched forward, his right hand extended.

"Let him alone, Jenks," Cope said. "He's more likely to bop me on the head than you."

"I was really hoping not to have to hit anyone at all. How are you, Ed? You seemed in a bit of a hurry last we met. I didn't have a proper chance to say hello."

They shook hands. Cope couldn't seem to decide whether to smile or to scowl, and his chin seemed to be trying to do both at once.

"I've been better, I have to admit, Othniel. Sorry I couldn't stay to chat the other night. You know how it is. How are you, you old bone digger?"

"I've been better, too. It's been a long time."

"Nearly twenty years, I reckon," Cope said. "The least I can do is get you some coffee. Jenks seems to have spilled his."

"I'll even drink it, if you don't poison it."

Cope laughed, surrendering his face to a smile. Marsh was a little surprised to feel his own face twisted into a smile. He arranged himself onto the proffered pickle barrel, which the surly scout vacated.

"Are you okay to get up and around, Jenks?" Cope asked, but the man seemed to think so.

He stood, but looked a little unsteady on his feet.

"Jenks, take the day off, and go take a nap. You look terrible. Get Boston to give you some of his brandy. But not too much."

The scout nodded and wandered off, shuffling slightly back and forth as if he had consumed too much brandy already. Cope walked behind him, and then quickly returned with another tin cup, full nearly to the brim with hot coffee. The days were getting colder as winter approached, and Marsh sipped the brew with appreciation. Cope rolled up another barrel and perched on it. A young man with a noticeable limp appeared from the middle tent and walked up, glancing at Cope as he approached.

"Ah, Charley," Cope said. "This is Professor Othniel Charles Marsh, of Yale University. You saw him the other night but there was no time for introductions."

The young man gave a sly smile and politely shook Marsh's hand.

"I have heard quite a bit about you," he said, which was no doubt the most polite way he could formulate to express it.

"Believe about twenty-five percent of it and you'll be close to the truth," Marsh said.

Sternberg laughed, and Cope did too, although only Cope seemed to realize that he actually meant it.

"I will leave you two to talk," Sternberg said. "I'm going to the river to wash up a little bit."

"He's a good man," Cope said after Sternberg limped away. "That bum leg doesn't keep him from anything. He'll probably end up surpassing us both."

Marsh sipped his coffee and watched the young man go. He had never been very fond of field work, and it always surprised him to see someone who was willing to overcome great obstacles to do it. He was glad people like this Sternberg lad existed.

"I must say I'm a little surprised to see you here, Othniel," Cope said. "I didn't think you got out in the field much these days, first of all, much less had time to run around with Indians."

For a second, Marsh thought this was all a mistake. He should not have come here. Behind Cope's smiling exterior was a man who would stop at nothing to defeat and humiliate him in front of the scientific establishment, or just whoever happened to be handy. He had once put the wrong head on a dinosaur skeleton, and Cope had pointed it out for months afterwards in letters to scientific journals. Then Marsh remembered the things Grieg had told him. This whole thing was bigger than their old rivalry. If there was any time to bury the hatchet, this was it.

"Edward, it goes without saying that there are strange things going on out here. There are strange people out here in Montana."

Cope regarded him for a long moment.

"That's true. You would not believe some of the characters I ran into at Fort Benton. I had to dicker like a salesman to get a decent price on my horses. And—"

"That's not what I'm talking about, Edward."

"Then what are you talking about, Othniel? There's nothing particularly odd here that I've seen, except for that skull you cobbled together to fool me."

Marsh couldn't resist a slight smile. He sipped his coffee and looked around the camp while Cope fumed at the memory. Marsh considered using pickle barrels as seats to be strange enough, but Cope was always one to cut corners. It was a drab little camp, although an enticing smell lingered in the air; Cope must have a good cook, and now Marsh had none at all. Marsh was turning his gaze back to Cope when he spotted the little man, nearly hidden behind the open flap of the furthest tent. It was a twin to the dark man Sam Sharp had brought down off the mountain. To someone who didn't know what the little men looked like, the figure would seem like a shadow, and Marsh had nearly missed him. He imagined he could see the creature's beady red eyes, but he knew his own eyes were not that good. So what Grieg said was true. Cope was working with that stranger.

"You're playing with fire, Edward," he said, matching Cope's hard gaze with his own.

"What do you mean, Othniel?"

"O.C."

"I forgot. You don't like your own name. What do you mean, O.C?"

"I mean the little man over there by the far tent," Marsh said, keeping his voice as low as possible. Grieg had said the creatures could hear across great distances, in addition to their talents with light. "I mean the deal you've made with that other paleontologist. The one whose camp you were leaving in such a hurry the other night."

Cope just frowned. He was probably trying to think of a way to deny everything, but Marsh had him dead to rights.

"You don't know what you're doing."

"And you do, I suppose."

"Yes. I do."

"And I suppose you can explain it to me."

"I'll do better than that, Edward," Marsh said, leaning in so far that Edward started to lean out. "Just wait right here. Don't move."

He slid off the pickle barrel and walked casually away, giving Cope a little wave as if he was popping off for the afternoon. Cope, his brows knit in puzzlement, gave a little wave back. The little dark man, as far as Marsh could tell, stood still and did nothing. Marsh came wandering back in five minutes, carrying something slung under his arm, something draped in white cloth. Marsh walked up to Cope, listing to the left under the weight of his cloaked burden.

"Are you bringing me some dinosaur bones?" Cope asked. "You shouldn't have."

"I didn't," Marsh said.

He whipped the cloak off the object, to reveal it as

the limp body of a little dark man, the red lights behind
its eyes out for good. Marsh grabbed it under its arms
and wiggled it in the air at Cope's visitor. That got the
fellow's attention. He jerked to attention and started
to advance into camp. Marsh wasn't sure, but it looked
like the hole in his forehead was getting ready to light
up and send out its mysterious beams. The creature
was too slow to evade Al Stillson's prying fingers. Stillson
jumped from behind the tent and jabbed at the base
of the small man's neck with the sharp end of a
paleontologist's pickaxe. The little man struggled for
a second, then jerked to attention again, then fell over
flat on its face in the dust.

Cope jumped off his pickle barrel.

"What did you do that for? Did you kill him?"

"You can't kill them," Marsh said, waving the man's
flaccid arm for emphasis. "They're not alive."

"What do you mean they're not alive?"

Cope paced back and forth, torn between examining
the motionless man face down on the ground or the
motionless man in Marsh's arms.

"Swenson just said the little guy was an associate of
his, dressed in some kind of special equipment."

"Swenson?"

"That's his name. The man whose camp your Indians
sneaked into. He said his name is Swenson and he's a
paleontologist from Sweden."

Marsh laughed, which seemed to confuse Cope even
more.

"Sweden."

"What's so funny about Sweden?"

Marsh wiggled the little man's arm again, and then
set him down on the pickle barrel. He slumped there
for a moment and then crashed to the ground like a
drunk falling off a barstool. A spray of bright gold wire
appeared at the edge of his neck.

"Look at him!" Marsh said. "Do you really think they can build things like this in Sweden? Are there some secret Swedish advances in science we don't know about?"

Cope, fascinated, knelt and examined the body of the thing. He poked a tentative finger at the wires.

"It's electrical? I've never heard of anything like this."

"That's nothing," Marsh said. "These things can generate light beams that can lift a man up in the air. The Sioux who went into Swenson's camp reported seeing a green light. I think that's how your Swenson manages to dig up the bones so fast. He uses this light to lift them up out of the ground."

Cope stared up at him, too astonished to even ask questions.

"And did you wonder how Swenson can move his camp so fast? *You* saw his tent, I didn't. The Sioux said it was huge. They said it looked very heavy. Do you know how he does it, Edward?"

Cope shook his head.

"His tent can fly."

Now it was Cope's turn to laugh, although his laugh was less a sound of scorn than one of nervous uncertainty. He slowly rose to his feet, never taking his eyes off Marsh.

"It can fly? That's some tent."

"It's not really a tent. It's a ship. A ship for flying through outer space."

It was probably really best to hit Cope with all of this as fast as he could, before his analytical mind could start to pick things apart.

"Through space?"

"Yes. Your man Swenson isn't from Sweden at all, Edward. He's not even from the planet Earth. He's from a planet we can't even pronounce, and he's going to take the fossils there."

Cope's astonishment and uncertainty was now giving way to giddiness. He probably thought his oldest enemy was going stark raving mad, and he was being given the pleasure of witnessing it.

"He's from another planet?"

"Yes."

Cope stared hard into his eyes for a long moment, then doubled over with laughter, doing everything but slap his knee to indicate what he thought of this theory. Marsh let him go on, and sipped his coffee while Cope staggered around in the dust, laughing and sputtering. Finally Cope saw he was not getting a rise out of Marsh and straightened up.

"You are kidding."

"I would not kid about this with you, knowing that you would think me insane."

"You always had good powers of analysis, O.C., and that is exactly what I think. I could find it much easier to believe that the Swedes have gotten way ahead of us in the field of electricity than I could to believe that Swenson is from outer space. You've gotten too soft up in your lab there in New Haven. This harsh climate out here is too much for you."

Now it was Marsh's turn to glare.

"I was leading expeditions not two years ago, so you can't say that's it."

"So why are you saying these things?"

"Because I met a man from outer space of my own, and he's competing with your man from outer space to get the same bones that we want."

"Well, O.C., I would certainly believe any man who came up to me and declared himself to be the resident of another planet. I can't think of why anyone would lie about something like that."

"Edward—"

"Unless he was insane, of course."

"Al, please go fetch Mr. Grieg," Marsh said.

Stillson was standing by the downed body of the little dark man, and nodded his assent. Before he could get five feet, they heard the sound of horse hooves coming into camp.

"Look what I found boss," the lanky scout said.

He had his rifle trained on Grieg, who slumped miserably in the horse's saddle, his bound hands tied to the horn.

"Never mind, Al," Marsh said. "I see Cope's man has saved us the trouble."

"Jenks, I thought I told you to take a nap," Cope said. "This man is apparently not a threat, he's just nuts. Thank you for your continued diligence, but you should really take a nap now so you'll feel better."

Dart reluctantly lowered his rifle. It was a long gun but he handled it as easily as if it were just a branch he had snapped off a dry tree.

"It's not even lunch time yet," Dart said. "I can't sleep when it's this bright out. I feel a little better. I think I'll go hunt."

"Well, it's up to you. But leave this one to us. I think I could handle him if I had to."

The scout nodded and wandered off. Cope looked at Marsh and flicked a thumb up toward Grieg, whose shiny face was nearly hidden in the shade of his broad-brimmed hat.

"This is your outer space man?" he asked.

"Why don't you ask him yourself?"

Cope put his hands on his hips and squinted up at Grieg.

"Hello there. Where are you from, sir?"

"Iceland," Grieg replied.

"Well, you're in good company out here. Our lovely wild west seems to be teeming with you Nordic types," Cope said, and then turned back to Marsh.

"I do not believe Iceland is located in outer space."

"Grieg, you can tell him," Marsh said. "He's the only one left who can help us."

Grieg sat quietly atop the horse.

"It would help if you would untie me," he said. "And let me get down off this horse."

"Tell me where you're from, first," Cope said.

Grieg let out a high-pitched whistling sort of sound. "It is nowhere I can explain to you, but it is in outer space."

"You give me this answer, and you expect me to untie you?"

Marsh grabbed Cope's arm.

"Edward, just let him down. We need to talk to him."

Cope brushed Marsh's fingers away.

"You're the one who has him tied up."

It took only a quick flick of Stillson's knife to free Grieg's hands, but the small man had difficulty getting down from the horse. He seemed to grasp the concept of putting a foot on the stirrup, but did not seem to realize that the saddle would shift when he did so, and that the horse might move a little during the whole process. He ended up falling into Cope's arms.

"Don't you have horses in Iceland?" Cope asked after he had helped Grieg stand on his own feet.

"He told you, he's not from Iceland," Marsh said.

"I must admit I did not quite catch where it was he said he was from."

Grieg whistled again, which did not clear things up very much.

Cope hunched down on his knees and looked closely at Grieg, pulling his hat roughly off his head to get a better view.

"You are short and you are thin," he said after a detailed examination, which Grieg endured with a stoic face. "Your skin is very pale. Your eyes are a bit larger than normal for someone of your size. Your skin is very smooth, too, I see. Extremely smooth. May I touch it?"

"No."

"Very well."

He handed Grieg back his hat, and Grieg stuffed it back down over his bushy black hair.

"Yet none of these things particularly mark you as a creature from outer space. Why is that? I would think that someone from another world would look different. Yet you obviously can pass for a human. Some ladies I know would consider your complexion an improvement over theirs."

"The environment on my planet is similar to the environment here, except it is a good bit warmer," Grieg said. "Do you not think that a similar environment would produce similar development in its inhabitants?"

Cope straightened up to his full height, which was not very tall, although it was taller than Grieg.

"That does make some sense. But life here has evolved along certain lines, and it's making a big assumption that the same lines would have arisen on your planet, no matter what the environment. You said your planet is hotter—it seems that even a slight shift in temperatures could greatly affect the outcome, to the extent that you should not look as much like me as you do. Now, Professor Marsh here and I have our disagreements about how evolution works, but I think we could agree on that."

Marsh nodded. It was amazing to think that Grieg should look so much like a human of Earth. He was small and pale, that's true, but so was Al Stillson, and no one was mistaking him for being something he wasn't.

"Perhaps you do not know as much about the course of evolution on this planet as you think," Grieg said.

"Look, this is a very fine discussion, but I think we should go on to other things," Marsh said.

Cope waved his words away.

"No, no, no. Just be patient a minute, O.C. You must admit you have come in here this morning and given me a great deal to think about. I am just trying to sort out some of this wild information. Mr. Grieg, what did you mean by that comment?"

Grieg looked uncomfortable, which his stonelike face registered only as a very subtle frown.

"I meant only that the course of evolution on this planet has not been influenced by natural means alone."

"You speak in riddles. You would not make a good professor, like our friend Mr. Marsh here," Cope said. "What do you mean by that?"

"It's the reason he's here," Marsh broke in. "His ancestors conducted some sort of breeding experiments here during the dinosaur days, and he says he's here to collect the bones."

"That is correct," Grieg said. "And this other collector, who is from a civilization that is an enemy of mine, is here trying to get them before I can get them."

Cope crossed his arms and frowned.

"Don't you think that's a key piece of information you should have shared with me, O.C.?"

"I was going to."

"When? At the turn of the century?"

"It doesn't matter, Edward."

"I think it does. What does this other fellow want with the bones, if his civilization didn't have anything to do with them?"

"It is complicated," Grieg said. "It involves a ruling by the _____. That is sort of a government that has been set up by different civilizations. They keep track of which civilizations conducted research on _____ and _____, things of that manner."

"It would be helpful if you would use words we could understand," Cope said.

"You have no words for these things," Grieg responded, a tone of haughtiness in his voice. "Not yet."

"All right. Let's assume you are not suffering from a particularly inventive form of insanity, and that indeed everything you have told me is true. You intend to take the bones away from this planet, do you not?"

Grieg paused.

"Yes, some of them."

"That is the same thing the other space creature is doing. Why should we help you get the bones, when you will take them away, just as he plans to do?"

Marsh ground his teeth together. That was a good point, and one he had not yet dwelt on.

"You should help me because the bones rightly belong to my people, not his," Grieg said. "As a scientist, surely you can understand that. We did the work on them, and yet he is trying to take credit."

"The end result, for us, is the same," Cope said.

"I will make you an offer," Grieg said. "How many bones did my competitor say he would give you?"

"Fifty percent," Cope said.

"I will give you seventy five percent of them, then," Grieg said. "Plus you will have the satisfaction of knowing you have done the proper thing."

"That sounds fair," Marsh said.

"Not so fast. I would get half if I cooperate with Mr. Swenson. If I cooperate with you, I presume I have to split my goodies with Mr. Marsh here, which means I'm getting only thirty seven and a half percent of the take. Plus, I could be dealing with a lunatic. Mr. Swenson has some nifty technological things at his disposal, but so far he has not claimed to be from outer space."

"I believe I can clear that claim up for you," Grieg said.

He pulled a round metallic device from his pocket. It had an array of small lights at the top, but Grieg refused to let Cope or Marsh get a good look at it. It was so small that it fit in his small white palm, and to conceal it from sight he had only to make a fist.

"I believe we are near the river," Grieg said. "Please walk there with me."

Marsh and Cope followed him down to the river without speaking, Al Stillson stumbling along behind. Stillson had said the man seemed to have some sort of boat moored on the Judith. Was that what Grieg was taking them to see? Charles Sternberg was on the bank when they got to the river, having just finished shaving at a shady spot under a tree. He wrapped his mirror and razor in a towel and frowned in confusion as they approached.

"What's going on?" Sternberg asked Ed Cope as the group approached.

"Oh, nothing much," Cope answered nonchalantly. "This gentleman is just going to prove to us that he is from outer space."

Sternberg laughed, but then stopped when no one else joined him in mirth.

"Are you serious?" he asked.

"Have you seen anyone else along the river this morning?" Grieg asked him.

"This is Mr. Grieg," Cope said.

"Hello, sir," Sternberg said. "I haven't seen anyone, just the reflection of my own face in the mirror."

"Very well."

Grieg stuck out his hand and seemed to push a button on his little metal device. He performed the task with a minimum of drama, as if it was something he did all the time, as regularly as Sternberg shaved. There was a hissing noise twenty yards down the river, and then something big and round rose into view. It looked like a whale was surfacing in the Judith River. The noise continued and, unlike any whale that Marsh knew of, this thing could fly. A quivering fish slid along its back and fell back into its aquatic home with a plop, while the thing continued to rise, hovering just above the surface of the river, dripping water like a newly washed fruit. As Marsh stared at it longer, it looked less like a fruit than an egg. It was round all over, its front tapering to a soft point. It seemed to have no doors or windows or external extrusions anywhere along its sixty-foot length.

"This is my _____," Grieg said. "I travel through space with it."

"I'm glad I already put away my razor," Sternberg said without taking his eyes off the wet craft. "I would have cut my head off when I saw this."

Cope appeared no less amazed.

"I want to go inside it," he said, but Grieg shook his head.

"I have shown you too much already," he said. This sight is the best thing I can offer you. I cannot let you inside. You will have to see this and believe, and take my word."

"Where *are* you from?" Sternberg asked the little man.

"Iceland," Grieg replied without pause, and this time everyone laughed except Sternberg.

"Charley, I will explain everything to you later," Cope said. "Why don't we all go back to the camp and I will get Boston to cook us up a fine dinner. We can talk things over."

"I must get into my ship," Grieg said. "You talk as you see fit. I need to track my opponent, to see where his camp is located. I will think up a plan and come to you when I have found him. I fear that we will not have much time. He will leave soon."

Without further ceremony, Grieg walked straight to the edge of the pebble-strewn bank and then stepped across open air to a door that suddenly appeared in the ship's side. He vanished and a moment later the egg splashed back into the river, the brown eddies of the Judith covering it as surely as if it had never been there.

"I don't blame him for having that thing," Sternberg said, breaking the silence of the astonished group. "That water is cold."

TWENTY FIVE

"Well, O.C., I cannot believe it has come down to this," Edward Cope said, and Marsh nodded his head.

It was late, and everyone else had gone to bed. Cope and Marsh decided to stay up and talk and drink a last pot of Boston Mickle's bitter coffee. They discovered they could stay tolerably warm if they kept next to the fire, and if they kept their voices low, they wouldn't keep anyone else awake. Boston Mickle had expressed no interest in staying up with them, and Jenks Dart had responded to company with his usual disdain. Only Al Stillson and Charles Sternberg had tried to sit up and listen to the masters talk, but Stillson was exhausted from the previous night's efforts and Sternberg soon followed suit and gave up, letting the two old opponents sit by the fire alone.

"You know, O.C., I'm still not too clear on what is happening here," Cope said.

"Amen to that," Marsh replied. "You should only worry if you do suddenly figure it out."

They laughed like old friends.

"No, but really," Cope said. "Why come to me? Why not just hook up with this weird little spaceman of yours and leave me out of the picture?"

"I tried that," Marsh said.

It was late and he was very tired, but the fire was

warm and Cope didn't look so threatening all of a sudden.

"That's why the lad Stillson and I are so tired. We tried to raid the man's camp last night. It didn't work. We didn't get anywhere near it. One of my men got shot up as a result, and another one disappeared. I don't know if he ran off or if your man Swenson took him somewhere. Everybody else quit my employ after that, even the cook, and I can't say that I blame them."

Cope looked at him and nodded slowly. He had spent the evening playing cards with Sternberg, and intermittently discussing what the Montana countryside must have been like back when it was covered with sea and surrounded with the thunderous roars of dinosaurs. He felt a flash of envy for what Marsh had attempted, but then again he was grateful that no one in his camp had been shot.

"So, anyway, I don't have anyone to help me anymore, just that boy and Grieg, and he's not much help."

"What happened to those Sioux you were dealing with?"

"They left to join Sitting Bull when he passed by. I guess they're up north somewhere now."

"Oh. I'm glad he didn't stay around, or my cook would have left, too. He's petrified of the Sioux."

"They aren't so bad."

"That reminds me," Cope said. "I never congratulated you on what you did for Red Cloud there in Washington. That was a terrible thing the Army was doing, and you did the right thing."

Marsh looked to see if Cope was needling him, but Cope's eyes were serious.

"Why, thank you, Edward. I appreciate that. The Sioux were very helpful to me here because of it, but now they've gone. You are all the reinforcements I've got."

Cope smiled and sipped his coffee. It felt like it was lighting a fire at the back of his eyes.

"You may be in worse shape than you thought," Cope said. "I don't have too much to offer. My scout is behaving strangely these past few weeks. My cook will not be useful for this type of operation. My chief aide is a wonderful paleontologist but he's crippled and deaf in one ear."

"There are times we must go with what God gives us," Marsh said.

"That is true. But God seems to have stacked the deck against us this time. Actually, O.C., talking about Indians gives me an idea. I had a dinner with some of the River Crows not too long ago. I pulled out my false teeth and they got a real kick out of that. They went back and told their tribe all about it and one man, I think his name was Jack, even rode a few miles just to watch me do it again. I don't think they have the same sort of affection and respect for me that the Sioux do for you, but they might be willing to help."

"What would we need to give them?"

"Give them? Nothing, probably. We could just tell them that Swenson is planning to raid their tribal lands and they won't care much for that. We could even tell them he's working with the Sioux. They do not get along with the Sioux. That would be enough, right there."

"At this point, I am for whatever works," Marsh said. "The snow will be coming here soon, and we won't get anything."

He tilted his head back and saw a fuzzy spray of stars above him.

"Look up there, Edward. Do you really think Grieg and Swenson came from there? It seems so fantastic."

Cope wiggled his rear end around so he could look up better.

"It does. But they are two strange jaspers, that's for sure. I have never heard of anyone from Sweden or Iceland who owned a big egg that could levitate over a river, or who paraded around with little men who run on electricity. If you have, you have either taken to drink or you are going to better scientific conferences than I am."

"I have not done either," Marsh said. "I think that for the time being we should take them at their word."

"Part of their word. I don't believe Grieg's story any more than I do Swenson's. They haven't told us why they really want the bones. Do you trust Grieg?"

"No."

"And I don't trust Swenson. He knocked my man Dart on the head, and it's quite a feat to sneak up on Jenks. And you say he has run off with one of yours. He will definitely protect himself when he feels threatened."

"Grieg seems kind of quiet and shy," Marsh said. "And you know sometimes those are the worst."

"Being one myself, yes," Cope said, and they both laughed.

"Something has occurred to me," Cope said after they had paused and sipped more coffee. "Swenson offered me half of the bones. Grieg offered us eighty percent, or whatever it was."

"Yes."

"But this is our land. I don't care if Grieg's ancestors came down here and helped Mr. Darwin's theory along. This is America, and those are *our* bones."

"I agree."

"So why don't you and I listen to what Mr. Grieg says. We'll take his plan and we'll get our Indians to help us and then we'll keep the bones to ourselves. We'll get the bones. One hundred percent."

"And how will we do this?"

"I do not know. Swenson is a formidable man, and who knows what Grieg has up his sleeve. We'll just have to play it by ear."

"That's as good a plan as any," Marsh said. "You know, something is bothering me about all this, about Swenson and Grieg being aliens. If they were around so long ago, down here doing these experiments, they are a very old people. They could be three or four million years old, maybe older. If they were already here doing these things when the dinosaurs were here, they could be ten million years old. Why aren't they more advanced?"

"They seem pretty advanced to me."

"Well, I know, but they still aren't quite what I would expect when I picture what we'll be like in millions of years."

Marsh leaned over and looked sternly at Cope.

"Edward, we shouldn't even be able to recognize them. We should have no idea what they are doing. Yet Swenson has this ship of his that we can recognize as a form of transportation. Grieg has one too. Yes, they're well beyond anything we have, but they're not so far advanced we can't recognize them."

Cope stared vacantly at the fire, and nodded. He remembered.

"You're right. But maybe I know the reason why they aren't more advanced. Swenson touched me on the side of the head, and I had these visions. I can't explain it. But I saw things, visions of what looked like a future city. There were huge towering buildings and things I can't even describe. And there was pain and destruction. I think I saw the aftermath of some kind of war."

What was it Swenson had said?

"I asked Swenson about it and he said, 'There is always war,' something like that. Maybe he and Grieg's people have been going at it for thousands or millions of years. Maybe that has slowed them down."

"I had not thought of that," Marsh said. "Somehow I expected more advanced people to be more peaceful, but maybe not. How destructive."

Cope nodded in agreement. He picked up the end of a thin log and poked the lignite to wake up the fire.

"I have to say it, O.C., it kind of feels good talking to you like this. It's been a long time."

"It has."

"Remember that day in New Jersey?"

They had spent an afternoon wandering the New Jersey marls, finding dozens of bones, the opposite of the sort of luck they were having now. Edward Cope, the young hotshot from Philadelphia, able to name and describe a seemingly endless profusion of species, supported by family money. Othniel Marsh, a Yale man, angling for a professorship, also supported by family money. Cope continued to describe species at an amazing rate, and Marsh did get his professorship, but he had to pay for it himself. Had to agree to pay his own salary from his rich uncle's money so Yale would take him. But it had been worth it. It had all been worth it.

"That was a beautiful day."

"It was," Cope said. "All those fossils there, even in a place with so many people. And then we come out west and find even more, with no people, just a couple of spacemen."

"When did you know you wanted to become a paleontologist, Edward?"

Oh, if only he could see the young Cope, running from fence to trees to meadow in Pennsylvania, looking under every rock for insects and lizards, interested even in the things that flew before his face in the summer.

"O.C., I don't really remember a time when I *didn't* want to be one. I wanted to be a paleontologist even before I knew what one was. It wasn't enough for me to just look at animals, I wanted to compare them and see which ones came from where. What about you?"

"I was the same way. I remember when they were digging a canal close to home. I went up there and the mud was just studded with trilobytes."

Cope smiled at the thought of the tarantula-like fossils of ancient sea creatures.

"Trilobytes! Those are great. I would have loved to have trilobytes when I was a kid."

"Oh, they were great. Big across as your fist. I dug up as many as I could carry. It's a good thing I didn't fall into the canal or I would have drowned, as many of them as I had in my pockets."

They grew silent and smiled politely at each other, thinking of childhood and trilobytes.

"You know, Edward, as similar as we are in some ways, you'd think we could get along a little better than we do."

"You would think that," Cope said. "I did enjoy that time in New Jersey. I just wish you had stayed out of Kansas when I was digging there."

"I had every right to be there," Marsh said, trying to keep his voice low and level, to retain the tone of warmth and camaraderie they had cultivated.

"Well, maybe so, but there had to be somewhere else you could dig. And then you turn up here, right in my way."

"In *your* way!" Marsh said, unable to rein in his annoyance. "I got that bone in the mail. I had every right to come out here and see what I could find."

"The bone was addressed to me!" Cope said, his voice also rising in the night. "You were instructed to forward it, not look at it."

"You bribed it away. That's not fair."

Sternberg, apparently forgetting who was paying his salary, shouted "keep it down!" from his tent, and Cope and Marsh lapsed into silence once again, but this time no smiles were in evidence.

"And anyway, you're wrong about evolution," Cope muttered after a minute.

Marsh, who had resumed staring at the stars, glared at him.

"Lamarck has already been discredited. I don't know why you cling to those absurd notions of his."

"Natural selection is the weak link of Darwin's theory. It's so obvious that species don't rely on deviations."

"Not deviations. *Variations*. Darwin is right, and you know it. You just won't give up your old theories. You won't admit Lamarck is wrong and you are wrong and Darwin is right. and I am right."

"Because you are not."

Marsh realized that their voices were climbing again, so he took a long sip of his now-cooled coffee.

"This is terrible coffee, by the way," he said.

Cope took a sip and then spat it onto the fire.

"I do have to agree with you on that."

Marsh flung the rest of his coffee into the fire, causing it to sputter in protest.

"Even the fire doesn't like it," Marsh said.

A ghostly face appeared on the other side of the flames, rising round and orange like a tiny sun. Cope and Marsh saw it simultaneously, and together they kicked up a small dust storm attempting to scramble to their feet. It was a floating pumpkin, its eyes only sunken black blots in its orange face. Neither Cope nor Marsh had a gun, so Marsh did the best he could by flinging a tin coffee cup at the ominous vegetable head.

"It's me," the pumpkin said. "Grieg."

Marsh put a hand to his chest, trying to restrain his racing heart.

"Thank you for the warning. We weren't expecting you back tonight."

"I wasn't going to come back. But the man you call Swenson has landed. He has changed his schedule and will now be working in the daytime. That means he doesn't have much time left."

Grieg was pulling a large sack behind him. He was dressed in his usual thick dark clothes, but it was a windy night and he had lost his hat. His hair swirled like an ebony fire around his reflecting face.

"Why would he change his schedule?" Cope asked. "I was hoping to get a little sleep now."

"There won't be time for that," Grieg said. "I believe that what you call snow may be on the way. A bad storm. He is probably trying to beat that, and I need to beat it, too."

"You come all the way through space and you're afraid of snow?" Marsh asked, but Grieg ignored him.

"What's in the sack?" Cope asked.

"Sheets. I took the liberty of removing them from your cart over there. We're going to need them."

He dropped the sack and extended his palms to the fire, shivering when the warmth hit his skin.

"What do we need sheets for?" Marsh asked. "Are we going to dress up as ghosts?"

He was beginning to think his original idea was right, and Grieg actually was insane, egg-shaped spaceship or not.

"I will explain it to you later," Grieg said.

"All right," Marsh said, not bothering to hide the disgust in his voice. So the advanced man comes down from space, worried about snow and planning to use sheets as an integral part of his great plan. Maybe millions of years was not enough evolution after all.

"Edward, how quickly can you talk to the Crow and see if they will help?" Marsh asked. "It sounds as if we're definitely going to need them."

Marsh squinted into the remnants of the night, as if he could see the Crows' camp.

"I don't know. I don't even know if they're still there. It would take about two hours to get there and back. It will be light by then."

"What are you talking about?" Grieg asked.

"Mr. Cope here knows some Indians he thinks will be able to help us. More people. More manpower."

"We do not have two of your hours," Grieg said. "I will transport you to these Indians. We must leave now."

He slung the sack over his shoulder, staggered momentarily under the weight, and then began walking away from the fire.

"You're going to take him on the spaceship?" Marsh asked, trudging behind the suddenly delighted Ed Cope.

"Yes," Grieg said.

"But I should go, too. You can't take just Cope alone."

"You stay here," Grieg said over his shoulder. "Wake up the others and get everything ready. We especially need sheets or some kind of cloth like that. I will be back very soon."

"I really should go, too," Marsh said again, his voice rising like a child's.

Cope turned and put his hands on Marsh's lapels.

"Now, now, O.C. I will tell you everything about this little man's ship. Just trust me."

Before Marsh could respond, Cope whirled and followed Grieg out of the camp, off to explore the craft of an allegedly advanced society. Marsh stood and fumed for a full minute. He then began stomping around the fire, muttering to himself. His foot struck something, and he suspended his rage long enough to look down. It was black and floppy and rubbed against his foot

like a living thing. Thornton Grieg's lost hat. Marsh
picked it up. It was thick enough for a Russian winter,
much less one in Montana. Grieg would no doubt be
very happy to get it back, especially with his dreaded
snow on the way. Marsh tossed it onto the fire and
went to wake the camp.

TWENTY SIX

It was hot enough to boil an egg inside Grieg's egg.

"It's stuffy in here," was the first thing Edward Cope said once they stepped inside the craft.

This was, to his knowledge, the first time a human being had set foot aboard a conveyance owned by a creature from another world. Cope had been hoping to think of words a little more dramatic, to show the solemn majesty and gravity of the moment, but those were really all that came to mind. For his part, Grieg did not seem in the mood to engage in any historic banter. He led Cope on a brisk walk to the ship, and called it to the surface of the Judith with all the brisk carelessness of a man summoning his cab outside a tony Philadelphia restaurant.

Cope did take some care on the steps, which had been invisible when he had watched Grieg ascend them from the bank. Now he saw that Grieg was actually walking on what appeared to be a tiny suspension bridge of sorts, only it didn't sway. It seemed to be made of blue light, but it didn't flicker. Likewise, it had seemed from the shore that the doorway suddenly appeared from nowhere in the side of the ship, but as he followed behind Grieg Cope saw that there was a thin line marking its boundaries. There was no magic here after all, just advanced technology at work. Cope was not sure if that made him feel better or worse.

The inside of the ship was smaller than he expected it to be. It looked rather drab and spartan. There was a rounded central space flanked by a long hallway that ran fore and aft of the ship. The front end was lighted, the back dark. Grieg did not give him much of a chance to look. He tossed his sack on the floor of the open space and tugged on Cope's sleeve to pull him along to the front.

On the way, Cope saw something white out of the corner of his eye. It was behind a panel that was open only a crack, but as they walked to the front of the ship the egglike craft tilted slightly forward with their weight and the panel's sliding door opened just a bit more. Feeling like a voyeur peeping into someone's closet, Cope took one step closer. He stopped still when he saw what it was, his breath caught in his throat. It was Grieg's skin, hung up like a suit of clothes inside a closet. Grieg's own face stared back at him, although there was no life behind the eyes. It was a costume. He could put it on and be Grieg.

"Come on," the real Grieg said, and pulled him along before he could see any more.

Cope decided it would be better to limit his snooping.

"Sit there," Grieg said when they entered the small room at the front of the ship.

He motioned to a flat bench that ran the length of the room. It was not very comfortable but was the only place to sit, so Cope obediently perched. Grieg checked to make sure he was seated and looking forward, and then began poking at small buttons and knobs in front of him. A thin opening appeared before them, showing him the stars and the first hint of sunshine peeking over the horizon. Cope instinctively leaned back, expecting a rush of air in his face, but the opening was apparently just a window and his moustache went undisturbed.

"Where are these Indians of yours?" Grieg asked when the egg was airborne and moving.

"East of the river, close to where it meets the Missouri," Cope said, not sure that would help. "Do you know where that is?"

Grieg punched at something and a series of lines appeared in the air before him. Some were straight and others squiggly. The map reflected nothing that Cope knew, but it seemed to make sense to Grieg. He stared at it for a moment, nodded, and then the map disappeared and he resumed punching at buttons and knobs in front of him.

"How does this craft work?" Cope asked. "What sort of fuel does it burn?"

"Nothing that you would know anything about," Grieg said. "Please look out the window only."

Cope did, but there was not much to see, just an orange paste on the horizon surrounded by the night. It was interesting to see the sunrise from this angle, but he was more interested in deducing something about Grieg's spacecraft. Imagine having such a thing! The science of paleontology would be revolutionized. No more spending days getting into the back country with recalcitrant horses and recalcitrant helpers. Just you, a couple of good men and this ship, and all the bones in the world could be yours. He could even bring Mrs. Cope and Julia along. They would no longer have to experience paleontology only through his letters! Then again, it really wouldn't do for everyone to have one of these flying things. If everyone had one, everyone could go everywhere. The desolate plains of Montana would soon be as peopled as the streets of Philadelphia, and the bones would be buried underneath city streets. It would really be best if he had the only one, at least for a while. He could get enough bones to last him a whole career in a very short time.

Grieg seemed to be busy with his myriad, inscrutable controls, so Cope began to casually look around without turning his head too much. Grieg did not seem to need to control the craft like one might control a team of horses. His poking and prodding of the numerous blinking lights before him did not seem to have much relation to the real operation of the mysterious craft, which moved on its way as smoothly as a boat slipping across still water, only much faster. The front of the craft was so small, Cope could not imagine how Grieg had been able to stand it for what he imagined to be an unbelievably lengthy trip to Earth.

On the wall next to him was a panel of different-colored squares, each one glowing from within in a way that would drive Thomas Alva Edison mad with envy. There appeared to be some sort of writing on the panels, but it was certainly nothing he could make out.

"I asked you not to look around," Grieg said, and a surprised Cope leaned back in his seat. "But if you are so curious, please push the button that is green."

"Why?" Cope asked, suddenly suspicious.

"It will give you a better idea of how the ship functions, if that's what interests you."

Of course, it did, so he pressed the panel. Shafts of darkness seemed to descend from the ceiling all around him. He could see nothing at all, not Grieg, not the inside of the ship, not his hand in front of his face. He could feel the seat under his rump but couldn't see it. He reached his hands out in front of him but couldn't feel anything, although the darkness was so complete as to be almost palpable. He could still hear, though, as Grieg's voice made clear.

"Please don't attempt to get up," his ghostly voice

said, seeming to come from everywhere and nowhere. "I believe it might make you ill."

"Am I blind?" Cope asked, resting his futile arms at his sides.

"Only until we get where we are going," Grieg said. "I asked you not to look around. So just relax."

The trip took a maddeningly long time. Cope was not the sort who could entertain himself just by thinking. He liked to look at things, to feel things, to assess their function and their place in life. Sitting in Grieg's black box allowed him to do precisely none of those things. He amused himself instead with fantasies of taking over the ship, and tossing the flailing Grieg into the river below. As a member of the Society of Friends, he really should not have such violent thoughts, but he told himself that as they were only fantasy, they were acceptable.

When next he could see anything, he was looking out the front window, down at the upturned, astonished faces of the River Crows.

"These are your Indians?" Grieg asked, the black curtains of blindness having been snapped away as quickly as they came.

Cope merely nodded.

"Then get off here, and return to the camp. I cannot carry you all, so I will carry none of you."

"How will I get down there?"

They were hovering a good fifty feet above the ground. Cope heard the occasional plinks of arrows hitting the craft's hide. The Crows were astonished, but not so in awe they wouldn't take an experimental shot or two at the shape above them.

"Look down," Grieg said.

"I am," Cope said, peering out the window.

"No," Grieg said, motioning for him to look straight down below his chair.

A round opening had appeared below him, making him tuck his feet back.

"What are you doing?" Cope shouted over the sound of the air blowing past the open hole. He dug his fingers into the meager padding of the bench. "Are you going to throw me out?"

He could see the Indians massing below him. In another minute, one of them would think to put an arrow right through that big round target, and he would be the bull's eye.

"Just step down," Grieg said. "Trust me."

"Trust you?" Cope shouted. "You said you were from Iceland!"

"I can go higher, but that would make the climb less pleasant for you. Trust me. Just step into the hole and start walking down."

Cope was getting very slightly nauseated looking through the opening. Either the ship was rocking like a boat in a harbor, or he was getting dizzy. Still, he had done worse. He closed his eyes and stepped off into nothing. His foot descended through air for a longer period than he would have liked, but eventually it did hit on something solid. Cope opened one eye and looked down. He was standing on a step made of the same faint blue light as the steps that had led him to the side door of the craft. That little bridge had been enough to keep him aloft, and this one seemed up to the task. He took a deep breath and began stepping down. Each time it seemed that his foot would descend forever, but each time there was a pressure that buoyed him up. He looked up after a few steps and saw Grieg's shiny face looking down at him.

"I will see you back at the camp of Mr. Marsh," Grieg said. "And hurry."

After only a few more steps he was on the ground, surrounded by the Crows. He had been afraid to look

down, afraid that he would fall or see an arrow headed
his way. The Indians stood right in his face, squinting
at him. They were all men here; they had sent the
women and children to the periphery of the camp while
they saw what sort of monster flew up in an egg and
walked on air. Cope saw a tall, familiar head pushing
its way through the crowd.

Chief Twobelly made his way to the front and stood
before him, spearing him with an intense gaze broken
only when the chief looked up to watch the egg fly
away into the morning sky.

"Remember me?" Cope said, and shoved his false
teeth out with his tongue.

The Indians gasped, except for Twobelly, who had
seen it before. Cope sucked them back in and then
repeated the move. Twobelly stared at him for a long
moment and then pointed into the sky.

"That is a trick," Twobelly said. "I have since heard
how it is you can stick out your teeth. But how do you
fly through the sky in the moon?"

"It will take a long time to explain to you," Cope said.
"I need your help."

Twobelly frowned at him for a long time. He scanned
the faces around him. They frowned, too, and Cope
was starting to think perhaps Grieg should have stuck
around a little bit longer.

"Our help to do what?"

It did not seem like the time to explain he needed
assistance to raid the camp of a person from outer space
in order to rescue the bones of animals that died out a
million or more years ago.

"A man is taking away some Thunder Horse bones.
I need to get them back. He may also be digging for
gold, and he may try to dig on tribal lands."

Twobelly's eyes gave no indication of what he was
thinking. His face was as unreadable as Swenson's.

"That is not our fight," Twobelly said at last. "That is the fight of the Sioux. We understand their anger, but that is not our fight."

"But if he is against them he could also be against you!" Cope blurted out. He wanted to give a more reasonable argument but the lack of sleep suddenly hit him and his tongue flapped of its own accord. "He may take your land."

"You are already doing that," Twobelly said, his braves nodding angrily in agreement. "But we will come with you. I am curious about anyone who can make the white man ask for help. Can this man fly through the air as you have done? Does he travel in the moon?"

"He does," Cope said. "And he has demon warriors that fight with him. I will need only brave men."

Twobelly gave a slight smile.

"That is the only kind I have."

O.C. Marsh walked to the horses to retrieve the bag that held his clothes. He had left most of his supplies in a wagon back at the old camp, halfheartedly hidden under some trees, but had thought to bring a few things in a wadded-up bag that rode on his horse's rump like a giant tick. Marsh ran his fingers over his jaw and took stock. He could use a good, long hot bath, a leisurely shave and a fresh suit of clothing. He could also stand to clean his glasses, which, when he bothered to wear them at all, bore what seemed to be a fairly comprehensive collection of the dust and dirt indigenous to Montana. He sighed at the thought he would have no time for any of these, save cleaning the glasses, and he was least enthusiastic about that.

He rounded the edge of the camp and began trudging up the hill, taking care not to slip on loose gravel and keeping one eye out for Cope's scout. The man looked like he would draw a gun on his own grandmother.

Marsh heard the snorting breath of the steeds and hoped that Stillson had fed them, as ordered. He was tired and in no mood to fight with an ornery horse. The trail was just leveling off enough for him to see the horse's heads when he nearly tripped over a bundle in the path, a bundle bigger than a man laid out end to end.

Marsh squinted at it; now he wished he had cleaned his glasses, after all. It looked like a cloth used to cover fossils, only this one had a faint green light dancing over its surface, like water sluicing back and forth over a shallow pond. He knelt down beside the thing and reached out a tentative finger. Tom Dyson and Sam Sharp had given him the full tales of being hit by green light from Swenson's little electrical men, but this light seemed harmless enough. He narrowed his point of contact down to one index finger and sent this proud soldier all the way through to the fabric. It touched the cloth and the green light disappeared.

Marsh gave a grunt of surprise and lifted the cloth. Underneath was a pile of bones, undoubtedly ancient but strangely clean as a whistle, as if the beast had died on this spot and rotted away under a strong wind. There were no chips of stone clinging to the mineralized bone, no scraps of anything at all. He pulled more of the cloth off and looked at what he had. It appeared to be a squat plant-eater, with a much smaller frill than what Cope had reported finding on his Monoclonius. The beast did not appear to be much larger than a mastiff or a Saint Bernard, although it was considerably older than either one. It was most definitely a dinosaur, and it had been left on Cope's doorstep as a thank-you for his promised treachery.

Marsh looked around. It had been left here for Cope, only Cope wasn't here and hadn't seen it. Only the horses had seen it, and they weren't talking. Cope had already received one such fossil, all cleaned and ready to go, and had even been given the bonus of a ride in a spaceship. And now here was another fossil, also museum ready. He quickly tossed the cloth back over the bones and started tugging at the skeleton. The thing was heavy, whatever it was, but it wasn't very large and there happened to be a goodly sized patch of scrub right next to the trail. Hiding the bones wouldn't be cheating. He had agreed to split whatever they could get from Swenson's spaceship. Cope had already gotten one fossil; splitting things fifty-fifty, this one was his.

TWENTY SEVEN

They approached like flowers swirling on the wind. The white sails of cloth rested on the air and then slowly drew down to their ankles, only to be lofted again by the next twirl.

"Are you sure this will work?" Cope asked, his own white bolt of cloth hanging over his head and down to his ankles. "This plan of yours seems a bit thin."

Grieg had found another big floppy hat that kept most of the sun off his face. He hunched in the back of one of Cope's fossil carts, that he had said they would need to carry off all the bones once the plan was put into action.

"Please, just try," Grieg said. "Twirl as you walk to his ship. They will not know how to react. You will get in."

The mysterious Swenson had turned up, not in a valley this time, but on the edge of a plain three miles from the river. His metal ship was nestled at the base of a rocky promontory that started off impressively but tapered off to a small piles of rocks topped with scrub. It seemed that he no longer cared if anyone saw his ship, only there were very few people around these parts to see it, broad daylight or no.

"He is in a hurry," Grieg said. "He will leave soon. We do not have much time."

"Okay, okay," Cope said.

He pulled his white cloth down over his face and moved it around until he located the eye holes that allowed him to see out, but which also caught at his eyelashes and guided dust straight into his eyes.

"Who cut these things?"

Cope joined the line of twirling white sheets. He was not much of a dancer, he learned as he began to dip and swirl across the landscape. He had trouble moving in anything like a straight line, but when he kept his eye on the other swirls of white he would catch his boots on a patch of scrub or a rock, and several times the graceful flower of his sheet stopped moving while he fell to his knees. Six of the Indians were already ahead of him, and he didn't want to be the last one through, so each time he got up and kept going. While on his knees one time, he spotted another clump that had paused up ahead. That must be Marsh. He mustn't let Marsh get through ahead of him.

By the time he reached the invisible barrier around Swenson's ship, a sizable hole had already been dug and the Indians were slipping through one at a time, still clad in their sheets. Once inside, the swirling began again. They looked like kids playing a game, although he couldn't hear any laughter. One of the white blots was going through with some difficulty, and required a little pushing from behind. Marsh. He had beaten Cope after all. Cope pushed his way through and then caught a breath before beginning to move again. He had not moved his hips like this in years, and his twirls seemed to be a little halfhearted. Still, crazy as the whole thing seemed, it was working. He saw one of Swenson's little electrical men standing at attention, watching the twirling figures but doing nothing. One of the white twirling shapes, an Indian one, judging by the energy of his swirls, danced around behind the little man. Two brown arms appeared, bearing an arrow broken in half. Before the little man could put up a struggle, the Indian had pulled aside the small leatherish patch at the back of his neck and disabled him. The electrical man slumped to the ground without so much as a twitch.

That Thornton Grieg was not as crazy as he had seemed. He had explained that the electrical men had been trained to expect a certain thing on the surface of the Earth, and if they encountered something different they were not prepared to change their behavior. He had used a word to explain how they were prepared, but it was one of those nonsensical whistling words that he spoke, for which the English language currently had no equivalent. "Trained" was as close as Cope and Marsh could come. Grieg had said it was not quite accurate, but he couldn't think of anything better. Regardless of the words used to describe it, the plan of getting past the electrical men was a success. Grieg said there was no creature on the Earth that was man-sized and white and shaped like a mushroom, so the sheets he had found around Cope's camp were perfect for disguising the true nature of the humans intent on doing mischief in Swenson's camp. Both Cope and Marsh pointed out that some human myths contained references to ghosts, which were shaped like the sheet-clad men Grieg had in mind; after thinking for a minute, Grieg had tossed in the twirling motion, and everybody was satisfied.

Cope looked around the camp, feeling a little foolish for wearing a sheet over his head and standing around another man's camp in broad daylight. Swenson would most likely be gone at this hour, Grieg said, off scouting locations. Cope was glad of that. The ghostly disguise was working so far, but he still would have been somewhat embarrassed to run across Swenson while dressed in his unearthly garb.

"Are all of the little buggers down?" Cope shouted, seeing several of the little men sprawled on the ground.

The Indians stopped twirling and a few tentatively raised their sheets over their heads.

"It looks that way," said the rotund sheet, who indeed turned out to be Othniel Charles Marsh. "I think we should go in."

The tallest white sheet, which was Chief Twobelly, walked up to Cope.

"We will stand out here, as you asked," Twobelly said.

Cope was torn about letting the Indians inside the ship. One part of him wanted the fierce Crows around for protection, especially since the ship had already apparently swallowed up one of Marsh's men. Another part thought that only a scientist should be allowed inside a craft built for traveling through space, no matter what the risk. There was no telling what the Indians might touch, and no telling what that could do. He had decided to compromise by keeping them outside, but near the door. That compromise also worked for Twobelly, who had explained that his men were not particularly eager to get inside any sort of big animal that could fly.

Cope and Marsh shucked their sheets but kept them splayed over one arm, in case they encountered more electrical men inside. They walked to the side of the craft, where Grieg said the door should be located. Swenson's ship appeared much bigger up close than it had the first time Cope had seen it, and he thought it was big then. Its central cone rose forty feet or more in the air, and even in the shade it seemed to shine. Standing beside it, Cope had the feeling he was about enter an odd sort of temple. There was no evidence of a door in what looked like smooth metal, but the control panel was indeed where Grieg said it should be. Grieg had drawn them a very detailed picture of what the door mechanism looked like; he had gotten a few details wrong, but overall it was a very good likeness.

"I don't understand why Grieg can't just get in here himself and do this," Cope said as he squatted next to the small flat panel that was covered with a dozen small controls that looked like the buttons of a cheap coat.

"He said he couldn't be seen anywhere around here or it could cause an incident," Marsh replied, squinting over his shoulder at the buttons.

Cope held the chart in his left hand while he ran his right hand lightly over the buttons. Marsh tried to peer at it but Cope wasn't sure he wanted him to know exactly how it worked, so he wiggled it about just enough to keep Marsh from getting a good look.

"I started to say it could cause an international incident, but I guess it's bigger than that," Marsh said.

"Unless he's insane, and then the joke's on us," Cope responded.

He moved the drawing of the button pad back and forth, making sure he was holding it the right way. Grieg had diagrammed how the buttons should be pushed, and in what order, but his written instructions were inscrutable. Apparently they were not sticklers for penmanship on his home planet.

"Well, the ship is here, and those little men," Marsh said. "I guess we should take his word about the incident. He and the people from Swenson's planet are at war, he said."

"I think he's just lazy and wants us to do his dirty work," Cope said. "Which we are. Hold still, here goes."

He took a deep breath and, after consulting the drawing one more time, punched the buttons. Nothing happened. Grieg had said he wasn't sure if the code he had figured out was the right one, and he had not been able to even explain to Cope and Marsh how he had deduced it. Apparently he had not deduced it. No door was opening; the side of the craft looked as smooth and undisturbed as before.

"Well, this is a problem," Cope said, rising to his feet and cocking his elbows.

As he did so, suddenly the side of the ship let out a hiss and the door vanished, sliding swiftly to the right until it disappeared. It was a big door, maybe five feet wide and ten feet high. Cope and Marsh exchanged glances.

"Did Grieg say to stand up first?" Marsh asked.

Cope consulted the drawing once more.

"No. Let's not stand here arguing about it. Chief Twobelly? Could you keep a few of your men right out here?"

Three sheeted figures twirled over and took up a vigil at the newly opened door, although Cope noticed they didn't get too close. Two other figures walked up, not bothering to make their sheets swirl.

"Is it okay to take these things off?" Charles Sternberg said. "It's getting a little hot under here."

"Yes," said Al Stillson.

"You can take them off, but keep them handy," Cope said. "We're going inside."

"Can we go too?" Stillson asked, and Sternberg pulled off his sheet and nodded to show his desire to join them.

There was no real reason to deny them entry, except Cope still wanted only scientists onboard. Sternberg would come closer to fitting that description than would Stillson, who would probably steal the place blind. Cope had not forgotten that the young man had been, until recently, a double agent. Still, he couldn't let Sternberg in and not expect Stillson to follow. He would have liked to keep Marsh out, too, but that was not an idea he was even going to broach.

"Let Mr. Marsh and myself go first," Cope said. "We'll

scout around for a minute and then let you know what we see. We will need your help with a little push, though."

The door began several feet off the ground, which was probably no problem for the lengthy Swenson but which presented some difficulty for the more modestly sized Cope and Marsh, who also bore the burden of some extra weight around the middle. Cope rested his hands on the bottom of the door, not failing to note that the metal lip of the door was strangely cool to the touch. Sternberg made his hands into a stirrup and gave Cope a push up, just enough for him to get his knee inside the floor of the ship. So Marsh had beaten him through the ghost wall, but none other than Edward Cope was the first one inside the ship, and was the only one to have flown on Grieg's craft. This deal was working out to his advantage after all.

He heard some grunting and panting behind him and turned to extend a hand to the flailing Marsh, who was showing why strenuous field work was no longer his forte. Finally Cope, Sternberg and Stillson, after considerable amounts of pushing and pulling, were able to shift gravity in their favor and Marsh stood shakily to his feet, aboard a spaceship at long last.

There was not much to see, at least not right inside the door. There was barely enough room for both of them to stand. Cope and Marsh were surrounded on three sides by featureless metal walls, topped with a featureless metal ceiling. At first, it seemed that there was no way out of the small cell of a room. No ladders went anywhere, and no other doors were visible.

"Surely the ship is bigger than just this," Cope said, shrugging down at Sternberg.

"I certainly hope so," Marsh said with a laugh. "But maybe he needs the rest of the space for all the bones he's collecting."

They peered around the room, looking for a way out. Cope noticed a small blue patch on the floor, which otherwise was a dull silverish color. Before he could bend to examine it, Marsh, not looking where he was going, stepped on it. Without a sound, he vanished.

"Othniel?" Cope asked, jerking upright with surprise.

Stillson and Sternberg gasped at the same time and the sheeted Indians, who had been watching quietly, took a few steps backward.

"What happened to him?" Stillson cried out.

"I don't know," Cope said.

He moved his hands through the air where Marsh had been, but O.C. had vanished completely. What was that blue patch? Had it somehow carried Marsh deeper into the ship, or had it destroyed him? Cope hoped O.C. was all right, but he found himself a little jealous at the thought that Marsh was now seeing something he wasn't.

"Don't do it," Sternberg said. "This is not worth it, boss. Let's just go."

"Oh, Charley, you know I can't do that," Cope said. "Pray for me."

He stepped on the blue patch. When he blinked again, he was somewhere else inside the ship, standing next to Marsh. He took a quick breath, relieved that he wasn't vaporized. Marsh gave him a quick glance and then resumed what he was doing, namely gawking. They were standing in a room much larger than they would have imagined a spaceship to have. It was a space bigger than any Cope had seen on Grieg's ship; a concert hall compared to a closet. A concert hall at Christmastime, to be exact. The room was festooned with small lights of all colors, some twinkling, some still. They stood at the edge of the room, a position that still allowed them to see it all. The ceiling began a little ways above their heads and then soared up twenty feet or more. A series of translucent panels started on each side of them and ran the length of the room, gradually widening out to leave a circular space in the middle. Viewed from above, the layout might look like a giant eyeball.

"This is fabulous," Marsh said, taking a tentative step into the room, being careful not to put his foot down on another blue patch.

"I'll say," Cope replied, following in Marsh's footsteps. "This can't be the workroom of a scientist. It's too clean."

His own office back in Philadelphia was chockablock with papers and drawings and even bones, so much so it often appeared that some odd creature had wandered into his haven and then exploded. Cope knew from hearsay that Marsh was also a packrat of great renown, whose personal fossil collection threatened to buckle the floors of any building unlucky enough to carry it.

"Oh, but he is a scientist," Marsh said. "Edward, come here."

Cope walked behind Marsh and joined him in perusing one of the translucent screens, which turned out to be full nearly from top to bottom with drawings and graphs. They also contained the twinkling lights, and this one had a goodly collection of them all by itself.

"Look here and here and here," Marsh said, pointing to the lights. "The sun, Mercury, Mars, the Earth. It looks like a map of the solar system. Very convenient for any spaceman intent on visiting us."

"As long as he isn't going further west," Cope said dryly, pointing to a couple of lights that shouldn't have been there. "Look here and here. What are those?"

"I don't know," Marsh said.

"Look over here," Cope said after he had walked on past, determined to see everything there was to examine in the room.

The next panel was less ambiguous. It contained tiny

drawings of monkeys that grew into apelike creatures and apelike creatures that slowly grew erect and turned into humans. The figures seemed to twinkle within the clear sides of the wall, as if they were three dimensional figures embedded under glass. Aside from their strange location, the procession of hunched figures was nothing that Charles Darwin couldn't draw.

Cope left Marsh to squint at the apes and wandered to the next panel, which bore more figures. He drew in his breath when he saw them, but not because they were more beautiful, even though they were. These figures shone like tiny emeralds behind their glass prison. They were pictures of dinosaurs. There were nearly more of them than he could count, all arrayed before his eye like a parade of jade. He wanted to soak up the detail, but the miniature beasts were so hard to see. Were they creatures from Swenson's world? Or from his own? Some of the shapes looked familiar, but most seemed to be leaned over further than he would have pictured. Perhaps they were not from Earth, or perhaps his own perceptions of how the creatures walked had been mistaken.

"Look at those!" Marsh said over his shoulder. "And look at this!"

He pointed further down on the clear wall, where the myriad of shapes began to dwindle like sugar poured through a funnel. There were fewer dinosaur icons on that end of the strange wall, and they were smaller, too, as if the representations were meant to signify, by their own number and size, the dinosaur extinction. Or maybe not. Cope squinted closer at a picture one inch from O.C. Marsh's outstretched index finger. It looked like a tiny man, a tiny green man, but he couldn't be sure. He had good vision, but it was hard for him to try to focus so close. Marsh, being nearsighted, was better able to stare at such tiny things.

"What is it?" Cope asked.

Marsh's finger touched the tiny drawing, and he drew it back quickly as if he had not intended to skip over the examination of the nearsighted and go straight to that of the blind. As he moved his finger away, the little picture seemed to shimmy and without so much as a sound a green man appeared before them. He stood about five feet tall, but looked like no one they had ever seen. His skin was made up of scales, his belly lighter than his back and sides. His eyes looked like the yellow seeds of some exotic fruit.

Cope and Marsh bumped into each other as they moved away from the lizard man, too surprised by his silent appearance to even speak. His eyes did not follow them, and his belly did not move in and out as he breathed.

"What on earth are you?" Cope asked after the lizard man failed to introduce himself, or indeed make any sort of movement at all.

Cope and Marsh waited for a long time for some sort of answer. Then Marsh stuck out a hand and waved it in front of the creature's yellow eyes. It did not blink. He feigned a quick punch right at its face. Cope shouted, "O.C.!" but the creature didn't twitch a muscle.

"Is he dead?" Cope asked at last. "Or in some sort of state?"

"I don't think so," Marsh said. "I don't think he's really here at all."

He reached over to the clear wall and touched the tiny picture again. The lizard man disappeared as quickly and silently as he had come.

"How does that work?" Cope asked, and Marsh shrugged.

"Well, if we can't figure it out, let's at least bring him back and have a look at him."

Marsh hit the picture again, and the lizard-man

returned, as still and silent as before. Cope reached out a hand to touch him. His hand touched scales, but he could feel no pulse, no sign of life. As a test, he even touched one of the glassy eyes. The creature did not blink. The lizard man showed no sign of life, issued no complaint at being so poked and prodded. Cope held the back of his hand before the lizard man's slit of a mouth. No breath ruffled the hairs of his hand.

"Now I am convinced," Cope said. "This is just some sort of model."

"But of what?" Marsh asked. "He's standing upright. There's no tail. His hips look simian, not like a lizard's at all."

Cope withdrew his hand and rested it on his hip. Marsh was right. The lizard man's hips were a little bit wider than a human's, but bore no resemblance to the splayed hips of modern lizards.

"He's not lizard hipped or bird hipped, either," Marsh said.

He was right about that, too. Dinosaurs had been divided into two groups, those with what were called lizard hips and those with what were called bird hips. This creature was too upright for either one of them, and its front pubic area was too smooth—too human— to be based around the extending front bone of a lizard-hipped dinosaur.

"Look at him," Cope said. "He looks like a little man. He's got ribs where a man's would be. His legs look like a man's. His arms look like a man's. If you took away all those scales and put a little hair, you'd have a man."

"Sometimes a little hair is all a man needs," Marsh said, leaning over the creature and displaying his own prominent bald spot. "But you're right. He's like a lizard that jumped the tracks of evolution and ended up a homo sapiens, almost."

"And there is how it happened," Cope said, pointing back at the board with its myriad of tiny pictures.

The array of dinosaurs on the far right end slowly whittled down until it arrived at the tiny picture of the lizard man, which now stood before them, defying their agile minds with its silent mysteries.

"Only it didn't happen here," Marsh said. He swept a finger at the board. "By the time we got to here in the fossil record, there were no dinosaurs. It was all mammals and reptiles, but no dinosaurs."

He stared at the lizard man.

"Especially none that looked like that."

"Then maybe it didn't happen here," Cope said, but then they both heard a voice, a human voice.

"Dr. Marsh. Oh, Dr. Marsh, please help me."

Marsh jerked his eyes away from the lizard man. He punched the creature's picture and it vanished again, as if its presence made it hard to focus on where the voice was coming from.

"Over there," Cope said, but Marsh was moving before him.

"I recognize that voice. That's Digger Phelps," Marsh said by way of explanation. "That's my missing man."

They walked past more translucent panels, but Marsh didn't even turn a head to see what was on them. Cope tried to get in a sideways glance, but he didn't want to let Marsh get too far out ahead, and he also was keeping an eye out for those blue patches. He knew which one had gotten him here, and didn't want to step on another one by accident and suddenly appear somewhere else.

"Digger!" Marsh shouted.

Cope winced, not sure it was wise to make too much noise on Swenson's mystery ship.

"Doc! In here!"

They had made it to the far end of the open room.

Digger Phelp's voice seemed to come from inside the far wall.

"Dammit!" Marsh said. "Where is he? There's no door here, Edward."

"Maybe there is," Cope said.

There was a small panel visible on the wall, right about the height of a man's hand. It didn't glow like the buttons had on the outside of the ship, but maybe the idea was the same. Cope reached up and pushed the button.

"Digger!" Marsh said as a door opened on the wall.

Digger didn't look so good. Then they heard a thumping sound behind them. Cope felt goosebumps rise on his arms with each footstep. Maybe lizard man was walking after all, angry about being poked and examined. He was nearly relieved when he saw Charley Sternberg, but that feeling quickly vanished.

"Come quick, sir," Sternberg said, shoving the words out between panted breaths, polite even in near-panic. "We appear to have some trouble."

TWENTY EIGHT

Sitting Bull had grown to like the small folding telescope that George Burgess brought with him from the east. Since coming west, Burgess had used it mainly to spot birds or occasionally to look up at the stars. Sitting Bull saw him peering through it in Canada, and had demanded to have a look. He had more practical uses in mind, such as using it to spot Canadian Army men or to look out for potentially dangerous Indian tribes.

Now he was using it to spy on their objective, the large silvery disk that sat on the other side of the plain, looking almost like it had crashed into the distant scrubby pines. They had traveled for days to get back to Montana and had then searched for days more to find the elusive metal tent of the strange white man. While the men waited behind them out of sight behind a ridge, he peppered Burgess with questions about it, questions Burgess was in no position to answer. He had not gone inside the ghost wall with the other Sioux; he had never set eyes on this thing, either.

"What are these?" Sitting Bull said at one point, and handed Burgess the telescope.

For an instant, Burgess was seized with the memory of sharing the telescope with Alice Stillson. He remembered the cold night on the sandstone, when they had warmed each other only with their naked bodies. Where was she now? She was almost certainly still with Professor Marsh, but he hoped she was nowhere near this disk. Things were going to get dangerous there very fast. Everything out here was too dangerous. He should turn away from his roots. He had to admit to himself that he was doing Sitting Bull no good, doing the Sioux no good. He should take Alice Stillson back east, and they could live together forever. What sort of house would they have? Not a big one. Maybe just a small, cozy one, down the street from some shops where they could stroll.

"Do you see?" Sitting Bull asked impatiently.

Soon Burgess would be with Alice Stillson again, but for now he drove thoughts of her and their cozy house from his mind and looked where Sitting Bull directed.

It looked like the large disk was being attacked by flowers. White, spinning objects drew closer to it, as if blown across the plain by the wind. Burgess had to admit he did not know what those were, either. He was sure that Sitting Bull was beginning to think that all his years back east had not taught him very much. He was as ignorant of some things as someone who had never cracked a book. He started to hand back the telescope with an apologetic shrug when he saw one of the flowers lose its blossom, turning into a dark-skinned man. A dark-skinned man with long, long hair. Burgess figured he should probably say nothing, but a part of him wanted to impress Sitting Bull with his knowledge, and that part spoke first.

"I believe those are Crows," he said.

Sitting Bull snatched away the telescope and stared through it, letting out a long, slow gust of breath. Burgess knew what he was thinking, even though his face never lost its typical frown. He had come all this way back into the United States to steal away the weapons of the white man, and now the hated Crow were going to get them first.

"We have spent enough time here looking," Sitting Bull said, confirming Burgess' fears. "Now we go in."

The Crows were getting restless. Marsh and Cope had vanished through the door, but nothing else seemed to happen after that, so they took to wandering around, sheets folded over their shoulders. Some of them devoted time to examining the large metal craft, but it was something that defied close analysis. Its skin was smooth, with virtually nothing that could break off or be worked loose. The ship was best appreciated by backing up and looking at the whole thing, as it sat on its belly at the edge of the plain. Some of the Crows did that instead. Al Stillson watched them for a long time, gathering pictures in her mind for use in her book. Their hair was black as licorice and astonishingly long, almost as long as the sheets they carried. Her own black locks were crudely chopped short, but even at its fullest she doubted her hair could ever be as long as theirs.

"Sometimes they put grease in it so it shines like water," Charley Sternberg said.

She twitched. She hadn't seen him come up.

"Are you worried about them?" she asked, and he knew she wasn't talking about the bored Crows.

"A little bit. Who knows where they went? I didn't even know it was possible for them to disappear like that."

They took a seat at the edge of the pines, where Swenson's ship and the plain spread out before them. The steep hills began rising across the plain, and carried on from there down to the river. Silvery clouds were massing there, as if the spiky tops of the hills were supporting them for a rest before they headed across the plain.

"Whatever is going to happen will have to happen soon," Sternberg said, scanning the sky.

He looked older when he frowned. He had slicked his own hair down with something, but it did not make it shine like water. It made him look like a St. Louis banker, not a River Crow.

"Why do you say that?" Stillson asked.

"Look at those clouds. It will snow here soon. I'm surprised it hasn't already, it's nearly November. The snow will be on the ground most of the winter, and nobody will dig anything up."

"I don't know," Stillson said, pointing to the fat silver ship. "Anyone who could fly that through space shouldn't be worried too much about a little snow."

"That's probably so," Sternberg agreed, nodding mournfully. "That's probably so."

Stillson looked at Sternberg. He was squinting into the sun and she could not see his eyes.

"Mr. Sternberg, you don't seem to be having a very good time out here."

He turned to Stillson and made his inadvertent scowl into a real one, extending his lower lip so far down it nearly touched his chin. Stillson laughed, and he joined her.

"I was having a good time, before. I like to get out and dig, even if we don't find anything but a couple of teeth. But this, this is not the sort of thing I had in mind."

He gestured at Swenson's ship, and then waved his hand over to one of the motionless electric men.

"I like to dig for bones and then figure out what those bones are. I don't like to tangle with creatures from outer space, and I don't like all the sneaking around we've been doing lately. When I started digging bones, there weren't many people out here interested in it. It looked like I was going to have the whole of the west almost to myself, to excavate as I pleased. But I guess the bones are so attractive here that not only did Mr. Marsh show up, with you and all his crew, but even beings from other planets are showing up to join in the fun."

"It wasn't quite what I was counting on, either," Stillson said. "My only regret is that I never got to do any of the sneaking around. I just had to wait back in camp and hear about it."

Sternberg laughed.

"I wouldn't worry about that too much if I were you, young man. I think you'll get your chance, the way things are going."

A sudden shouting came from one of the Crow, who tossed his sheet back over his head and pointed at the low hills in the distance.

"Now what?" Sternberg said, standing up and shielding his eyes with the back of his hand. "Stillson, what is he pointing at?"

Stillson saw nothing at first. Then she saw what looked like a series of black dots appearing on the horizon. By this time, the Crows were already all up and whooping at the top of their lungs.

"What is it?" Sternberg said. "Who's coming?"

Whoever it was, they were coming fast. Stillson chewed her lower lip nervously. As they got closer, she could see they were Indians, and there was something familiar about them. The Crows were whooping and shouting as they scrambled around, getting to the hole under the ghost wall. They had left all of their weapons on the other side, and would have to exit one at a time, all while bearing down were—

"Oh, my God," Stillson said.

"What? What?" Sternberg asked.

"It's the Sioux. They're coming back. You better go warn Mr. Cope. We're going to have trouble out here."

"What about you?" Sternberg said. "You better come inside with me."

Stillson walked to the very edge of the ghost wall, making sure to stay out of the way of the agitated Crow, who were shouting at each other to hurry up and get through. She stared as hard as she could at the advancing Sioux, looking to see if that one familiar face was among their number. The Sioux kept coming, the thunder of their horse's hooves preceding them, but she just couldn't tell if Sitting Lizard was one of them. She wasn't sure if she should want him to be or not. She longed to see him, longed to kiss him again. But then again, if he was riding with this crowd, he was about to be in a fight, and could get hurt. That would be worse than not seeing him at all.

"Oh, please be careful," she said in a compromise prayer.

Just then the arms and legs of the electric men started twitching, and they let out identical high-pitched shrieks.

"Ahhh!" Stillson shouted.

She clapped her hands over her ears, but the sound was still painful enough to make her gasp. She looked back to see Sternberg staggering at the edge of the ship, trying to climb up to the blue patch even as he kept his ears covered. Stillson ran to help him, avoiding the Crows who were now shouting in pain as they twisted in the ghost wall tunnel like worms.

"What does this mean?" Stillson shouted as she gritted her teeth against the noise and gave Sternberg the needed push.

"Maybe the Sioux aren't the only ones coming back," he shouted, and then he was gone.

Jenks Dart sat midway up the branches of one of the scrubby pines, glad to have found one of the few branches that was capable of supporting a man's weight.

He was wrapped in part of a green tarpaulin from the camp, not one of the white sheets that the Crow were wearing. Putting a white sheet over your head and running around in the middle of a plain on a clear day seemed to him to be one of the stupidest things you could do out west. There were altogether too many Indians around these days for his taste, although the Crow seemed friendly enough. The Crow were not the ones he was worried about.

He was supposed to have taken part in the idiocy below him, but had made no effort to do so, and Ed Cope had left him alone. If Cope did not seem particularly surprised that he had elected not to join the group, he did not seem particularly bothered by it, either.

Dart rested his rifle across his knees. From the ground below, the tarp would render him invisible, and his rifle would appear to be just another branch. His view of the plain was blocked by whatever that huge silver thing was, but he could still see enough to satisfy himself. It helped that he was not really sure what he was looking for. He just thought that anytime white men were colluding with Indians out here, he should probably know what was happening. So far, not much, at least as he could tell. The Crows that he could see did not seem terribly active. Cope and the other scientist, O.C. Marsh, were somewhere out in front of the silver disk. Stillson and the man from Cope's camp were off to his left, leaning on their elbows and talking.

If being out here made him so nervous, he should probably keep moving, head off to California where nobody knew him. He was not sure what work there was to do there, but there was bound to be something. There would be too many questions if he headed back east, but if he headed west nobody would bother him. They would think he was just off the wagon from Ohio.

He had thought he could stay in Montana and everyone would go away once the Indian wars were over, but suddenly it seemed everybody was here, getting in each other's business. The Crows were always after the Sioux, the Army was always after the Sioux and sometimes the Crow, and now, if all that weren't bad enough, bone diggers from back east were stomping over every bit of land, ready to excavate creatures better left buried.

Shouts from the Crows brought him out of his reverie. They were jumping around and pointing excitedly off to the right. Dart squinted to where they were pointing, and saw men on horses, approaching fast. Not just men—Indians. He looked for a minute more to be sure of what he saw. Not just Indians—Sioux. And not just Sioux. Unless his eyes were playing tricks on him, parading phantoms of his past before his eyes, the leader of the descending horde was none other than Sitting Bull.

Dart sat stunned in the tree as tears came to his eyes. For an instant he wondered if the big Indian he had seen in Cope's camp was among the arriving mass. The man had promised him money for letting him take the bone. Then he realized this opportunity was bigger than just money. This was his chance to rid himself of the nightmares. God was going to have mercy on him and give him another chance. He felt the spirit of George Armstrong Custer move through his veins, into his arms, down to the fingers that tightened around his rifle stock. He had failed General Custer before, cursed him as a fool, and the man had died. Money was no longer a concern. It was now in his power to take revenge.

Before he could start moving back down the tree, he heard a twig snap below. He was seized by a sudden terror. Had the Sioux managed to sneak up behind him? He turned his head around, slowly, silently, and peered down below into the trees. A tall man with long blonde hair moved purposely through the pines, headed for the silver disk. It was the man he had seen at Ed Cope's camp. What was his name? Swenson. This was his disk, this was his camp. Dart watched him in fascination. Swenson moved with the ease of a cat. He reached down and touched a silver wand that was sticking out of the ground. At least it looked like a wand, or some kind of lever. He had not noticed it before, but he had not been looking for it. It emitted an eerie green light from the top, although he could see no trace of flame. After touching the strange wand, Swenson kept moving through the trees and disappeared from his view.

Ed Cope had been raving about some kind of invisible wall that surrounded Swenson's camp. Dart knew the man was a Quaker, but assumed he had just had too much to drink the night before. But maybe what he said was true. He remembered watching the Sioux crawl, one after another, into the man's camp. The Crows had done the same thing today, only they had done it wearing white sheets. They had both dug holes and squirmed through them, so maybe there was something to this invisible wall after all. He looked down at the green wand. Swenson had touched it before moving through the wall. Maybe it was some kind of doorway, or maybe it was a part of the wall itself. Whatever it was, he should at least have a look at it.

Dart scrambled down from the tree, taking care not to drop his rifle, and walked to the green wand. It was only a small piece of metal, about a foot tall, with a round knob on the top that somehow produced a glow without fire. He looked at the path Swenson had taken. He could walk through the trees to within four feet of the disk. He could see no way into it from ground level, but if he climbed on the pines it would be easy enough to jump on the flat shelf that encircled the disk. From there it would be a quick walk to the front of the disk.

If he kept his head down, he could look out on the Indians without being seen. He would be up in the air, high above their heads. He swallowed hard at the implication of his thoughts. He would be up high, behind what looked like a thick piece of metal, looking down through open air at the Sioux. At Sitting Bull. He would have a terrific shot, and they would be unable to shoot back.

He reached out and grabbed the top of the green wand as he had seen Swenson do. He steeled himself for a sharp pain, but felt nothing. Before he lost his nerve, he straightened up and walked right through the invisible wall, heading for a marksman's perch on the front of the silvery disk.

TWENTY NINE

"What is he doing to me?" Digger Phelps asked in a quavering voice that looked out of character for his hard face.

Charles Sternberg couldn't blame him for his fear. The man was encased in a chamber in the wall that looked like nothing so much as a medieval Iron Maiden torture chamber, although one that was somewhat modernized. Ed Cope had left the ship to see to the mounting problems out there, but O.C. Marsh stayed, staring with concern and consternation at his employee.

"How are you feeling?" Marsh asked.

Phelps did not look like he could be feeling anything but pain. His arms were kinked at the elbows and his hands turned as if he was a begging dog. Dozens of tiny red light beams played over his face and body, standing in for a true Iron Maiden's spikes.

"Digger, this is Charley Sternberg," Marsh said. "He's with Mr. Cope's team. Believe it or not, we're working together now."

Sternberg nodded at Phelps.

"Never thought I'd say pleased to meet you to a Cope man, but pleased to meet you," Phelps said. "Excuse me if I don't shake hands. This doesn't hurt at all, but I can't move and my leg itches something fierce."

259

"Excuse me," Marsh said, and reached his head into the small space on either side of Phelp's head.

These were more strange lights, and he wanted to see where they originated.

"Don't," Phelps said, but it was too late.

Marsh staggered back from the chamber, holding his eye and letting out grunts of pain.

"Oh, God, my eyes are bad enough," he said, pulling his hand away to reveal a wet, red eye. "How does it look?"

Sternberg stared at Marsh's eye, but so no evidence of damage.

"Not good, but it looks like it will recover."

Marsh put a palm back over the eye and walked back to where Phelps stared miserably from the wall.

"Don't put any part of your body in there," he cautioned to Sternberg.

Sternberg ran through a mental list of his own defects—bad leg, one ear only good for deflecting wind around his head. He had lost too much already to go risking any more body parts.

"I won't," Sternberg said. "But how will we get him out if we can't touch him?"

That was a good question, and Marsh appeared stumped for a moment. He took his hand away from his eye, which looked watery but a little better.

"Everything seems to function on remote switches around this place," Marsh said, almost to himself. "Yes. It's easy once you know what to do. We just need to find the right button or switch."

"There's this," Sternberg said, pushing the small panel that was right at eye level. He hadn't noticed it until Marsh mentioned switches, but then there it was.

Phelps instantly disappeared behind a door that seemed to merge invisibly with the wall.

"Hey!" he yelled from inside.

Sternberg hit the switch again, and Phelps was back, his eyes rolling back and forth rapidly.

"Don't do that," Marsh said. "But you've got the idea. Digger, could you see anything when Swenson put you in here?"

"Swenson?"

"The man who put you in here. Could you see anything of what he was doing?"

"For a while, yes. He put me here and then walked off to that end of the ship and started doing something. There was some kind of thing that came out of the wall. It sort of looked like a desk, but it sort of looked like the wall, at the same time."

Phelps motioned as best he could with his eyes, a pitiful sight that made him appear to be having a spasm.

"All the way over there?"

Phelps attempted to nod with his eyes.

"Charley, you stay here," Marsh said. "I'll go see what I can find. What was going on outside that got you so excited?"

"A bunch of Sioux Indians rode up on horses. They don't get along with the Crow. It looked like they were about to fight. I hope Edward can calm them down."

"The Sioux? Sioux you say! I'm the one who ought to be out there talking to them. They'll listen to me."

He stood with his hands on hips, looking ready to follow Cope out the door. Then he tossed a glance to his employee, and gave a quick sigh.

"But maybe Ed can handle it, although he's just as likely to get them all riled up. Do what you can here, Charley, I'll be just across the room."

He padded across the room, leaving Sternberg to stare into the panicked eyes of this man Phelps. It could just as easily be him in there, or so he thought.

"How did you get in here, anyway?" Sternberg asked.

"It's a long story. I avoided all those little guys. I

managed to get up to the side of the ship and then he got me."

"Swenson?"

"How do you know his name?"

"I've met him."

"You've *met* him? How did you meet him?"

"He came to our camp."

"I go sneaking around to get in here and avoid that man and get myself frozen and stuck in this cage and you go have tea with the man? What is the thinking here?"

"We didn't have tea," Sternberg said, trying to ignore Phelp's sarcasm. He supposed if he was locked in a box in a wall, he would be more than sarcastic. "I'll see if I can find any switches along here."

"Don't push anything," Phelps said. "Let the professor find the door."

"I can help," Sternberg said, but he decided not to argue.

It was a moot point, as he wasn't finding much of anything to push on the wall. This ship of Swenson's was antiseptic. It was probably the cleanest room he had ever seen in his life. He walked down the wall a few feet, so intent on looking for a switch or any sort of feature on the wall that he nearly didn't notice that Swenson himself was standing right in front of him.

"Hello," Swenson said in a soft voice. "I believe your name is Charles Sternberg. I was not expecting to see you here."

Sternberg opened his mouth to shout for Marsh, but found he couldn't make a sound. He saw that Swenson had a small metal object in his hand, which he kept pointed at his visitor. He strained to push air from his lungs or make any sort of sound to alert Professor Marsh, but the metal object seemed to make sure that nothing happened. He looked across the room, but couldn't see Marsh.

"So how are you? It's been a little while. I see that you are not content to just break our agreements. You must break into my ship to get whatever else you can."

Sternberg could not argue with that, even if he could speak.

"I believe I may have some use for you," Swenson said.

He did not speak in a threatening manner, but Sternberg felt a chill run through his body just the same.

"I'll make you an offer, Charley. I see you have a malfunctioning leg. I believe you may also have an ear that does not work. I can fix those for you, Charley. I can help you, and you can help me. You see, I like to study the physical ailments of your—of people. In return, I can help repair those ailments. It will be painless, I assure you. All I need for you to do is step just slightly to the left. Just about one foot to the left."

Sternberg looked to his left. It was getting a little hard to move his neck. He saw nothing at first, but then noticed a bump in the wall; the same sort of unobtrusive switch that opened the door Digger Phelps was hidden behind. Alf Swenson, it seemed, desired to put him in the same sort of immobility as Phelps. What sort of physical ailments did Phelps have? Swenson said it was an offer. That meant that maybe he could refuse. But Phelps didn't seem to have given his approval. He had not appeared the least bit enthusiastic about whatever treatments he was getting.

Fix his leg, though, did the man say? His leg had not worked properly in fifteen years, since he was a wee boy of ten. He could still remember the day he busted it for good. He wasn't doing anything heroic, wasn't even working. Charley-boy was just fooling around with an older friend, chasing him around the barn, and finally up into the barn, up to the second floor. That boy—what was his name?—had climbed up on some hay in the very peak of the barn, and Charley went after him. He didn't see the hole in the top of the ladder; his friend was laughing and kicking down hay, and it covered the gap that Charley fell through, fell twenty feet through down to the hard floor. That was it for the leg, which the doctor thought was just sprained, but which never quite worked again. And then four years ago the leg had gotten wet and frozen when he worked out on the ranch in Kansas, and the knee had tightened up, which kept him in the hospital at Fort Riley for three whole months. It was a bad leg.

Sternberg stared Swenson in the eye; no way to keep Swenson from knowing he was at least thinking about it. He flexed the twisted muscles in his leg, remembered again the run through the hay and the laughter that had ended so abruptly. It was a bad leg, but it was his leg, stiff or no, and that's just how it was. His ear never did work, but that was his, too, and if God did not wish it to function, he would just as soon not hear anything with it.

He tried to say, "no thank you," but his mouth was still not up to the task. He slowly shook his head.

"How disappointing," Swenson said, although he did not point the metal box away. "I said, please step one foot to the left."

So this was not an invitation to be refused after all. Sternberg's bad leg lifted slowly, moving of its own accord, or rather Swenson's accord. He had trouble lifting it on the best of days, and now here it was moving by itself. He felt his weight shift to the left although he tried to lean away to the right. His right leg began its own halting movement.

Suddenly Swenson's attention was diverted by a shout from behind. Sternberg's right leg dropped to the floor. He neck was free, too, and he turned just in time to see Digger Phelps shoot from his wall chamber and speed away across the room, dodging between the translucent walls. He heard voices coming from the other end of the room, echoing off the high ceiling. Swenson uttered a word he didn't understand and began stalking swiftly past him. That was his mistake. All of Sternberg's weight was on his left leg, which allowed him to quickly shoot out his right leg and catch Swenson in mid-stride. The man went down hard, his long hair brushing past Sternberg's face.

"Mr. Sternberg! Please come over here!" Professor Marsh shouted, and Charley waited no time at all in responding to the call.

Swenson was shuffling to his feet, but Sternberg made good time, shuffling hurriedly on his stiff leg that would now never be fixed, cutting back and forth between the walls. He had not really had a good look at them on the way inside. He noticed now they were full of tiny pictures of all sorts of creatures. He might have stopped to look at a few of them had Swenson not been breathing down his neck. The long-legged Swenson had nearly caught up with him by the time he rounded the last wall, but things seemed to still be working in his favor. Professor Marsh was hunched over a small button-studded table that extended from the wall of Swenson's ship. Digger Phelps was resting his rump on the far edge of the table, a lazy smile on his face and a pistol in his hand.

"You should have gotten rid of my shooting iron, Mr. Swenson," Phelps said. "Or at least not put it away when I was looking."

Sternberg walked to the other side of the table, consciously putting it between himself and Swenson. The long-haired man eased his run as he neared the table.

"Just keep slowing up there, Mr. Swenson," Phelps

said, keeping the gun trained on Swenson's stomach. "I am not that good a shot, but I believe I could hit you."

"What are you doing?" Sternberg whispered to Marsh, who was hunched over the table, frowning and running his hands over the desk, but not actually pushing any buttons.

The table was covered with more than buttons, he saw when he looked down on it. It had plenty of those, but under them it also had some sort of line drawing of the ship's interior, showing dozens of lines radiating out from the center of the craft.

"Shhh," Marsh whispered back. "I am trying to figure out where the bones are."

"Did you say bones, Professor?" Digger asked. "I know where they are. I saw where he put them."

For someone who had been stuck inside a wall, Phelps had certainly been paying attention, Sternberg thought. The thought seemed to occur to Swenson, too.

"You certainly are an attentive man," Swenson said as he took a step forward.

"Stop or I will shoot!" Phelps said, straightening up and pulling his rear end off the table. "I will shoot!"

He did not. As Swenson got closer, Phelps stopped moving at all, although he kept the gun aimed at his tormentor.

"Oh, no," Sternberg said, but before he could duck Swenson had aimed his metal object his way.

The words froze in his throat. He could still move his eyes for some reason, and looked at Marsh. Marsh had never even looked up from the button-studded desk. His frowning form bowed before it, looking like a concert pianist preparing for a recital.

"Now then," Swenson said. "I see that you all seem to be arrayed against me. First you work against each other, now you work against me."

He did not look particularly angry, or even surprised. He almost looked bemused.

"But now none of your are going anywhere, and you most certainly will not get any bones. I should have saved myself the trouble and just done this in the first place."

Swenson must have come in the back way, as he had apparently not thought to check the front door. Edward Cope suddenly appeared, standing on one of the blue patches. He shouted at the group, without pausing to notice that Swenson was even present, not to mention that he had frozen everyone.

"There's been a shooting and now the Indians are going to fight!" Cope yelled. "Come quick, Marsh, and calm your boys down or there will be nothing left of any of—"

He just then seemed to notice Swenson, who obligingly turned the metal object on him and froze him right in the middle of his sentence.

THIRTY

George Burgess sat nervously on his horse, watching as Sitting Bull shouted at a tall Crow Indian. The Sioux had come galloping up, but as they neared the strange giant disk the Crow began to be in a better and better fighting position than they had been previously. Sitting Bull had given the order to to slow down, and by the time they actually reached the disk, and the Crow, they were clopping along in a downright civil manner. The Crow, for their part, seemed ready to bluster but not ready to fight, and when an agitated Edward Cope appeared, waving his arms around, everyone seemed ready to accept his frantic appeals for peace.

Burgess saw Alice Stillson looking up at him. She was still in her garb as a boy so he could not yet jump off the horse and embrace her, not without drawing some unwanted attention. She looked beautiful, dirty face and all. She was standing entirely too close to the action, though, right behind Ed Cope. He motioned for her to walk off to the side in case anything should happen, although at this point things were more peaceful than he would have imagined.

Of course, there was a difference between being peaceful and being friendly, and neither side had quite made it to that far shore. Burgess pulled on the reins and tried to calm his unsettled horse, which pranced from side to side, bumping his legs into those of the other braves, which did nothing to gain their confidence in his horsemanship. He was not paying full attention to his restless steed because he was trying to follow the dialogue of Sitting Bull and the Crow chief, whose height was impressive even though he was not on a horse. He didn't need one. He was nearly as tall as the slumping Sitting Bull, who had not yet gotten off his own horse. The conversation veered between Sioux and whatever language the Crows spoke, with occasional chunks of bad English thrown on top. He could not get most of it, but the gist seemed to be that Sitting Bull wanted the Crow to get away from the silver disk, and the Crow chief was saying that it was really none of Sitting Bull's business what the Crow did. These basic points seemed to be made early on but were repeated with what he took to be slight variations and occasional threats, to the point that all the assembled braves first clutched their rifles and looked tense and ready but eventually got bored, and began shuffling their feet and looking around. Even Edward Cope, who stood with his arms crossed off to the side, out of harm's way, looked like he was considering going back into the silvery disk from whence he came.

Burgess decided it was safe to turn away from the standoff and examine the silver disk. It was like nothing he had ever seen, a metal top plunked down on the plain as if left by a giant boy who might remember it at any moment and come back to set it spinning. It seemed to have no windows or doors, but he was pretty sure Cope had come running out of it. Maybe he had just been hunkered down underneath it somewhere. A tiny speck of light stabbed into Burgess' eye. Something was moving on the disk now, on the lip that encircled the whole thing. It shone like something metal, only a type of metal that reflected sunlight differently

than did the disk itself. The disk just seemed to glow
in the sun; this thing flashed. Burgess remembered
his telescope and raised it to his eye, glad that Sitting
Bull had not yet decided he wanted to keep it for
himself.

There was a man on the lip of the disk, and he had a
long rifle. Burgess' mind raced. He knew that rifle.
He had seen that barrel up close. It was the man from
Cope's camp, the one who had let him steal the dinosaur
leg bone. What was he doing? Guarding Edward Cope?
Cope appeared to be in no danger. Was he mad about
his money? Burgess had completely forgotten about
his promise to get Marsh to pay the man. Burgess
squinted harder, trying to will the telescope to bring
the picture in closer. The man was not just lazily holding
the rifle over the disk. He was getting into shooting
position, and he looked serious. Burgess pulled the scope
away from his eye and looked with a sinking heart at
where the bullet would be headed—right at Sitting
Bull. He looked through the telescope again. No
mistake. The man was ready to fire.

With a fierce shout, he drove his heels into the flanks
of his horse. The beast lurched forward, amazed to be
given the signal to charge after being held back for so
long. Burgess rode past the other braves and had made
it to Sitting Bull just when a distant pop sounded in
the air. He wanted to shout a message to Sitting Bull
to back away but suddenly his body would not cooperate.
He saw the ground reaching up to claim him, noticed
the texture of the dirt and the scrub grass with
something like amazement before the darkness came.

Her whole future was snatched away from her in just
an instant. Sitting Lizard was back, but she had not
even had a chance to do more than toss him a few
enticing looks before the noise came, and then he

disappeared in a sea of jumping horses and shouting Sioux. Ignoring shouts from Edward Cope, Alice Stillson ran headlong into the undulating mass of people and found the man she loved.

Sitting Lizard was lying on his back on the dirt, oblivious to the horse's hooves that threatened to crush his skull at any instant. He was wearing Sioux garb finer than anything she had ever seen. He would have looked irresistibly handsome were it not for the dark hole in his chest and the blood spurting from it, fountaining out in rhythmic time with the beating of his heart. His eyes fluttered like birds, but he managed to keep them open when he saw her kneeling over him.

"Hello, Alice," he said.

The noise around them was at an ungodly pitch, as the two tribes prepared to go to war, but she heard the words as clearly as if they were the only two people on the plain.

"Hello, Sitting Lizard," she said, her words strong despite her quivering chin. "You look so handsome. You are so brave."

"I don't feel so good," he said.

She held a hand over his heart to staunch the blood, which flowed around her palm like a river coursing around a sandbar. It would have its way, it would not be slowed. Their remaining time together on earth would now be measured by the amount of blood he had left in his body. Sitting Lizard seemed to realize that.

"Damnit, Alice. I wanted to take you back to New Haven," he said in ragged gasps. "This is no place for you. I wanted to take you back east and we could raise our kids and when they are old enough we could walk down to the museum and attend the lectures—"

His ragged breaths gave way to gurgling coughs.

"We can still do that," she said.

He was fading, and she was losing sight of him. It seemed he would vanish entirely through the film of her tears. She blinked furiously to clear her vision, sending salty water to mingle with the dark blood that covered his beautiful beaded buckskin. She did not tell him her own dreams, where they stayed in the west and raised their children in its beautiful austerity. Their museum would be the open doors and the dust on the ground and the snow on the mountains. If he did not want that, that was fine, she would go to New Haven with him. She would do whatever he wanted, if he only would stay alive.

"Alice," he said, his coughing subsided. "How—how will you write about me in your book?"

She laughed, and he laughed with her, and it felt so good to laugh with him that it was a long moment before she realized that his laughing had stopped and he was gone. A man nearly six feet tall was gone because of a hole in his chest barely larger than the tip of her little finger. He was gone before the battle, gone without a fight, gone without saying goodbye.

Alice Stillson slumped back on her heels and felt the future drain away from her. It receded silently in the distance, and gradually the din going on right around her returned and dragged her back into the present. She prayed that a horse would kick her in the head, kick her back into the future, but none did. He was gone, and her punishment now was to remain alive.

"Stillson! For God's sake, boy, let's move!"

She felt Edward Cope's hands grab her shoulders and pull her backwards. Her arms and legs would not cooperate with him, and she heard him grunt with exertion. She watched numbly as Sioux braves now squatted near Sitting Lizard's body, picking him up and moving him away from what was ready to be a field of battle. She would not tell them that Sitting Lizard was planning to put his Indianness behind him, revert to being George Burgess, and become a white man wrapped in a brown man's body. The Indians carried him lovingly away. The man who had saved Sitting Bull. He was gone from her and her world once and for all. He was one of them whether he liked it or not.

Cope dragged her from the fray. Her legs began to work again, and she stumbled with him closer to the disk. The shouting was tremendous, ferocious, and seemed worse than any actual fighting could be.

"What were you thinking, Al?" Cope asked once they had crawled back under the ghost wall and had gained the shade of the silver disk.

He stood before her and then he saw. Her tears had poured down her face with sufficient velocity to wash away the dirt that usually lived on her cheeks. Her hat had blown away or been knocked away. Edward Cope no longer saw a dirty boy. He saw a young girl in love with a dead man.

"I see," he said. "I am so sorry. Young lady, I will pray to God to help you however he can. But right now I have to get back inside this ship and see if I can stop this madness."

Jenks Dart actually closed his eyes when he made the shot, something he knew he was not supposed to do, but he couldn't help it. When he opened his eyes all he saw was chaos, but it did appear that one Indian who had been on his horse was now no longer on his horse, so he had hit something. The Sioux were moving around so much it appeared they were being stirred by a giant invisible hand, and he could not tell if the one he had hit was Sitting Bull or not. He could not see Sitting Bull, so he assumed he had been successful.

He, Jenks Dart, was the man who had killed Sitting Bull. Surely that was enough to offset the cowardice he had displayed in running away from the battle at Little Bighorn. He could call it cowardice now, having avenged it. Historians would now refer to that as a momentary stain on his otherwise stellar career. Maybe they would even recognize his actions as being motivated by the hand of God. He had not really run away from Little Bighorn. He had only saved himself from getting killed there so that he might later avenge the death of General Custer and smite Sitting Bull.

Whatever future historians might think, he decided he had better get away from this place quick, or he would be known as the man who killed Sitting Bull and was then torn to pieces by his angry Sioux. Dart slid away from the lip of the disk, but he did so too quickly. Its surface was more slippery than he remembered, and he found himself sliding back toward the trees at its far edge. The disk seemed to be tilting, as if it was a beast trying to throw him from its back. He scrambled for footing, losing his grip on his rifle in the process. He made a desperate grab for it, but it slid faster than he could move, and disappeared off the far edge of the lip. He was now sliding pretty rapidly that way himself, and could hear the rifle bouncing off tree branches as it fell to the ground.

Dart had picked up considerable speed by the time he reached the far edge of the disk. He gathered his legs under him as best he could but didn't manage to slow his progress much, and nearly got the wind knocked out of him when he hit the pine trunk that he had used to climb onto the disk in the first place. He clung to the tree for a long moment until he could get his breath back, and then started climbing down. The Sioux and Crow were making a hell of a racket on the other side of the disk, and he hoped no one had noticed him. He would not take a chance and stick around, however. Once on the ground he scouted around for his rifle, but it was dark in the shade of the branches and he couldn't see it. He heard twigs snap. Indians usually could creep through the woods almost silently. If they were moving so fast as to snap twigs, that meant they were probably not coming to shake his hand. They were coming to kill him, and quick. He abandoned the search for the rifle, but thought of something else. He reached down and touched the odd green-lighted lever to get through the ghost wall, and then decided to take it along. Maybe if he took it with him it could be used to set up a miniature ghost wall around him, something he would probably need. He was not sure he could wrest it from the ground, but it moved easily in his hand. When he pulled it free, the green light faded out. He wasn't sure what that meant, but neither did he have time to stick around and figure it out. He jammed it in his belt and ran through the trees.

He had left his horse on the other side of the small patch of woods, right where the more mountainous terrain began. With a small sigh of relief, he saw the horse was still there, idly munching on scrub grass as it waited for him.

"Hey, there, Scout," he said as he ran up to the horse.

He untied the horse from a small sapling and vaulted neatly into the saddle, ready to make some tracks. The noises from the woods were getting louder, and he heard excited words being exchanged in an unknown tongue. Just as he began to ride away he saw an Indian face stick out from behind a tree at the edge of the woods, and then heard more shouting. He spurred Scout in the sides, perhaps a little harder than he should have; but now he was running for his life. Dart felt cold sweat beading up under his vest as he skirted the treeline and then headed for the hills as soon as he saw an opening.

The ground here was clumpy and rocky and littered

with good-sized clumps of sandstone, meaning he couldn't make time as well as he could have on the other side of the woods where the plain began. But that was also where the Indians lurked. He might as well just shoot himself.

"Steady, boy, steady," he muttered to Scout as they climbed the narrow trail that led between two low hills.

It was steeper and more narrow than it had looked going in, but he had no choice. With any luck it would broaden out and allow him to make more speed, and also fulfill a double duty by hiding him from anyone looking across the landscape. It was nearly impossible to track anyone in the ravines if you weren't in them yourself. His wish came true, and Jenks breathed a quick prayer. The ravine had bottomed out nicely, and recent storms seemed to have swept all the big rocks from the center of the path. Scout was running as fast as if he was on an open plain. He was home free. Jenks Dart had killed Sitting Bull and had gotten away with it.

He almost laughed out loud, but then he heard the thunder of hooves above him, and a dreadful war cry penetrated the gully and echoed off its high sides. He saw a steady cloud of dust moving along the ravine wall above him. The ravine floor was flat and smooth, but apparently its walls were, two, and at least one Sioux was able to keep pace with him. He saw a glint of sunlight on a rifle barrel, held extended in one brown hand. They couldn't aim, not at this speed. He would have to offer another prayer, one calling for the ravine walls to suddenly go higher, or vanish altogether. If the ravine floor and walls met again, he was a dead man.

He kicked Scout harder and the horse snorted in complaint, but tried vainly to accede to his wishes. It simply couldn't run any faster. Dart peered ahead as best he could. God had abandoned him. One hundred yards ahead, the ravine wall curved around to the right before gradually sloping down to flat ground. The Indians could get right in front of him, and his own rifle was lying uselessly on the ground back at the disk.

Only one thing to do; turn around. It would buy him some time, and maybe the Indian up on the wall would stumble and fall off and break his neck. Dart pulled back on the reins and turned to look back over his shoulder when he heard the popping sound and felt a hot jab of pain enter under his ribs. The pain was so quick and so deep that he almost laughed. It felt like a metal finger had reached out to tickle him but had gone too far and plunged itself into his body. So there was an Indian behind him, too. He was not in a very good position all of a sudden.

Dart groped at his waist for a knife when his fingers closed around something else—the metal spike he had stolen from the silver disk. It was part of the ghost wall. It was worth a try. He pulled back on the reins as hard as he could and the horse, confused about its course of action, managed to trip and send him flying headlong across the ravine. Dart skidded painfully across the dirt and rocks, which had looked so smooth from atop Scout but which were considerably rougher on contact. He heard Scout sputter and whinny, but did not wait to see how the horse was doing. One more shot and he would be done for. He scrambled to the edge of the ravine, plunged the metal spike in the ground and pushed the green button. Then he waited.

He couldn't see anything for a long time, until the dust began clearing. Then he saw Scout regain his feet, apparently none the worse for wear. It was too bad he couldn't put Scout inside his own personal ghost wall, because the Indians were sure to steal him. But it

couldn't be helped. If the ghost wall even worked, that
is. He held one hand to his bleeding side and peered
through the settling dust. Two frowning faces appeared.
The Sioux had once had feathers in their hair, but now
they were flattened back from the chase. They were
not here to taunt or fight with him. He could tell by
the way they gripped their rifles. Their purpose was
to kill him and move on.

The first Indian walked up to him, stopped about
five feet away, aimed his rifle at Dart's chest and fired.
Dart flinched and closed his eyes, but felt nothing. He
opened his eyes again. The Sioux stared back at him,
amazed. So the ghost wall worked. All he had to do
was stick it in the ground and it somehow sealed him
against the ravine wall. The Sioux stared for a moment
longer and then fired again. Dart kept his eyes open
this time, didn't blink even when he heard the roar of
the barrel at close range. Nothing happened, except
the Indians became so confused they looked almost
comical. Dart was tempted to stick out his tongue at
them, but he really didn't feel up to it right now. The
bullet that was already inside him was moving around,
and it hurt. One of the Sioux stuck out a hand and felt
the ghost wall, which made him frown and babble to
his companion. Dart worried momentarily that they
might spot the ghost wall spike, but it was wedged near
a rock and had become covered with dust, and they
didn't look at it. He knew that some of the Sioux knew
how to dig under the wall, but these apparently didn't,
and even if they did the packed ground of the ravine
was too hard for them to uproot. He smiled, just a little.
He was home free.

The Sioux took turns shooting at him some more,
with the same result. Their bullets simply bounced up
in the air. Dart thought it would be nice if one of the
returning bullets would hit one or both of the Indians

in the tops of their heads, but he was not likely to be that fortunate. He was lucky enough already.

He crawled back until he was resting somewhat comfortably against the ravine wall, and waited. The Sioux watched him for a long time, but eventually they grew bored and got back on their horses and rode away, taking Scout with them. They probably only rode a little ways, and he wasn't going to be fooled. He would wait a good while longer. He bandaged himself as best he could, urinated off to the side where he couldn't smell it so much and went to sleep. He slept there that night and waited through the whole next day, and finally at sunset of the second day he tentatively reached out to the spike and took down the ghost wall. Without making a sound, he stood up and looked around. They were gone. He had no horse, but he was alive. His injury was not so bad, and the bleeding had stopped. He walked for miles, taking care not to go back towards the plain, but down to the river. He got lucky there, too. An Army boat was heading downriver, and the men had heard of him already. They cheered when the learned that the man who had killed Sitting Bull was among them. He fell into a woozy, drunken sleep that night, with happy shouts and congratulations ringing in his ears. When he awoke, he was not alone. It seemed the men weren't the only ones proud of his deed. A young woman had found it worthy of celebration as well, and he lost himself in her kisses. He had a long, joyful slide down the Missouri River.

And then the bullet reached his heart.

One of the Sioux poked the other and nodded to where the bloody white man lay. His eyes had been moving rapidly back and forth under his lids, but now were still. They had fired numerous shots at him but he had not been harmed, but now he was dead anyway.

His magic had not saved him. They had been prepared to wait forever for him to come out from behind his magic shell, but he had died inside it instead. The first Sioux to shoot stuck out a hand, but still encountered a wall he could not see, one that could block bullets. The white man was protected, even in death. At least he was dead.

THIRTY ONE

An annoying alarm sound reverberated through Swenson's ship. Othniel Marsh winced, but he couldn't move his hands to cover his ears. Angry shouts echoed up from below, and the ship seemed to rock slightly. Swenson, still pointing his silver device at his four captives, walked a few feet to the north wall of the main room and touched a panel. There was no glass there, Marsh knew, but it was as if Swenson had suddenly opened a huge window at the front of the ship, one that showed the outside world beyond and below where they stood. What Swenson saw did not please him. Throngs of Indians were running directly around the ship, and even underneath, passing out of the viewing range of Swenson's mysterious window. The ones running underneath it had long hair; must be Crows. The ghost wall was obviously down, and the two warring tribes were now squaring off right under the ship, with the Crow using its metal bulk as a refuge.

Swenson said a couple of words no one else in the room could understand, but it was pretty clear what they meant. He set his silver device on the edge of the table, pointing it at his captives as best he could, and then pushed Marsh away from the table. He moved him as one might move a statue; he walked him backwards on his immobile feet until Marsh was resting against one of the picture-studded walls. Marsh cut his eyes over to the frozen figure of Edward Cope, and saw that Cope would be laughing out loud right now if he could. Swenson then turned his back on the group and began poking at the table. The mysterious window grew larger, showing more of the fighting below the craft. Looking at it made Marsh feel nearly physically ill. He was looking at the floor and looking *through* the floor simultaneously, and found it difficult to concentrate on the floor and the rampaging Indians below it at the same time. He decided to take the safe course and close his eyes.

Swenson muttered more unintelligible words and then said, "Stay here," as if any of his motionless guests had a choice.

Marsh opened his eyes a crack. Swenson was gone. He had left his silver freezing device on the edge of the table, but he had also left the window open. Marsh closed his eyes again. The ship rocked briefly, no doubt because virtually the whole Crow tribe was now underneath it, hiding while taunting the Sioux.

"It moved," Digger Phelps said through his nearly frozen lips.

"I felt it, Digger," Marsh replied, keeping his eyes shut. It seemed a little harder to move the muscles in his face now, for some reason.

"No, I don't mean that," Phelps said. "It moved. His little thing moved."

Marsh peeked again. The silver device had, indeed, shifted position somewhat, and was now pointing mostly at Marsh, Sternberg and Cope.

"I think I can move my finger," Digger said. "I think I can hit one of the buttons on this table."

"Do you know what you are doing?" Marsh said through lips that would barely move.

"Who cares?" Cope said through similarly stiff lips. "Do something."

Phelps concentrated and, sure enough, his fist and index finger moved toward the buttons. It came to the closest one and pushed it down. There was a tremendous grinding sound from somewhere in the bowels of the ship, and suddenly the floor to Marsh's left began to move. A long plank out of the floor suddenly began to sink down to the ground. It was the real ground, too, and was a real opening, not the mysterious sort of window Swenson had already opened. Marsh cut his eyes to the left until they hurt, and thought he could see a few puzzled Crow faces looking up into the belly of the ship. Edward Cope had the misfortune to the standing on the very strip of flooring that was now being lowered, but fortunately for him the floor was a little slick.

"Oh oh," he said through clenched teeth. "Do something that will let us move!"

He slowly slid down with the flooring, moving in a fluid line like an ice skater, right into the midst of the astonished Crows. Phelps could do little more than move his index finger just a tiny bit farther. The first button had been a doozy, and Marsh could hardly wait to see what would happen next. Phelp's exploring digit hit the second button, just as the ship rocked again. The strip of flooring had hit the ground, forming a sort of ramp, but it tilted the disk slightly on contact with the less-than-level earth. Marsh felt himself teeter backwards on his concrete legs, and was glad his crooked elbow came in contact with the wall behind him and held him up.

Suddenly he found himself shooting straight up into the air. The round ceiling of the ship's inner chamber loomed above like the dome of the sky. One instant he had been looking at the floor, the next he was facing a completely different way. Something was underneath him, something big. He teetered on it like a see-saw board.

"Good God!" Phelps shouted, and Sternberg let out a gasp of surprise.

"What is it?" Marsh asked. The dome was moving before his eyes as he swayed.

"It's—" Sternberg said, but he didn't finish.

"What?" Marsh asked. "What?"

Whatever it was, it had a ridge that was digging into his spine. Something had to give. Fortunately, it did. The thing underneath him moved, and the ship tilted with it. Marsh heard a metallic clinking sound as Swenson's silver freezing device fell to the floor, releasing him from its spell. He pitched heels over head for the floor, but managed to reach up and grab something to keep from falling. It felt like a rock cliff. He could see only darkness before him.

"Good lord," he said, and then the thing moved again.

He had two choices; jump to the floor and take the risk of being crushed by whatever this was, or climb up and figure out what to do later. He didn't know how high up he was, so he opted for the latter. The side of the thing was lumpy hide and he managed to find toe holds easily, although his shirt got scruffed. At last he scrambled to a sitting position and realized what he had done. The thing beneath him had a huge flaring crest and a horn as long as his arm. Its eyes were the size of billiard balls. He, Othniel Charles Marsh, paleontologist extraordinaire, was doing nothing less than sitting on the back of a dinosaur. A living, breathing and, apparently, somewhat angry dinosaur.

"Phelps!" he shouted. "This is a dinosaur!"

"I know!" Phelps shouted back. "I know!"

He and Sternberg had used their newly-regained

mobility to hide themselves behind the button table, lest the dinosaur in question see them and take out its frustrations on their considerably smaller bodies.

Marsh gazed down on the beast with delight. It seemed to stretch twenty feet or more, and its front end was crowned with a horn as long as his forearm and a good bit sharper. A frill of bone swept around the horn and continued until it culminated in the studded ridge that Marsh was now using to rest his hands. This was the thing that had kept him falling to the floor.

"Beautiful," he said, while the beast turned its head from side to side to get a good look at him.

It was obviously herbivorous. Its upper jaw ended in a beak that would not have looked out of place on a parrot, and the single horn could serve only a defensive posture. Marsh got so carried away looking it over that he almost didn't notice that the beast was moving, and moving fast. It saw the ramp that descended to the ground. It saw daylight and it wanted out.

"Stop it!" Charley Sternberg shouted, but there were no reins on the creature.

Marsh shouted in surprise and then hung on to the dinosaur's bony frill with renewed force. The beast snorted as it gained speed, and it very nearly trampled Edward Cope as it accelerated down the ramp. Cope, who had also come unfrozen and was walking his way back up, had to jump off the side of the ramp and fall ten feet to the ground to avoid being impaled on the creature's horn.

"Where are you going with my Monoclonius?" he shouted as the beast hit the ground with an audible thump.

So that's what it was; a living, breathing version of the monster Cope had already written up in the scientific lexicon. Had he the chance, Marsh would have enjoyed the irony. Cope would get credit for discovering this extinct animal, but he would get to ride it across the plains of Montana, the very area it once ruled. This thought occurred to him like a flash of lightning, but he did not get to savor the idea because he was trying to keep from bumping his head on the underbelly of Swenson's space ship. The Crow, who were indeed hunkered under the disk, now scattered back into the open to keep from being pounded into the ground by the Thunder Horse. Marsh was vaguely aware that arrows and bullets were flying through the air, but in a few short instants it seemed that everyone was running. The Crow ran from underneath the ship. Some mounted Sioux warriors were thrown to the ground as their frightened horses jumped away from the Monoclonius. The others abandoned their attack on the Crow and began running alongside the monster, gaping in awe.

For its part, the Monoclonius seemed to have no fixed idea except to run in a straight line as fast as it could. For such a big, heavy beast, this thing could *move*. It whipped across the landscape like a tornado, sending shock waves echoing across the plain. The temperature had dropped dramatically, and he noticed that the sky had now been conquered by clouds. The beast moved so fast the ground appeared white, Marsh thought, until he realized snow was falling, replacing the drab hues of the land with its harsh opaqueness. The wind stung Marsh's eyes as he hunkered behind the bony frill as best he could, praying the beast would not make any unanticipated moves. The bony ridge of the Monoclonius' back felt like it was sawing him in half, but he felt no pain, only exhilaration. He became aware that the Sioux moving alongside him were whooping with joy. If he weren't so afraid of falling off, he would have whooped right along with them. It was like riding a locomotive. It was like riding a thundercloud in Heaven. It was like riding a horse of the Valkyries. It was like nothing else on earth.

A group of Sioux had assembled ahead. Apparently their wonder at the beast had now cooled. Seven or eight of them had lined up with arrows and rifles at the ready, preparing to bring the Thunder Horse to its knees. Marsh waved at them but they didn't move. The idiots would kill the thing without even realizing what it was. It should be moved to a more proper home, somewhere within traveling distance of the Peabody Museum at Yale University. It should not die in Montana; not again. Marsh stuck a tentative leg out from behind the frill and kicked down at the creature's eye, then quickly got back in his place. The creature slowed just a bit and turned its head to the side, then continued on its way. Marsh squinted through the icy air. The Sioux were still ready. A few dozen more yards and they would conduct a test of how well dinosaur hide could stand up to modern weaponry.

He kicked down with his right foot again, and very nearly fell right off the creature's back. This time he got the beast at the very edge of its eye, and it snorted in pain. Marsh pawed furiously at its back and regained his hold just as the monster began a wide arc turn. The Sioux shouted in surprise and anger, although Marsh did not hear any shooting. He did not know if they realized he was the poor man on its back, and did not know if they would care. He wanted to be the only man to have ever ridden a Monoclonius, not the only man to be shot off the back of one. The Indians jumped back on their horses and took off in pursuit, which gave the Monoclonius some incentive to reverse its course and run back toward the silver disk.

Marsh could see that the Crows seemed to have vanished. They had not seemed particularly eager to explore the disk, much less to fight with the Sioux, so perhaps they had seized the opportunity to get away. Marsh thought the Monoclonius would see the disk and veer off in yet another direction, but the vast creature's legs seemed to move faster than its brain. It was running straight at the disk, tracking a line as straight as a locomotive's. The disk was coming up fast, faster than Marsh could wish. He could nearly make out Alf Swenson's face. Swenson was jumping up and down and shouting, and did not seem at all pleased. The monster showed no sign of slowing down despite Swenson's histrionics. As a matter of fact, he could swear it was gaining speed. Did it intend to plow right through the middle of the ship? Had it gone mad?

He tucked his head behind the looming frill of the Monoclonius and waited for the end. He had always assumed that he would die when his belly got the worst of him. A heart attack, most probably. It would probably come late one night when he was relaxing at home after a long day. Or maybe he would just keel over in his laboratory, fossil in hand. It had never even crossed his mind that he might perish in a collision between a thundering dinosaur and a space ship. He would die betwixt dinosaur and space ship, and his body would be lost under the first snow.

The pain in his rear suddenly ceased. He could no longer feel the scaly hide of the Monoclonius under his grasping fingers. The incessant booming of its feet—feet he had never actually been able to see—stopped as well. He seemed to be flying. Was he dead? This was not so bad. Was he traveling to heaven? He soon discovered that he was not. He was merely traveling down a few feet, back to Montana. Marsh looked down.

The Monclonius was gone. It had been uncomfortable, but he missed it now that the snowy ground was looming up to meet him. He hit the earth hard, sending the thin layer of snow back into the air. The sky seemed to shudder above him as he scraped along underneath it. Fortunately he had landed on one of the few flat parts around, one free of both rocks and scrub grass under its white covering. He could feel his coat disintegrating from his back and shoulders, but at least the dirt and pebbles had yet to reach his skin. The coat was expensive and well made. He had not appreciated that sufficiently until now, until he was on the skidding tour of the west.

Marsh slowly dragged to a halt. Perhaps the Monoclonius had not been as tall as he thought. Once he seemed to stop moving, Marsh opened his eyes, and then blinked as snowflakes greeted them with their cooling embrace. He wiggled his fingers and toes. They still seemed to operate. He drew in a breath, got no complaints from his lungs or ribs. He had ridden a dinosaur and had lived to tell about it. Marsh was just enjoying that memory when a strange creature hovered over him. A dog? He blinked again. It was Alf Swenson, his face cast in a frown.

"It was not real," he said.

"It felt real," Marsh said, the only response he could think of at the moment.

"It was not, and now it is gone. I am leaving too. I am fed up with your kind disrupting my work."

"Where is everyone?" Marsh asked.

Had they missed his glory ride? He had especially wanted Mr. Cope to see it. He had wanted Cope to see the whole thing. Marsh slowly leaned up. Swenson made no move to help him. He saw the Sioux milling around in the middle of the field. They were staring at the broad track he had made in the dirt, but they did not seem to want to come too close to the disk. Maybe they were afraid they, too, would disappear, like the Monoclonius.

"Where is Edward Cope?"

"I believe he is inside my ship."

Marsh's head was starting to hurt now.

"Then I believe your work may be disturbed a little further."

THIRTY TWO

"Did you see that?" Edward Cope said as he stomped up the ramp leading into Swenson's ship. "Did you see that? Othniel was riding a dinosaur! Othniel was riding *my* dinosaur!"

"We saw it," Charles Sternberg said.

"Get up from behind that table, both of you! It's gone. Where did it come from?"

"I don't know," Digger Phelps said. He rose to his feet slowly and warily, as if afraid the beast would come back in search of a new rider. "He must have pressed one of those little pictures."

He pointed to the picture-studded wall near where Marsh had been standing. Cope paced over and scanned the wall. Sure enough, at roughly elbow height there was a tiny representation of what looked very much like Monoclonius, complete with flesh and skin. Cope reached a tentative finger towards it.

"Don't!" Sternberg and Phelps shouted together.

"Please don't, boss," Sternberg said. "It is not a pleasant animal to see at close quarters."

Cope heard muttering behind him, coming from the ramp. He saw a black-haired head coming up the ramp. It must be one of the River Crows. Then he saw that the hair was not very long. It was Al Stillson, back in form as a boy, although she no longer fooled his eyes.

"Al," he said. "Come here."

He saw other dark-haired heads appearing. These were the actual Crows, Chief Twobelly among them. Cope put one arm around Stillson and walked her to the table where Sternberg and Phelps waited.

"Is it a good idea to let them in here?" Sternberg asked as the Crows began to wander around the ship.

"Why?" Cope asked. "You think they might poke the wrong buttons and mess things up?"

Sternberg gave a quick laugh.

"Surely no one would do that."

The Crows were fascinated by the ship, but showed no compunction to touch anything.

"Be careful of those blue patches on the floor," Cope shouted to Twobelly. "Do not step on them."

The big chief nodded, although not in comprehension. Cope had to admit the warning did not make much sense. One of the Crows would just have to test it out for themselves. It really wouldn't matter much if they did; they would just end up outside, and could walk back around to the ramp. It might even be fun.

"Now what do we do?" Sternberg asked. "Where is Professor Marsh now?"

"He's outside," Stillson said in a flat voice. "I saw him talking to the tall man Swenson."

"Swenson!" Cope said. "And where is the Monoclonius?"

"I don't know. It disappeared and Professor Marsh fell down. And then I saw Swenson talking to him."

"Thank you," Cope said. "We don't have much time. Swenson's not going to stick around here. We need to find the bones."

"The bones?" Phelps said. "I think I know where they are. I saw Swenson doing some more things with this button board. I think he used this button here to get to the bones."

He reached out his finger to press the button.

Sternberg and Cope reflexively took a step back. When Phelps pressed the button, the wall behind him let out a grinding sound and a notch appeared in the wall. On the floor before it was another blue patch. Some of the Crows were startled by the noise, and two raised their rifles in a defensive posture. One of the Crows accidentally stepped on the blue patch that led to the outside door, and promptly vanished, which led to much muttering around those remaining.

"He'll be all right," Cope shouted to the baffled Twobelly, who was looking where his warrior had disappeared. "Stillson, would you mind staying here with them and keeping an eye on them? I think it's best if they not play around with this button table here."

He made his voice as soft and gentle as he could. Stillson seemed to be off somewhere far away, by herself. Cope wanted to hear her whole story, of why he was really a she, but there was not time.

"Come, gentlemen," Cope said. "Let's find some bones before Mr. Swenson gets back."

Phelps stepped on the patch and disappeared. Sternberg looked back at Cope.

"This is really not what you had in mind when you wrote to me, is it?" Cope said with laugh. He patted Sternberg on the shoulder, a pat that also had a little push in it. "Go on. I'll be right behind you."

Cope blinked and saw they were in a different part of the ship, although the room was recognizable. It was as round as the one they had just left, but not as tall. It appeared to be largely empty, although there were some round objects along the wall whose function he didn't care to contemplate. He had seen enough wonders. This thing was advanced, but it was still a ship, and it still had to carry its bones somewhere.

"I think we're in a room below the other one," Phelps said. "It looks like the same sort of shape."

"Look at that, Mr. Cope," Sternberg said. "There are more of those see-through walls."

There were, although these were much smaller and were next to the walls of the room, not out in the middle. They didn't appear as finely made as the ones in the upper room. There was something haphazard about them. Cope was tired of looking at tiny pictures, but there seemed to be nothing else here. These were not pictures, but seemed to be letters of some kind, of a language he couldn't hope to read. Then he looked again. They were pictures, after all. They were pictures of tiny, tiny bones, as if left by lilliputian dinosaurs.

"I know how this works now," Cope said. "Don't worry. We'll have our bones yet."

He began touching the pictures. Shafts of light beamed from each one as he pressed it, and the bones began piling up, appearing out of thin air. They apparently were in some kind of order, starting from the far end of the room and working back to where the three men stood. With each push, the complete or nearly complete skeleton of a dinosaur would appear, jumbled together but just as clean as if it had been picked over in a laboratory for months. Sternberg and Phelps appeared stunned until Cope said, "Help me!"

They all began touching the bone pictures then, and each time would turn to see the real things appear behind them. Sternberg never seemed to tire of looking over his shoulder, although he had a good idea each time of what would be there. Cope glanced at him with admiration. He was a great kid. He really loved bones.

"This is a lot easier than the way we do it, huh, Charley?" Cope asked, and Sternberg just laughed.

"It's not working anymore," Phelps said at one point. "I touch the little drawing and nothing happens."

Cope looked at his own finger to see that it was true. He would touch the tiny rendition of the bones, but no shaft of light appeared and nothing happened. The tiny bones stayed tiny.

"Mr. Cope," said a loud voice from nowhere. "Please return to where you were. Stop interfering with my bones."

"Who is that?" Phelps asked.

The speaker was invisible, but the voice was certainly loud enough.

"That's Swenson," Cope said.

"Where is he?" Phelps asked. "How can he talk if he's not here?"

"How can we jump around this ship just by stepping on blue floors?" Cope responded. "How can we push buttons and bones appear?"

"That's true," Phelps said. "After all that has happened, I don't know why I'm surprised."

"Swenson could float in here upside down and on fire and I wouldn't be surprised anymore," Sternberg said. "We'd better do as he said."

"I want my bones," Cope said, striking a fist against his hip in frustration. "That's what all this is about."

"Time's up," the disembodied voice said.

A piercing whistle sounded through the room, causing all three to cover their ears in a hurry.

"Go!" Phelps said, and he and Sternberg ran for the blue patch.

Cope watched them run. The sound felt like it was curdling his brains, but he wanted his bones. He would not watch Swenson fly off into space while he was left empty handed. Sternberg looked back and motioned him on with his free hand; he only had to block one ear. Cope looked at the bones. Maybe he could carry a few, but not enough to be worthwhile. He would have to go face Swenson.

"All right," he said. "I'm coming, Swenson. But I don't think you'll like it."

He returned to the upper room to find Sternberg and Phelps standing next to Stillson. They were standing so still that Cope thought they were frozen again, but then Sternberg scratched his nose. The Crows were still roaming around the main room, and still had not seemed to touch anything. Swenson stood behind the button table, the silver freezing device in his hand, a fairly obvious threat.

"I am leaving now," Swenson said. "It is clear I will be able to get little more done here. You have done your best to ruin my work, even after I extended the hand of friendship to you."

He paused, perhaps waiting for Cope to express regret or to apologize. Cope folded his arms and did neither.

"I went so far as to draw up that map for you that I promised," Swenson said.

He held up a square piece of paper about as big as a sheet of foolscap, covered with lines and squiggles.

"It's not written in your language, but you could figure it out. It would be of enormous benefit to you. Now you can forget it."

He wadded the paper into a ball and dropped it on the floor behind his feet.

"I believe you may have some control over these dark-skinned men who are wandering around. Please ask them to leave, and then you leave as well, and you, Mr. Sternberg, and you, Mr. Phelps, and you, young girl."

"Girl?" Sternberg said.

"Never mind," Cope said. "What if we don't go?"

Swenson moved a thumb over the silver device in his hand.

"I could make you all leave. I am trying to let you go of your own accord, with some dignity. It's all over now. Please leave. I have left the front door open for you."

The ramp was still open, Cope saw. He also saw a band of Sioux coming up it, rifles and bows and arrows in hand. Swenson saw his surprised gaze and matched it.

"Now, this is too much," he said, but suddenly the Sioux, spying their enemy, let out ear-piercing whoops and stormed up the ramp. The Crow backed up to the far wall and assumed a defensive posture.

"Get out!" Swenson shouted.

He pushed a button on the table and the mind-numbing shriek that Cope had heard below now sounded through the room. It echoed off the high domed ceiling, which made it all the more intolerable. The Indians all wore faces of agony but did not back down. Swenson left it on for a few more seconds and then cut it off in disgust. Apparently he did not care for it either. One of the Sioux stalked around the translucent wall, his eyes trained on Chief Twobelly. Cope edged away and let him pass.

"Why are you doing this?" Cope asked as the man passed.

To his surprise, the Sioux warrior answered.

"We cannot let the Crow have the secret weapon," he said, and kept moving.

"What secret weapon?" asked Cope.

The Sioux did not answer, but continued his slow, deadly pacing. He carried a rifle, but was a bit careless about how he held it. As he passed the translucent wall, he managed to touch one of the tiny pictures with its butt. His forward progress was halted by the form of the lizard man, which suddenly stood between him and his foe. The Sioux straightened up in surprise. Swenson was not so shy about letting an audible sound of disgust loose from his mouth. He muttered several words in his alien language and poked a button on his table.

Twobelly had not noticed the stalking Sioux, but he did take notice of a man-shaped lizard. Cope saw what he was preparing to do and shouted for him to stop, but Twobelly was quick with his bow and arrow and managed to get off a shot straight to the lizard man's midsection just as Swenson's finger touched the button. The lizard man disappeared. The arrow continued on its way and struck the Sioux in the leg. The Sioux warrior collapsed grimacing on the floor, but did not let a shout of pain escape his lips.

Swenson pushed more buttons. The disk began to rock. Swenson was apparently no longer willing to wait for his ship to be vacated. The disk rose into the air, and tilted to the front. The wounded Sioux tumbled down the ramp, followed by Sternberg and several startled Crow. Cope hung on to one of the translucent walls, making sure he didn't press any pictures himself. The lizard man just stood there, unperturbed.

"Go," Swenson said. "I am leaving with you or without you."

"But you can't," Cope protested.

He saw Stillson, who had fallen on the floor, sneaking over to recover the wadded map Swenson had tossed down. Good girl. He could not remember if she was still on his payroll or not, but he would make sure she was well compensated for her thoughtfulness.

"I am leaving now," Swenson said.

The disk lifted a dozen feet off the ground and pitched forward suddenly. Cope lost his grip on the slick wall and slid to the open door. He looked down. It was snowing furiously now. The ground was covered with it, and he had a hard time telling how far below it was. He had been dreading the snow, which would put an end to the expedition, but was glad for it now. It would cushion the fall. The Crow and the Sioux had momentarily forgotten their differences and glared up at the hovering silver disk, angry to have been so unceremoniously dumped from it. They began firing rifles and arrows at the ship, but were fortunately shooting at the back side, not at the door where Cope dangled like a piece of straw in a bird's mouth.

The ship tilted again, and Stillson appeared just above him in the open doorway. He grabbed her around the waist and gripped the door, the tension pushing up the veins on his arm.

"I would say I enjoyed meeting you, but I really have not," Swenson said. "Goodbye, Mr. Cope."

The ship tilted again, but they did not fall.

"My foot is stuck," Stillson said. Tears squeezed out around her eyes. "It hurts."

"Swenson!" Cope said. "Let us down! Her foot is stuck."

"Go down there, and be attacked?" Swenson said. "I don't think so. Jump. It won't hurt you."

He pushed more buttons. The ship rose higher, but apparently not as high as he wanted. Cope looked down below.

"What did you do down there in the hold?" Swenson shouted at Cope. "The ship is too heavy!"

The bones. He and Sternberg and Phelps had summoned as many bones as they could from Swenson's picture wall.

"We filled it up with your bones," Cope said. "Dump them and you can take off."

"Dump them?" Swenson said. "I don't think so."

The Indians below were getting braver. An arrow came winging through the open door, missing Cope by less than a foot, and ricocheted off the domed ceiling. It came within one inch of spearing Swenson's hand to his table.

"That's it!" Swenson said.

He walked over and loosened Stillson's foot. He bent down until his face was mere inches from Cope's.

"You are a troublesome species," Swenson muttered through clenched teeth.

"Those bones are ours now," Cope said. "They belong here."

"They most certainly do not. I will shrink them again and take them away. Good day, Mr. Cope, Miss Stillson."

Cope had been barely hanging on, and it took Swenson the merest nudge to dislodge his grip. Cope and Stillson fell like angels being tossed out of heaven. The disk above them looked like something out of a dream, until they hit the ground and fell into six inches of snow, which buried them in its wet, fluffy shroud.

THIRTY THREE

Cope sat up in the snow and dusted it off as best he could. He turned and saw O.C. Marsh approaching. Marsh helped Stillson stand up, and made the futile effort of brushing snow off her shoulders. It was quickly replaced. The silver disk hung above them, and they looked up at it as helplessly as if it were the moon. It rose higher and higher in small increments every few minutes, resembling the Earth's satellite even more as it ascended.

"He still has all the bones, doesn't he?" Marsh said.

Cope nodded.

"I'm afraid so. He'll be off in a few minutes, I guess, and then they're gone."

"Well, we tried."

Cope looked at Marsh, and they both smiled. Cope considered telling Marsh about the map that Stillson had pilfered. Then he thought better of it.

"Yes, we did."

The ship continued its slow climb. It was now about two hundred feet in the air. The Indians had largely given up on the idea of shooting it down, but every now and then one would plink an arrow off its bottom. The door was now closed, and from underneath the ship looked like some sort of upended tea saucer. Sternberg and Phelps wandered over, and stood with them, gawking helplessly.

The Indians began shouting. Cope and the group looked to where they were pointing. It was not enough to have one impossibly advanced alien ship in the sky. Now there was another. If Swenson's ship resembled a saucer, this one was an egg. All that was needed was a cup, and a good extraterrestrial breakfast could be had.

"It's Thornton Grieg," Marsh said.

It was indeed his craft, fresh from its berth in the river. The egg floated closer to the saucer and red sparks of light began streaming from it like fireworks. The saucer rocked in the sky.

"I thought he was trying to lay low around Swenson," Marsh said.

"He seems to have given up on that idea," Cope said. "He strikes me as a desperate man, or whatever he is."

"Whatever he is, yes," Marsh said.

The sparks continued to fly from the egg. Swenson's saucer rocked more, and then a dark opening appeared in its underside. Something began to fall out. Cope squinted. He thought he could make out a ribcage. He laughed, which caused Marsh to look at him quizzically.

"He's dumping the bones," Cope said.

"Oh, no," Sternberg said. "That's terrible."

"What do you mean?" Cope asked. "That's great. The snow will break their fall. We'll get everything."

"But Grieg doesn't seem to know they're falling," Sternberg pointed out. "He's still shooting, or whatever it is he's doing."

Cope looked up again, blinking his eyes against the falling flakes. Sternberg was right. The bones were falling, all right, but they were falling right into the path of some of the red beams from Grieg's egg. After that, they were no longer bones falling, just bone dust.

"Great," Cope said. "Just great."

The red streaks stopped. Some of the bones did make it through, falling to the ground in a stream of spines and skulls. Swenson's saucer shot straight up, disappearing into the fluffy clouds that continued to lavish the ground with snow, oblivious to the fantastic shape that sped through them. Grieg's egg hovered for a moment more and then vanished into the clouds as well.

"Get the carts," Cope said. "Let's go get whatever we can."

"Maybe not," Marsh said.

The Sioux and Crow had resumed hostilities. They were shouting at each other, circling like lions. They were near the fallen bones. Anyone going in there was likely to find an arrow through his head.

"Think we can talk to them?" Marsh asked.

"We'd better do it fast," Cope said. "This snow is going to hide everything pretty soon."

THIRTY FOUR

Thornton Grieg did not look at all happy. He sat across the table from Othniel Marsh, glowering as best his inexpressive face could glower. It was flat-out cold now, a veritable winter wonderland outside the big tent, and Grieg shivered despite his heavy coat.

"Where are they?" he said. "I know you have them."

He meant, of course, the bones, but Marsh actually did not have them. There were not a great many to have, as it turned out. Most had been pulverized by the red beams from Grieg's ship, but Marsh thought it might be inappropriate to point this out. A few things had been found, but by the time the Crows and Sioux had been calmed down sufficiently for a fossil search, the snow had obliterated most of the marks where they had fallen. They would lie there until spring, at which time the melting snow would carry them down the ravines and into the river. Perhaps a few would stay put, but most would probably be lost. The ones they had recovered were split somewhat evenly, after a good bit of haggling, and were already on the way back east, safe from Grieg.

"I'm afraid they were lost in the snow," Marsh said flatly.

He folded his fingers into a little church steeple. He was trying to remain calm, but the uncertainty about what he was going to do was unnerving. He hoped Grieg was too upset to notice the thick string that played across the floor and rested on the edge of the table. He most definitely hoped that Grieg would not look up to see the clumsy mechanisms above him. He had not had time to rig up something more sophisticated, but so far Grieg was proving suitably inattentive.

Cope had already gone back to Philadelphia, forced to leave by the snow and by a pressing speaking engagement. They had shaken hands like old comrades, but had not made plans to get together back east. There was no point in kidding each other.

"O.C., I must say this has been a very interesting time," Cope had said.

"Agreed," Marsh responded.

"When people ask me how things went out here in Montana territory, I think there are some key events that I will leave out," Cope said. "I will no doubt forget to mention people from other planets, and ships that can travel through space, and small dark men who run on electricity."

Marsh had laughed.

"Such things are already receding from my mind. I will probably forget to mention having ridden on the back of Monoclonius. Soon it will all seem like a dream."

"I'm not sure I would call it a dream," Cope had said, apparently miffed by the reference to Marsh's adventurous ride, the one thing he did not get to share.

Cope did not seem entirely happy to leave when Marsh was still there, but they both knew nothing paleontological could be accomplished now until spring, so he had reluctantly departed, with Sternberg in tow. Marsh was prepared to follow him, but, having no remaining help, had been obliged to stay longer. Then Grieg showed up and demanded a meeting. Marsh asked him to come back the next day, when he would

get what he was due. Grieg agreed. Marsh had hired
Boston Mickle from Cope, and had something in mind
besides his regular cooking. It had taken him, Phelps
and Stillson all night to set things up.

"We had an agreement," the miserable Grieg said.
"I saw the bones falling. You were right there. I know
you got some of them."

Marsh met his strange eyes briefly, and then looked
back at his steepled fingers.

"Let's get to that in a moment," he said. "Mr. Grieg,
I don't believe you've been entirely truthful with me
here."

"What do you mean?"

"You said that your people had conducted some
breeding experiments out here, and that's why you want
the bones."

An odd sound came from Grieg's head. It sounded
like his teeth were chattering.

"Yes," he said, getting his jaw under control. "That
is correct."

"But I was on Mr. Swenson's ship," Marsh said. "I
saw many odd things there that suggest that maybe
Mr. Swenson's people are the ones responsible for the
breeding programs."

"That is not true."

"Are you sure?"

"I am sure. Now give me the bones that are due me.
Keep some of them but give me the ones I want. I am
through playing with you, Mr. Marsh."

"Your people are not like Mr. Swenson's people, are
they?"

It was a bright day but the cold forced Marsh to keep
the tent flaps closed and instead rely on candles for
illumination. Grieg, as usual, looked porcelain and
ghostly in their light.

"We are similar in many ways," Grieg said.

"I am sorry, but I still think you're lying to me," Marsh said. "You cannot have any of the bones."

Grieg rose to his full height, which was not very impressive, and rested his fists on the table.

"I will force you to—" he started to say.

Marsh stood up as well, and pulled hard on the string. The string tightened in its pulleys and tugged in turn on the oversized stew pot that was precariously positioned in the peak of the tent. The pot tilted, pouring out a generous portion of Boston Mickle's sticky rice. The goop covered the astonished Grieg. He looked like Lot's wife from the Old Testament story, only he was a pillar of lumpy rice, not salt.

"Now!" Marsh shouted.

Stillson and Phelps whipped up the tent flap and ran to hold Grieg, who had fallen on the floor in surprise. They pushed him to the ground with folded sheets, so their hands wouldn't sink into Mickle's overcooked goo. Grieg pushed and struggled, but only managed to get his mouth free.

"What are you doing?" he screamed.

"Testing a theory," Marsh said.

Grieg was stronger than he looked. He managed to roll over, but Stillson and Phelps piled up on his back. He took a deep breath, and then rose to his knees. His attackers held on tenaciously, but Grieg gave a tremendous grunt and shoved them both aside. He turned to face Marsh, rice dripping from his face.

"Just as I thought," Marsh said. "You weren't the ones doing the breeding. You were the ones bred."

A new Grieg faced him from within the rice. Mickle's concoction, which Cope had discovered was good for wrapping bones, also proved good at pulling away the fake skin Grieg had worn like a too-tight suit. His eerily smooth skin was gone, replaced with green scales. The creature that faced Marsh was none other

than the lizard man he had spotted inside Swenson's
ship.

"Are you happy?" Grieg said.

His voice sounder higher pitched, almost fluttery.
Grieg pushed at the rice, which fell away from him in
sticky glops. It pulled away his human clothes as well
as the fake skin underneath them, revealing a branch
of the dinosaur family that Marsh had never dreamed
could exist—the dinosaur as man. The dinosaur as man
was not looking even remotely happy at the moment.
Grieg held up one hand, which Marsh saw ended in
some sizable claws, and stalked around the table after
him. Marsh abandoned all decorum and fled the tent,
tossing the flap down behind him to slow Grieg down.
Boston Mickle was standing just outside the tent, curious
as to how his rice had turned out.

"Run!" Marsh shouted at him.

It was hard to move through the snow, which was
now at knee level. There was really nowhere to run,
either, as the big tent and their small sleeping tents
were all that remained of the camp. The rest of the
land was now a snowy moonscape. Marsh had thought
up the rice trick but had not considered what might
happen after that. He continued to believe that an
advanced civilization would be slow to anger. It had
not really occurred to him that a lizard man could be
moved to attack.

He looked back. Grieg was outside the tent, heading
his way, tromping his green five-toed feet down into
the snow, not looking like the product of an advanced
civilization at all. Marsh realized that he was looking
at only the second dinosaur to tromp the plains of
Montana in millions of years. The first had been the
Monoclonius, a plant eater. The second was apparently
a carnivore; Grieg's mouth was open and Marsh ruefully
saw the spiked teeth within it. So he would not die in

a crash between a dinosaur and a space ship after all. He would be mauled to death by a lizard man, a dinosaur evolved into the shape of a man. He had to admit that was a little bit more fitting, but it was still not something he relished. He heard a crashing sound behind him and closed his eyes, waiting on the end. It did not come. He turned to see Grieg collapsed in the snow, his ribcage fluttering like the wings of a bird.

Marsh took a tentative step toward his foe. Was this a trick? Grieg was visibly shivering. It wasn't a trick. Grieg was a sort of lizard, after all, and it was very cold out, even for a mammal like Marsh. He slowly walked up to Grieg. Grieg's mouth was moving. Marsh bent down to hear what he said.

"So cold," Grieg said. "So cold."

"Where is your ship?" Marsh asked.

"In the river," Grieg said through his sharp, but chattering, teeth.

Stillson and Phelps walked up behind him, ready for more fighting that did not seem to be coming.

"I will make a new deal with you," Marsh said. "We will take you to your ship if you will leave."

"I want my bones," Grieg said.

"No. I don't know what has gone on between you and Swenson's people, but the bones are ours now. We live here. They belong to us."

"They are my people," Grieg said weakly.

He turned his head to fix Marsh with one of his yellow eyes.

"They are my people," he repeated.

Marsh shook his head.

"They are ours now. We take you back to your ship, you leave. Do you agree?"

Grieg stuck his head back into the snow. He nodded, smoothing out a semicircle that surrounded his green head like a halo.

"This isn't over," Grieg said. "My people will be back. My enemy's people will be back. We have both been looking for the original breeding ground. We did not think this was the place. That is why there was only one of him and one of me, just one of me following to keep an eye on him. But this is the place. Now that we know, many of us will be back."

His voice fluttered away. Stillson and Phelps picked Grieg out of the snow, carrying him by his hands and feet. Marsh helped roll him over and then supported his back. Grieg's scales felt odd against his fingertips. Grieg's hand moved slowly until his palm touched Marsh's temple, and then Marsh stopped.

Marsh saw Montana as it was. He saw the vast sea, saw the bulky creatures moving alongside it. He felt the air, thick with salt, heavy with moisture. He smelt the rotting cycads and the fragrant palms. He heard the crash of the waves, loud as thunder, rhythmic as the beating of a heart. He felt elation, the elation of knowing this was where it began. He felt despair, the despair of knowing it was all gone, all trodden under mammalian feet. Grieg's hand fell away and Marsh felt the cold air sting his lungs. He was back in modern Montana, far from the sea, and he was one of the conquering mammals.

"We will be back," Grieg said in a whistling whisper.

"We'll be here," Marsh replied, and began walking again.

EPILOGUE

Dear diary

Well I am heading back east now. Mr Cope is already gone and Mr Marsh leaves tomorrow. I will ride with him part of the way but not all the way. I do not think I will go to St Louis. Maybe I will go on to New York. I am not sure where I will go. I just want to be away from here. It is cold here and I do not feel very good. He is not here anymore so there is nothing for me here either. I have lots of money now. Mr Cope and Mr Marsh paid me so I do not have to worry about getting by for quite a while.

I am not sure what to do with the map. I had hoped to get it away without being noticed but Mr Cope saw me take it and he wanted it. I didnt think he should have it by himself so I told Mr Marsh about it and he wanted a copy too. They agreed that Cope would get the original and Marsh would get a copy drawn by me. They didnt watch me very closely though. The original looks like it was done in regular ink on regular paper. It looks sort of like that anyway and Mr Cope never did get a good look at it so he didnt know. I made two copies and then crumpled one of them up until it looked like the original. I gave that one to Mr Cope and the unwrinkled copy to Mr Marsh. I kept the original for myself and have

311

smoothed it out the best I can although it still has a lot of wrinkles.

What they dont know is I didnt quite draw their copies of the map the way it was. I drew the landscape just the same but I moved around the little marks that marked where the bones are. I moved some pretty far away and left others close to where Mr Swenson had them but the point is that neither map is very good. I am not sure what they are going to do with their maps but they are not going to get out of them what they think they are going to get out of them thats for sure.

Sitting Lizard gave his life out here. His blood is here but he only lives in my head now. That is not Mr Copes fault nor Mr Marshs but I think if they want more bones they should have to work to find them. I dont want to make it too easy on either one.

Love, Alice.

AFTERWORD

O.C. Marsh, Edward Drinker Cope and Charles Sternberg were all giants in the field of paleontology, and Cope really did discover the dinosaur *Monoclonius* in Montana in 1876 (though probably not in the way described here). That said, anyone looking to see where this tale runs off the rails of history will not be long disappointed.

These men are fictional characters, as they appear in this book, but I would like to acknowledge my debt to the following historical sources: *Cope: Master Naturalist*, compiled by Henry Fairfield Osborn, was invaluable, providing a look at Montana through Cope's own letters. *The Life of a Fossil Hunter*, Sternberg's autobiography, was also indispensable, as was *O.C. Marsh: Pioneer in Paleontology*, by Charles Schuchert and Clara Mae LeVene. To a lesser extent, I also relied on David Spalding's *Dinosaur Hunters* and Robert West Howard's *The Dawnseekers*. I am also indebted for various odds and ends to Frederick E. Hoxie's *The Crow*, Charles M. Robinson III's *A Good Year to Die* and Evan S. Connell's *Son of the Morning Star*.

Most early sightings of extraterrestrials involved tall, blonde Nordics or scaly lizard-type aliens. Thanks for that information must go to *Strange* magazine.